"My life is none of your business," Lori said.

"You made it my business when you kissed me the way you did tonight."

"I know I led you on," she said stiffly. "And I really am sorry."

Zack dismissed her apology with a wave. "Forget it. That's not the issue."

"Oh? Then what is, Mr. McBride?"

"If we hadn't been in a public place, we would've made love right then and there. It's gonna happen. Real soon."

"It most certainly is *not*," she said hotly.

"Yes, it is, darlin'. You know it and I know it, and I need to understand what's going on with you so I don't scare the hell out of you when it does."

HEARTS OF WYOMING:
Rugged and wild, the McBride family has
love to share...and Wyoming weddings
are on their minds!

Dear Reader,

Special Edition is pleased to bring you six exciting love stories to help you celebrate spring...and blossoming love.

To start off the month, don't miss *A Father for Her Baby* by Celeste Hamilton—a THAT'S MY BABY! title that features a pregnant amnesiac who is reunited with her long-ago fiancé. Now she must uncover the past in order to have a future with this irresistible hero and her new baby.

April offers Western romances aplenty! In the third installment of her action-packed HEARTS OF WYOMING series, Myrna Temte delivers *Wrangler*. A reticent lady wrangler has a mighty big secret, but sparks fly between her and the sexy lawman she's been trying very hard to avoid; the fourth book in the series will be available in July. Next, Pamela Toth brings us another heartwarming story in her popular BUCKLES & BRONCOS miniseries. In *Buchanan's Pride*, a feisty cowgirl rescues a stranded stranger—only to discover he's the last man on earth she should let into her heart!

There's more love on the range coming your way. *Finally His Bride* by Christine Flynn—part of THE WHITAKER BRIDES series—is an emotional reunion romance between two former sweethearts. Also the MEN OF THE DOUBLE-C RANCH series continues when a brooding Clay brother claims the woman he's never stopped wanting in *A Wedding For Maggie* by Allison Leigh. Finally, debut author Carol Finch shares an engaging story about a fun-loving rodeo cowboy who woos a romance-resistant single mom in *Not Just Another Cowboy*.

I hope you enjoy these stirring tales of passion, and each and every romance to come!

Sincerely,

Karen Taylor Richman
Senior Editor

Please address questions and book requests to:
Silhouette Reader Service
U.S.: 3010 Walden Ave., P.O. Box 1325, Buffalo, NY 14269
Canadian: P.O. Box 609, Fort Erie, Ont. L2A 5X3

MYRNA TEMTE
WRANGLER

Published by Silhouette Books
America's Publisher of Contemporary Romance

This book is dedicated to the old friends, Kathie Hayes,
Terry Kanago and Mary Pat Kanaley. And to the new friends,
Miss Cherry Pie and the Eel-Skin BICC Gang. Thanks for
sharing all the fun and tears. You guys are the best!

Many thanks for help with research to Debra Sims of
Douglas, Wyoming; Teresa Sherman of Spokane, Washington,
and to Larry Beeler of Busy Bee Ranch, Spokane, Washington.
Any mistakes are definitely the author's.

 SILHOUETTE BOOKS

ISBN 0-373-24238-7

WRANGLER

Copyright © 1999 by Myrna Temte

This edition published by arrangement with Harlequin Books S.A.

Printed in U.S.A.

Books by Myrna Temte

Silhouette Special Edition

Wendy Wyoming #483
Powder River Reunion #572
The Last Good Man Alive #643
*For Pete's Sake #739
*Silent Sam's Salvation #745
*Heartbreak Hank #751
The Forever Night #816
Room for Annie #861
A Lawman for Kelly #1075
‡*Pale Rider* #1124
†*A Father's Vow* #1172
‡*Urban Cowboy* #1181
‡*Wrangler* #1238

Silhouette Books

Montana Mavericks

Sleeping with the Enemy

*Cowboy Country
†Montana Mavericks: Return to
    Whitehorn
‡Hearts of Wyoming

MYRNA TEMTE

grew up in Montana and attended college in Wyoming, where she met and married her husband. Marriage didn't necessarily mean settling down for the Temtes—they have lived in six different states, including Washington, where they currently reside. Moving so much is difficult, the author says, but it is also wonderful stimulation for a writer.

Though always a "readaholic," Myrna never dreamed of becoming an author. But while spending time at home to care for her first child, she began to seek an outlet from the never-ending duties of housekeeping and child-rearing. She started reading romances and soon became hooked, both as a reader and a writer. Now Myrna appreciates the best of all possible worlds—a loving family and a challenging career that lets her set her own hours and turn her imagination loose.

McBride Family Tree

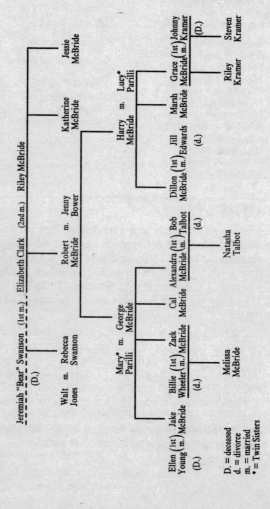

Jeremiah "Bear" Swanson (1st m.) Elizabeth Clark (2nd m.) Riley McBride
(D.)

Walt m. Rebecca Swanson — Jones

Robert m. Jenny McBride — Bower

Katherine McBride

Jessie McBride

Harry m. Lucy* McBride — Parilli

Mary* m. George Parilli — McBride

Ellen (1st Young m.) Jake McBride
(D.)

Billie (1st Wheeler m.) Zack McBride
(d.)

Cal McBride

Alexandra (1st Bob McBride m.) Talbot
(d.)

Dillon (1st Jill McBride m.) Edwards
(d.)

Marsh McBride

Grace (1st Johnny McBride m.) Kramer
(D.)

Melissa McBride

Natasha Talbot

Riley Kramer

Steven Kramer

D. = deceased
d. = divorce
m. = married
* = Twin Sisters

Chapter One

Sighing with relief, Lori Jones watched Rob Grant park his rig behind their boss, Wade Kirby's, then parked her own rig behind Rob's. After five days of hauling horses from Southern California to Northwestern Wyoming she could hardly wait to escape the confines of the big pickup and feel solid ground beneath her feet again. Judging from the impatient snorts and stomps coming from the trailers behind and in front of her, the horses felt exactly the same way.

Poor babies. Wade Kirby's movie horses were notoriously pampered creatures, but it didn't matter that the trailers were all top-of-the-line, luxury transport. The trip still must have been about as comfortable for the animals as if they'd ridden the entire distance standing up on a bouncing, swaying bus.

"Can we get out, Mom?" Brandon asked.

Lori gave her fidgety, ten-year-old son a tired smile. "Wade's talking to a couple of men up there by the ranch house. Let's sit tight until he finds out where we're going to unload."

"Wade'll talk all day," Brandon grumbled, tugging the brim of his beloved Dodgers cap farther down on his forehead.

"He won't this time, honey," Lori said. "The horses are too tired and cranky to wait very long."

"Me, too," Brandon said.

Lori chuckled at his disgruntled tone, receiving a scowl before Brandon allowed himself to loosen up enough to give her a small, wry grin. The sight of that grin warmed Lori's heart and at the same time, gave it a vicious wrench. It had been four years now. How long would it take for her son to learn to smile easily again, to laugh and yell and play the way other boys did?

In a vain attempt to stave off the inevitable stab of guilt, she turned her head away, focusing on the three men heading in her direction. Wade Kirby came first. She'd worked for him for five months now, the longest she had allowed herself to stay anywhere since the disaster. He was a decent man and a fair boss, and she loved working with his horses. Unfortunately she didn't know if she would dare to go back to his ranch in California when this job was over.

Though Wade was at least six feet tall and not even close to being skinny, the men following him were brawnier and topped him by a couple of inches. The one on the left had a gorgeous black beard and wore the traditional cowboy uniform of jeans, battered boots, a blue work shirt and a light gray, sweat-stained Stetson cowboy hat. The one on the right was clean shaven and though he wore the same basic outfit, he somehow managed to look as if he rode a desk rather than a horse.

In spite of their differences, the men looked so much alike, they had to be brothers. Both were extremely handsome in a dark, rugged sort of way, probably somewhere in their mid-to-late thirties. And they both studied her through the pickup's windshield with an assessing interest that made the fine hairs at the back of her neck twitch with alarm.

Oh, damn. Male attention was the very last thing she

wanted in her life. She hoped these two discouraged easily, but she doubted she would be that lucky.

Not that she was any great beauty. Men simply were perverse. When a woman wanted them around, they all vanished, and when she didn't, they stuck to her like strapping tape.

"Lori, Brandon, come on out and meet our hosts," Wade said, speaking to her through the open window in her door.

Since she could hardly refuse without appearing rude, Lori gathered up her courage and forced herself to climb down from the high seat. She heard Brandon's door open and shut on the far side of the rig and listened to the soft slaps of his sneakered feet in the dirt as he hurried to join her. She put her arm around his thin shoulders and hugged him against her side for her own comfort as well as his, then turned to face the strangers.

When Wade introduced her and Brandon, the desk rider tipped his hat back, offering her a friendly smile and a hand to shake. "Afternoon, ma'am," he said in a deep, smooth voice that probably would have sounded great on the radio. "I'm Jake McBride. Welcome to the Flying M."

"Thank you," Lori said.

While Jake turned to greet Brandon, the guy with the beard took off his hat, tucked it under one arm and combed his hair back with his fingers, then stepped forward and took her hand in his. "Name's Zack McBride, ma'am. I've got the best horse setup, so you folks'll be workin' over at my place."

Where Jake's voice had been pleasant, Zack's held just enough of a husky rasp to give a woman goose bumps from imagining what it would sound like when he felt... passionate. Dark as espresso, his eyes held a spark of intelligence as well as a twinkle of good humor. His smile was so appealing, it should have been registered as a lethal weapon. Add in his big, gorgeous body and his thick, glossy black hair with just a hint of gray at his temples, and...

Oh, double damn. She hadn't felt the vaguest flicker of

attraction toward a man since her marriage had turned sour. She certainly didn't want to feel attracted to this one, either. This was hardly a convenient time for her libido to decide it wasn't dead after all, but there was no need to panic.

On such short acquaintance her reaction to Zack McBride couldn't be anything more than a biological urge. She didn't know a thing about him other than what he looked like and where he lived. Yes, he was handsome as sin, but for all she knew, he might be the most egotistical jerk west of the Mississippi River.

She yanked her hand from his grasp and stepped back, wishing he would stop smiling at her and go away. All she wanted was a safe place to raise her son for a few months. She couldn't afford the complications having a man in her life would entail.

"It's nice to meet you, Mr. McBride," she said, putting as much coolness into her voice as she could.

His eyes narrowed, one brow arched in surprise while he studied her with an intensity that made her want to squirm. Before he could say anything, however, Jake turned away from Brandon and clapped Zack on the back.

"Why don't you ride with Lori and Brandon and show them the way to your place?" Jake said.

"Maybe you'd better ask Ms. Jones if that's all right with her," Zack said.

"Of course it is," Wade said, shooting Lori a puzzled frown. "We need to get the horses out of those trailers as soon as possible."

Lori gave a stiff nod of agreement and urged Brandon back into the rig, making certain he sat in the middle of the bench seat before climbing in after him. Zack walked around the pickup's front bumper and settled into the passenger seat. With only a slight hesitation, he directed her to a narrow, graveled road cutting across the ranch to the west.

The pickup's tires rumbled over a cattle guard. Lori tightened her grip on the steering wheel, bracing for the inevitable jolt that would come when the horse trailer hit the metal grid.

The muscles in her neck and shoulders ached with tension and weariness. She inhaled a deep breath, calling up her reserves of poise to help her cope with this awkward situation.

His voice soft and tinged with reverence, Brandon said, "Wow."

She glanced over at him, hiding a sudden, fierce rush of emotion with a smile. Brandon's cheeks were flushed, his eyes wide with admiration while he looked off to his left and then to his right, trying to see everything at once. He leaned forward, straining against the seat belt as if he could will the truck to go faster.

Turning her own gaze back to the narrow, twisting road ahead, Lori sympathized with him. On this trip they'd traveled across rugged mountains and green valleys, deserts and rivers swollen with the spring runoff from snow melting in the high country. Some of the scenery had been beautiful, even spectacular, but the Flying M Ranch looked about as close to heaven as mere mortals were ever likely to get.

Giant cottonwood trees lined the road, reaching toward a sky of such a brilliant blue that she found it difficult to believe it hadn't been created by the special effects artists. The same was true of the saw-toothed, snow-capped mountains towering over the valley in a protective circle. The cow pastures were incredibly lush and green; the sleek Herefords grazing in them looked a bit...smug, as if they had every reason to believe their fortunate circumstances would last forever.

"This is such a cool place," Brandon said.

"Thanks," Zack said. "The McBrides have been on the Flying M for four generations now. We're real proud of it."

Brandon looked up at Zack with a lack of fear that made Lori's breath catch. "I don't blame you."

She silently agreed. If she ever owned such a beautiful place, she would care for it with the same meticulous attention to detail as the people who lived here obviously did. That would never happen for her now, of course, but she

wouldn't let her natural envy prevent her from admiring the
evidence of hard work everywhere she looked.

The barbwire fences enclosing the pastures stood straight
and square, with a military precision that suggested those
wires would never dare to sag. The few remaining haystacks
were neatly fenced; the barns and buildings were all freshly
painted. Even the gravel road was amazingly free of potholes.

Yes, everything looked perfect here, she thought, barely
repressing a cynical laugh. She'd lived in a "perfect" place
before, and beneath the facade, she'd found nothing but misery and grief. Frankly, she would have felt more comfortable
if the Flying M had had numerous glaring flaws, out in the
open where she could see them.

Instead, it got better and better. The barbwire fences gave
way to wooden post-and-rail fences with rounded corners
rather than square ones. The livestock in the pastures changed
from cattle to horses. Black ones, white ones, bay ones, all
of them gorgeous and sporting the elegant conformation and
high-flying tails of Arabians.

"Oh, Mom, look," Brandon said, practically bouncing on
the seat, pointing to the pasture on his right. "They look
like—"

Lori shot him a quelling glance, then said softly, "Yes, I
know what you mean. They're beautiful, aren't they?"

His face flushed and Brandon immediately subsided, lowering his head and nodding his reply rather than speaking
again. Lori cursed silently, hating herself for squelching his
excitement, hating Hugh for making the squelching necessary
in the first place. To make matters worse, she felt Zack
McBride's disapproving gaze drilling into her from the passenger seat.

Well, let him disapprove of her. It was always easy for
other people to judge what they didn't understand. Besides,
he couldn't make her feel any guiltier than she already did.

"Take that next lane on your left," Zack said. "My place
is just beyond those trees."

Lori signaled for the benefit of the drivers behind her, then followed Zack's directions. His voice had become terse, his manner decidedly less friendly. She ignored the changes as best she could, reminding herself that anything keeping this man at a distance ultimately would be a blessing.

When all three rigs were positioned to Wade's and Zack's satisfaction, there was the usual flurry of activity—setting up the portable corral panels, lowering ramps from the trailers, setting out equipment that would be needed during or shortly after the horses were unloaded. Lori and Brandon had their own routine down pat. Within an hour, their eight equine passengers were munching hay and stretching cramped muscles in the temporary holding pen Lori had assembled for them, patiently waiting to have their protective gear removed.

"Whoa, damn you, whoa!" Rob Grant, Wade's newest employee, shouted from the next rig.

Lori straightened up, frowning at the fury in Rob's voice. This was his first road trip with Wade's horses, which made him an unknown quantity. He'd never done anything that warranted the immediate dislike she had felt toward him the first time they met, but she still had to repress an instinctive shudder whenever he stood close to her.

Perhaps it was just that he'd replaced Manny Rodriguez, a long-time partner in the business who had suffered a mild heart attack two months ago. In all fairness, Lori had repeatedly scolded herself for her attitude toward Rob. After all, it wasn't his fault that he wasn't as calm and experienced with horses as Manny. Nobody she'd ever met, including Wade, was as calm and experienced with horses as Manny.

But Rob still gave her the creeps.

"Dammit, I said whoa!" he shouted again.

Telling Brandon to stay with their charges, Lori hurried around the back end of the horse trailer. Lulu, a black mare who had quickly become one of Lori's favorites in Wade's herd, stood in the front entrance of the trailer, her eyes rolling in terror. Normally the calmest and most cooperative of horses, she was balking at the top of the ramp and trying to pull her head out of Rob's grasp. Small wonder. Viciously slapping the knotted end of the lead rope across Lulu's neck, Rob yanked on the halter and shouted at her.

"You stupid hayburner! Get going!"

Though she wanted to hit Rob over the head with that rope, Lori forced herself to walk forward with an easy, nonthreatening stride. She couldn't help Lulu if she frightened the poor little mare even more. Before she could get there, however, Zack McBride vaulted into the holding pen, stepped up onto the ramp, grabbed Rob by the back of his shirt and tossed him onto the ground with a flick of one hand. Rob landed on his rear on top of a fresh pile of horse dung.

"What the hell do you think you're doing?" Rob shouted.

Glaring down at the startled wrangler, Zack said, "We don't treat horses that way on the Flying M."

"That's not your horse."

"Does it look like I care?" Zack said. "If I see or even hear about you mistreating *any* animal on my land, I'll personally beat the livin' daylights out of you and throw your sorry butt off this place. Is that clear?"

"Yeah." Scrambling to his feet, Rob took quick, agitated swipes at his clothes. "It's clear."

"Good," Zack said. "Go cool off somewhere and let me settle this little gal down enough to unload her."

Rob opened his mouth, but a warning glance from Zack was enough to change his mind about arguing. His face crimson, he stomped past Lori, giving her the murderous glare he'd wanted—but hadn't quite dared—to give Zack. Lori had seen that kind of look in a man's eyes before, and it scared her spitless. And Zack…dear God, how violent was he? She might have stood there forever, frozen with fear, if his voice hadn't distracted her.

"There, there now, sweetheart," he crooned, offering Lulu his free hand to sniff. "The bad man is gone and nobody's gonna hurt you again."

Lulu jerked her head back as if she expected another blow. Zack continued crooning to her. Lori felt the oddest sensation from listening to that low, raspy voice. It was almost as if he were crooning those words to her as well as to the mare.

"Aw, darlin', I know you're scared, and you have every right to be," he said. "But it's okay, now. Zack's here. That guy was an idiot not to see what a fine little horse you are."

Lulu's ears rotated toward him and she lowered her head for a quick sniff.

"That's a good girl." Moving ever so slowly, Zack reached out for Lulu's shoulder. The mare's hide shivered and she danced away. He chuckled softly. "Well, aren't you a smart girl to be so cautious? Of course, you don't trust me yet. Why, we haven't even been properly introduced. Don't you worry, darlin'. I'd never force you to do anything you don't want to do."

Nostrils flaring, Lulu dipped her head and took a step closer to Zack. He wooed the mare with a patience few people had for their own children, much less for an animal. Lori watched in fascination while he waited for Lulu to trust him enough to allow him to touch her.

"Mom? Is everything okay?" Brandon called from the front bumper of the pickup she'd driven. Lori nodded and waved him away. He shrugged and walked back around the truck.

Unfortunately the sudden noise startled Lulu, who pulled away from Zack again, forcing him to start over. If he felt the slightest irritation at the interruption, he didn't show it. His voice remained serene, his touches slow and affectionate.

"That's my sweetheart," he said, smiling when Lulu allowed him to scratch around her ears. "Come on now, there's nothin' to be afraid of."

As if she understood his words and believed them, Lulu calmly walked down the ramp beside Zack. While he expertly ran his hands over her, checking for injuries, he lavished her with praise like a proud papa.

A lump formed in Lori's throat. She really wished she hadn't stood here and watched all of this. She couldn't afford any romantic involvements. She couldn't even afford to make friends with anyone. But...oh, triple damn.

After seeing Zack's gentleness with a frightened animal, it was going to be nearly impossible not to like him. A lot.

Zack McBride stole a glance at the woman standing outside the holding pen and wondered what she was thinking. Her face held little expression, but she studied every movement he made toward the little black mare with an intensity he didn't understand. From the moment he tossed that idiot off the ramp, it should have been clear to Ms. Jones that he had no intention of hurting the animal.

If anything, he probably ought to feel embarrassed at some of the sappy things she'd undoubtedly heard come out of his mouth. His family teased him all the time about being so dotty over his horses. Not that he cared about their teasing. They all had quirks of their own; at least his didn't hurt anyone.

He snuck another glance at Ms. Jones. Yup. She was still staring a hole through him. The quality of her stare didn't feel critical, exactly. There was a stillness about her that reminded him of a deer, pausing at the edge of the forest, nose raised to smell the wind. As if she would run at the first hint of danger.

He really didn't blame her. Ms. Jones had every right to act a little wary around him. Wherever she came from originally, she'd recently spent some time in Southern California. Any woman with half a brain would learn to be wary of strange men around L.A. Zack prided himself on being a fair judge of people, and she didn't strike him as a dummy.

Well, maybe she'd just never seen such a good-looking Wyoming cowboy before, he thought, firmly poking his tongue against the inside of his cheek. Oh, the folks around Sunshine Gap had always called him, his brothers and his male cousins "those good-lookin' McBride boys." And, false modesty aside, he'd have to say that women usually seemed to like his looks well enough; he'd never had any trouble getting dates back when he'd wanted them, anyway.

But Ms. Jones was hardly looking at him as if she planned to jump his bones. No, she was looking at him as if she didn't quite know what to make of him. Or maybe she just wasn't sure whether or not she should believe what she was seeing.

The mare lowered her head, practically begging for an ear scratch. "That's my sweetheart," he said, lovingly rubbing her velvety ears. "Come on, now, there's nothin' to be afraid of."

With no further hesitation, the horse followed him down into the holding pen, her hooves rattling the metal ramp with every step. When they reached the bottom, Zack patted her neck.

"Was that funny noise what spooked you, darlin'? Well, I don't blame you a bit for getting scared. You were a mighty brave girl to walk on that silly thing. But here you are, safe and sound, with all four feet on the ground again. Feels good, doesn't it?"

Zack ran his hands over the horse, checking for swelling joints or other obvious problems. Straightening, he looked over his shoulder at Ms. Jones.

"Mind if I take off her shipping boots?" he asked, indicating the padded wraps on the mare's legs.

Ms. Jones gave him a slight nod. "Go ahead. You won't get an argument from Lulu."

"Lulu?" Sputtering with laughter, Zack shot an appalled glance at the mare. "Oh, sweetheart, that's a terrible name for such a pretty little horse, isn't it?" Lulu rubbed her head against his arm and snorted as if in agreement.

Wonder of wonders, Ms. Jones actually smiled. If he'd thought she was attractive before—and he had—her smile did funny things to his insides. It made him want to see her smile again, maybe even try to make her laugh. He led Lulu over to the portable fence.

"You like that name?" he asked.

"Not really," Ms. Jones said, wrinkling her pert little nose with obvious distaste. She reached over the fence and held out a hand for the mare. Lulu snuffled in greeting. The woman smoothed Lulu's mane, affection in every stroke of her hand. "If she were mine, I would have called her something more exotic, like Kira or Jolie or perhaps…Ebony."

"Much better." Zack chuckled. "Lulu sounds like an old plow horse."

Ms. Jones lifted her shoulders in a what-can-I-say? sort of shrug. "Well, um, thank you for helping her."

"My pleasure." Zack's temper flared at the memory of the driver slapping poor Lulu with that rope. "I meant what I said to that kid, though. I'll personally toss him off this ranch if he ever pulls another stunt like that."

"I'll talk to Wade about it," she said, stepping back as if she suddenly felt nervous. "I assure you, he doesn't allow his horses to be abused."

Zack turned to look at the horses milling around in the pen. "I can tell that. He's got some fine stock here. He'd have to be a fool not to take good care of them."

"Were…were those your Arabians we passed on our way here from the big ranch house?" she asked.

"Yup," Zack said with a proud smile. "Those are my babies. Most of 'em are half or three-quarter Arab. They're beauties, aren't they?"

She smiled back at him. As smiles went it looked a little…hesitant, but it was sincere enough to light up her whole face. Zack's heart gave his rib cage a couple of hard whacks and his breath got hung up in his lungs. She wasn't really beautiful, especially not with her shoulder-length hair all bleached and her dark roots starting to show. He didn't know why any woman would do that just to be a blonde. In his opinion and experience, blondes were highly overrated.

Still, Ms. Jones was one striking woman. She had a sort of delicate air about her that made him feel big and strong and, well, yes…horny. Funny that should happen with her. She was long and lean, and had what his mom would have called a willowy figure. Not a bad package, really, but he'd

always been attracted to…curves before. Maybe he finally
was growing up. After an instant's consideration of that notion, he grinned to himself. Nah. Probably not.

It didn't matter anyway. She wasn't going to be here long
enough to be anything more than an acquaintance. Or maybe,
if he got real lucky, a…playmate.

"They certainly are," she said.

"Are what?" Zack said.

"Beauties. Your Arabians? We were talking about them?"

Feeling like a dope for going off on one of his mental
detours in front of this woman, Zack shook his head. "Oh,
yeah. Sorry. I was thinking about something else and lost
track of the conversation."

She uttered a soft laugh and waved away his apology.
"I've occasionally been known to do that myself. I'd better
check on Brandon. I'll come back here when I'm finished
with the others."

"You don't want my help?" Zack asked, splaying one
hand over his chest. "I'm hurt, Ms. Jones. Real hurt."

"They're not your responsibility," she said, ignoring his
lame attempt to flirt with her. "Brandon's probably almost
done. This bunch will be fine for a few minutes."

He was still formulating a response when Lulu abruptly
raised her head and turned both ears toward the road. Zack
glanced over to see what had captured the mare's attention.
Aw, hell. That was Gracie's pickup racing up the road, trail-
ing a rooster tail of dust. She only drove that way when there
was trouble. He unhooked Lulu's rope and stepped out of
the pen.

Grace drove up to him, shut off the engine and jumped to
the ground. "You've got to go to town, Zack. Warren
Fisher's really knocking 'em back at Cal's Place. Cal's gonna
keep him there as long as he can."

"All right, Gracie." Zack turned back to Ms. Jones. "Nice
meetin' you, ma'am. See you later."

Lori nodded, then watched, mystified while Zack jogged
over to a battered, four-wheel-drive vehicle, climbed inside

and roared out of the driveway. She looked at Gracie, wondering who she was and what her relationship to Zack was. On closer inspection, Lori decided she must be Zack's sister. Probably in her late twenties, Grace had the same dark eyes, the same raven-black hair. The shape of her face was even similar to Zack's.

"Hi," the woman said, offering a hand to Lori. "I'm Zack's cousin, Grace Kramer. You must be one of the wranglers."

Lori introduced herself and then Brandon, who had poked his head out again to see what was going on. Grace grinned and waved at him before turning back to Lori.

"What is he, about ten or so?"

"That's right," Lori said. "He was ten in April."

"I've got two boys," Grace said. "They're ten and twelve, and they'd love to have a pal. Bring him up to the house when you get a chance."

Warming to Grace's friendly, open manner, Lori nodded and thanked her for the invitation. Then she inclined her head toward the road where Zack had disappeared from sight. "Do you mind if I ask what that was all about?"

Grace laughed and shook her head. "Oh, Zack does a lot of things to support his horse habit. He's a paramedic, drives the ambulance and substitutes for the school-bus drivers when they're sick or out of town. He's also our only cop. Some folks call him the town clown, but he's really a deputy of the Park County Sheriff's Office in Cody. He just had to go deal with a drunk who likes to fight."

Feeling as if she'd been punched, Lori looked away, praying Grace wouldn't notice her distress. What had she done to deserve this? She couldn't think of a thing she was truly ashamed of, but maybe in a past life she'd been a heinous criminal.

It was the only explanation that made any sense. This couldn't be a coincidence. Nobody had *this* much bad luck, did they? If only she knew. At the moment, she didn't think she knew anything.

"Well, I suppose I'd better get home," Grace said. "It was nice meeting you, Lori."

Lori forced a smile. "Thanks. I enjoyed meeting you, too."

Grace climbed back into her pickup and stuck her head out of the driver's-side window. "Be sure to let one of us know if you need anything. I don't have much female company, so feel free to stop in for coffee whenever you want. The pot's always on."

Knowing she'd never be able to do any such thing now, Lori nodded, then watched Grace drive away, returning the jaunty wave Grace gave her. The instant she was sure the other woman could no longer see her, Lori rushed toward her own rig. Should she pack up Brandon and leave right now? Or wait a few days? What would arouse the least amount of suspicion?

She'd thought this job would be safe. She finally was doing what she loved, she'd finally met a man she might be able to like and he had to be a cop? What the hell was wrong with her karma?

Chapter Two

It took Zack over two hours to get Warren Fisher settled down and sobered up enough to risk taking him home. He spent half an hour at Warren's house, talking to him about getting back into treatment for alcoholism. After yet another half hour of making his rounds in Sunshine Gap as he always did whenever he made a trip into town, he drove back to the Flying M.

Passing a long line of silver trailers, he shook his head at the battle of emotions that erupted inside him every time he saw more of the movie company's equipment headed for the ranch. On one hand, the script his cousin Marsh had sold was based on their great-grandparents' romance and courtship, which was why *Against the Wind* would be filmed at the Flying M. Marsh had worked hard to become a Hollywood screenwriter, and Zack was proud of and happy for his cousin's success. And the production undoubtedly would bring plenty of money into Sunshine Gap.

On the other hand, Zack had serious doubts about the wisdom of bringing so many outsiders into this isolated, rural area. Since he'd gone through the police academy, he knew the law, the procedures and the equipment used to enforce it. But as the only law enforcement officer in Sunshine Gap, he really wasn't prepared to handle crimes more serious than disorderly drunks, speeders and the occasional burglary. They didn't get many serious crimes here, of course. But God only knew what kinds of problems those wacky Californians might bring along with them.

He also disliked having his daily routine on the ranch disrupted. At the rate the production company was hauling stuff in, they'd have a small city set up within the boundaries of the Flying M before the end of May, which was only a week off now. Most of the cast hadn't even arrived yet, and the traffic was already getting bad by Wyoming standards.

But, on the other hand, if they stayed on schedule, the whole mess would be gone by the end of July. In the greater scheme of things, two months didn't seem like a very long time to put up with a little inconvenience. Besides, he'd already met some interesting folks, and he'd probably meet a lot more before the filming was finished.

Take Ms. Jones and her son Brandon, for instance. There was a pair he'd like to know better. He'd always enjoyed kids and wished his ex-wife had been willing to have more than one. Melissa's birth had been rough on Billie, though, and he could hardly blame her for refusing to risk another childbirth experience like the first. He blamed Billie for plenty of other things, but not for that.

Damn, but it still hurt too much to think about his failed marriage or how much he missed Melissa, so he wasn't going to do it. Not right now, anyway. He'd think about Ms. Jones instead.

His fascination with her probably was just a hormone thing. According to his sister, Alex, he'd neglected his social life something awful lately. Zack figured that was true enough. To his way of thinking, there wasn't much point in pursuing an active social life in Sunshine Gap.

He knew every unattached woman even halfway close to his age in the county, and not one of them really revved his engine. At thirty-eight, he'd finished planting any so-called wild oats he'd ever owned. He'd wanted a home and family of his own, but since he'd messed that up big time, he'd decided to stick with his horses for companionship.

Dealing with horses was less boring, less painful and less expensive than dating women he didn't want to encourage in the first place. He'd had one disastrous marriage, and he was never going to try that again. No way. No how.

So, maybe Ms. Jones's appeal came from knowing she'd be gone after July. Better yet, he didn't know her whole dang family or her entire life story, and she didn't know him well enough to anticipate every single thing he was going to say. Which made her sort of a…novelty. Hell, that sounded shallow. And, it *was* shallow. So why didn't he just stay away from her? Well, he really didn't want to, and it sure would be nice to talk to a woman who really liked horses instead of hating them the way Billie had.

And there was always the boy to consider. Zack had seen the hunger for a man's attention in Brandon's eyes, and he seemed like a pretty nice kid. Where was Brandon's dad? Dead? Or was he one of those idiots who walked away from his own kid without so much as a backward glance?

If that were the case, it would be ironic, Zack thought, pulling into his drive. Here he was, wishing like hell he could be more of a father to Melissa, while his ex-wife thwarted him at every turn. And here Brandon was, desperately wanting a father in his life, and the jerk couldn't be bothered to face up to his responsibilities. Sometimes life didn't make any sense at all.

Zack parked beside the three-bedroom, modular home he'd bought two years ago. He caught a whiff of grilling meat coming from the direction of his guests' horse trailers. The automatic growling of his stomach told him it was long past suppertime. He decided to mosey on over there and see if the wranglers had any leftovers they wanted to get rid of.

He found them gathered around a small, portable picnic table and a grill set up near the horse trailer Ms. Jones had driven. Wade Kirby smiled when he spotted Zack and greeted him with an outstretched hand. Tipping his head to one side, Wade indicated the pasture where his horses now grazed.

"I can't thank you enough for stepping in to help Lulu." He enthusiastically pumped Zack's hand. "There's something I want to discuss with you. Have you got a minute?"

Zack shrugged. "Sure." His stomach growled again, and he said hopefully, "You got any extra burgers?"

Wade chuckled. "Of course. Come on over to the table." He turned and called to Ms. Jones, who stood beside the grill. "Hey, Lori, throw on a couple more for Zack, will you?"

She gave Wade a thumbs-up sign, but barely glanced in Zack's direction. Rob Grant got up and left when Zack took one of the folding lawn chairs Wade offered him, which didn't bother Zack a bit. Under the circumstances, he would have been surprised if Grant hadn't left.

Zack *was* a little bothered that Ms. Jones didn't join them, however. In fact, after handing him a plate of food without so much as a greeting, she carried her own plate about as far away as she could get and still keep an eye on the grill, sat on a stump and began to eat. Instead of hanging out with the men the way Zack's nephews would have done, Brandon chose to eat with his mother. No crime in that, of course. It just seemed a little…unusual to Zack.

When he'd put enough food in his belly to stop the hunger pangs, Zack turned to Kirby. "What did you want to talk about?"

Wade's mouth compressed into a grim line. "I'm sending Rob back to California. I took him on when my partner got sick, but if I can't trust him to treat the horses right, I don't want him on my payroll. That'll leave us shorthanded until the rest of my crew arrives. I wondered if you'd be interested in some work while we're here."

"I wouldn't mind the work," Zack said after giving the idea a moment's thought. "But I have other obligations that could get in the way. If I get called to handle a problem in town or drive the ambulance to Cody, I'd have to go.''

Wade frowned. ''How often does that happen?''

''More often than you might think,'' Zack said. ''My cousin Grace might be willing to fill in for me if she's free. And her boy Riley knows his way around horses. He's twelve and big for his age, and he can be pretty good help when he wants to be. He's not done with school just yet, but he will be by the end of next week. June third's the last day.''

''Maybe we could try that and see how it works out,'' Wade said with a thoughtful frown. However, after a moment, he shook his head. ''Actually, I have some doubts about this, Zack. I'm probably going to need someone more full-time and I'm not sure a boy could really handle the job. Brandon helps Lori, but some of these horses are temperamental. I wouldn't want a kid to be more than a helper.''

Zack nodded in understanding. ''I hear ya. Let me give it some thought. I can probably come up with a few local folks for you to check out. We've got lots of breeders in the area.''

''You know anyone who raises Appaloosas?'' Wade said. ''I've been looking for a mare.''

''Sure. There's a gal down in Pinedale who's built one hell of a good reputation in the past five years. In fact, she might even be interested in workin' for you for a few weeks. Name's Becky Dawson. No wait, I keep forgettin' she got married.'' Zack tapped his right temple, searching his memory for Becky's last name. ''Her husband's a doctor...Sinclair. Yeah, that's it. Becky Sinclair. She knows horses like you wouldn't believe.''

''That's how Lori is,'' Wade said. ''She's the best trainer I've ever had.''

Zack shot a glance in Lori's direction, then focused in on Wade again. ''Where's she from?''

''Originally?'' Wade shook his head. ''I don't know. Sometimes I hear a trace of a Southern accent in her voice, but she doesn't talk about her past at all.''

''Didn't she have any references when you hired her?''

"Nothing to do with horses," Wade said. "She'd been waiting tables in a restaurant in Reno, but the first time she stepped into a pen it was obvious she knew what she was doing."

"Didn't you ask her where she learned about 'em?"

Wade shook his head again, more vigorously this time. "As long as she does her job—which she does very well— the rest of it's none of my business."

"Know if she's married?" Zack said.

"Not for sure, but I doubt it. She's been working for us for five months and I've never heard her or Brandon talk about a Mr. Jones. If there *is* one, he keeps a real low profile."

That news made Zack unaccountably happy. He still had unanswered questions regarding Ms. Jones, but at the moment, her marital status seemed the most important one. Zack McBride did not mess with married women, period.

If Ms. Jones was indeed single, the rest of his questions could wait. Besides, it'd be more fun to find those answers himself by spending time with her and Brandon. Zack carried his plate to the little picnic table where Lori and Brandon were packing the leftover food into a big cooler.

"That was a fine meal, ma'am," Zack said. "Thanks for feedin' me."

She shot him a sideways glance. "You're welcome, Mr. McBride."

"Mr. McBride?" Zack shoved his paper plate into the garbage bag sitting beside the table. "We've got so many Mr. McBrides around here, you'll drive everybody nuts if you call me that. Do us all a favor and call me Zack."

Brandon looked up at him. "How many are there?"

"Seven if you count my cousin Grace's two boys. Nine if you count my dad and my uncle, but they're on a long trip, so you won't be meeting them."

Brandon's eyes grew round. "Wow, that's a lot."

"Well, there's really two families involved." Zack grinned at the boy. "See, my dad and his brother married twin sisters,

and they raised all seven of us kids together here at the Flying
M. We all act like brothers and sisters, but technically, some
of us are what you'd call double first cousins.''

"I've never heard of that,'' Brandon said.

Ms. Jones banged the lid of the cooler shut and gave her
son a narrow-eyed stare when he looked up at her. Some
silent communication passed between them. Brandon stiffened and backed a step away from Zack. The boy's sudden
withdrawal roused Zack's curiosity and rankled his temper.
What the hell was that all about? Couldn't the kid even talk
to anyone?

"I, uh, I've gotta go and do my…chores,'' Brandon said.

Ms. Jones wiped her fingers on the sides of her jeans and
called after him. "I'll be there in a minute, Brandon. Pack
anything you'll want for the night. The trailers should be set
up over at the other house by now.''

Brandon nodded and left. Zack watched the kid disappear
in the direction of the pickup, then looked back at Ms. Jones.
He caught a flash of her hair swirling out around her shoulders, as if she'd quickly turned her head away so he wouldn't
see that she'd been watching him. Right. Like he hadn't felt
her gaze drilling a spot on his left shoulder blade, anyhow.
Something felt a little off here.

She picked up the cooler. Ignoring her protests, Zack took
it from her and carried it to the back of the pickup. When he
lifted it over the side and set it down again, she forced a
word of thanks from between clenched teeth.

"If I thought you meant that, I'd say you're welcome,''
Zack said. "I didn't mean to step on your toes or break any
feminist rules, you know. That thing just looked too heavy
for you to carry.''

"I'm stronger than I look,'' she said, her tone as frosty as
February. "And I'm intelligent enough to ask for help when
I need it.''

"Fair enough. But you know, I'm startin' to wonder if
there's some reason you don't like me very much.''

She blinked, obviously taken aback by his bluntness, then

raised her chin and put even more frost into her voice. "I don't know what you're talking about."

"Sure, you do. You've shushed Brandon around me twice now. I get the impression you'd rather have him stay away from me. I'm thinkin' maybe there's a reason for that. Was there something I said or did that offended you?"

"No." She cast her gaze toward the ground and folded her arms across her chest. "I simply don't want my son talking to strangers."

"That's generally a good policy for kids," Zack said, though he doubted she'd answered him with complete honesty. He tipped his hat back and shoved his hands into his front jeans pockets. "But we were just making conversation and you were right there to protect him. It wasn't like I was tryin' to lure him away."

"I didn't say that you had."

Zack eyed her carefully, noting that she was holding herself stiffer than week-old roadkill. "No, it was more like you were afraid of something Brandon might say."

"Don't let your imagination run wild," she said with a laugh. "Occasionally, I'm a bit...overly protective of Brandon. It's all part of trying to be a good mother."

Hearing more than a hint of strain in her laugh, Zack decided to back off. "I understand, and I'd never criticize anyone for trying to protect their kids. I guess I'm just so used to people thinking I'm one of the good guys, it sort of shocked me to be treated otherwise."

"Mr. McBride—"

He flashed her a hard smile and interrupted. "Zack. Please, call me Zack."

She paused, then slowly nodded. "All right,...Zack. I'm sorry if I've offended you."

"No harm done." He hesitated just long enough to make her raise her eyebrows in query. "Would you mind if I called you something a little less formal than ma'am or Ms. Jones?"

She inclined her head in acknowledgment. Her smile was

a little tight, but he thought it looked sincere enough. "Certainly. Call me Lori."

"Lori," he said, testing the sound of it. "That's a real pretty name...Lori."

"Thank you." Her cheeks turned a delightful shade of pink and she shifted uneasily. "Well, I need to get Brandon settled for the night. It's been a long day."

Zack stepped back and tipped his hat to her. "Okay. I'll see you tomorrow then."

He turned and headed for his barn. Mysteries drove him crazy until he solved them, and he smelled a mystery surrounding Lori Jones and her boy. Sooner or later he'd figure out why she was so damn skittish. In the meantime, he still had his own chores to do, and he'd best be getting on with them. His babies sulked if he was late.

Lori watched Zack McBride walk away, feeling a too-familiar, gnawing sense of worry invading the pit of her stomach. She wished she could spend enough time around the actors to learn how to project whatever emotions she chose. Had she hidden her fear well enough? It was impossible to be certain.

Biting her lower lip, she went back to work. By the time she and Brandon had organized their trailer, she was exhausted and a headache thumped out a heavy rock-and-roll beat at her temples. When she tucked Brandon into bed, he looked up at her, his forehead creased with a frown.

"I'm sorry, Mom. I didn't mean to blab my mouth around Mr. McBride."

She smoothed a rebellious shock of hair out of his eyes. "It's all right, honey. You do your best, and that's good enough."

"He seems like a really nice man," Brandon said quietly.

"I'm sure he is," Lori agreed with a rueful smile. "Everyone we've met here seems nice. But we still have to be careful. You know how important it is."

Brandon swallowed, then nodded. "I know. I don't ever

want him to find us again. Do you really think he's still...alive?''

''Whether he is or not, we'll both be in trouble if we're caught. We're not going to let that happen, though. Are we?''

''No way,'' he said with a laugh. ''We're too smart, too sneaky and too cool for that.''

She held up a hand. He slapped her palm, completing the confidence-building ritual they'd created. Though it might seem silly to some people, Lori intended to continue the ritual for as long as she could. It had helped them get this far, hadn't it?

She kissed his forehead, then climbed to her feet and turned out the light above his head. ''That's right, partner. Get some sleep now. We'll have a lot to do tomorrow.''

''Night, Mom.''

She pulled the curtain across his bunk, walked to the small window above the sink in the kitchenette and gazed out at the darkness. The main ranch house sat on the other side of the barnyard, lights showing in most of the windows. Though well-maintained, it was big and old, and would never win any awards for architecture. But there was something about it that made her ache to go inside.

There was an aura of warmth and welcome surrounding the place, a solid sense of permanence radiating from it. It looked like a house Norman Rockwell might have painted for one of his *Saturday Evening Post* covers, an all-American house that represented safety, security, home. God, even though the initial terror had worn off, it had been a long, long time since she'd felt safe.

Would she ever feel truly safe again? Would Brandon?

Those questions reverberated through her mind over and over during the night, leaving her nearly as exhausted when she awoke the next morning as when she'd finally crawled into her own bunk. She was used to that, however, and rolled out of bed at the first sign of dawn. Staying busy was the best cure she'd ever found for the heebie-jeebies.

At lunchtime, she decided she'd chosen the right job to

keep herself busy. There was enough work here for three adult trainers. Since Wade had left to drive Rob to the airport in Cody, she had no time to worry about anything but the horses.

She didn't know what she would have done without Brandon's help. He loved the horses as much as she did, but she still felt guilty when she saw him heave a deep sigh and swipe the back of one hand across his sweaty forehead. A little boy shouldn't have to work so hard. In fact, she was sure they'd broken more than one child labor law today.

Massaging the small of her back with both hands, she inclined her head toward the pickup. "Break time, Brandon. Would you like a soda and a snack?"

"Yes, ma'am."

He fell into step beside her, and his quiet demeanor again struck her as being far too adult for a boy his age. Ten-year-old boys were supposed to be loud, obnoxious and well…goofy. Brandon barely knew how to play anymore.

It wouldn't do any good for her to worry about it, of course. After all, what could she actually do to change their circumstances? Not one blessed thing. Such helplessness enraged her, frustrated her, saddened her. But all she could do was go on taking one day at a time, sheltering Brandon from the worst bumps and bruises life had to offer as best she could.

When they reached the pickup, she flipped open the cooler, pulled out a can of Brandon's favorite soft drink and one of her own. He scrambled into the cab and grabbed the sack of fruit and granola bars she'd brought along, and together they sat in the shade provided by a large apple tree growing beside the pasture fence. A moment later, Zack McBride's dusty Blazer roared up the drive.

Lori automatically reached up to check her hair, realized what she was doing and forced her hand back to her side. After bathing and grooming horses all day, she undoubtedly looked horrible, but Zack's opinion of her hair or any other particle of her appearance didn't matter. It couldn't matter.

And yet, when he stepped out of his vehicle and looked straight at her, she felt a jolt of awareness she hadn't felt in years. It was as if she'd simply been going through the motions of living, but now that he was here, her real life could begin. Talk about having a wild imagination, she grimly told herself. If the man knew the truth about her....

While he ambled around the vehicle, the passenger door opened, and two smaller and younger versions of Zack jumped from the high seat to the ground. Lori heard Brandon inhale a soft gasp. He turned to her, his eyes full of questions for which she had no answers.

"Hi," Zack called, approaching them with a grin, the two boys hustling to keep up with his longer legs. "These are my cousin Grace's boys. They've been dying to meet Brandon ever since she told them there was another kid on the place."

Brandon and Lori scrambled to their feet. Three sets of dark eyes gazed at her from three handsome McBride faces. She surreptitiously brushed dirt and grass from her bottom.

"Afternoon, ma'am," the smaller boy said. His smile produced an adorable pair of dimples. "I'm Steven Kramer."

The bigger boy said, "I'm Riley. We'll show you around the ranch if you want to come with us for a while. Uncle Zack'll give us a ride over to the main barn and we'll pick up our horses. You ride, don't you?"

Brandon nodded. For an instant, he looked up at her, eyes wide with excitement and a silent plea to let him be one of the guys for a change. Then, as if that look had never happened, he straightened his thin shoulders and turned back to face the boys. "Thanks, but I need to help my mom right now."

Though she could have used his help and she would worry the entire time he was out of her sight, Lori couldn't stand for Brandon to miss this opportunity. She grasped his left arm and gave it a gentle squeeze. "You've done enough for today. I can handle the rest of this if you want to go with them."

"Really?" Brandon said, his voice husky as if he couldn't believe his good fortune.

Lori nodded. "I'll meet you back at the trailer at six-thirty."

"All *right,*" Steven said, giving his brother a high-five.

Both Kramer boys politely nodded to Lori and said, "Nice meetin' you, ma'am," before turning away and heading toward Zack's Blazer. When Brandon still hesitated, Steven called over his shoulder, "Well, come on, dude. See ya later, ma'am."

Lori waved an acknowledgment with one hand and nudged her son into motion with the other. "Mind your manners, Brandon. And be very careful."

"I will." He took off for the Blazer as if he feared she might suddenly change her mind.

Zack gave her one of his long, scrutinizing looks. "Wouldn't you like to come along?"

Telling herself she had to resist in spite of the invitation in his dark eyes, she warily gazed at him, forcing what she hoped was an impassive expression onto her face. "No, thank you. I have work to do."

"Anything I can help with?" He propped one hand on his hip and used the other to tip back the brim of his hat.

"No, thank you," she said again, hoping he would simply accept her refusal. She really hated confrontations.

"You sure?" He leaned closer to her, searching her face in a way that suggested he hoped to find a weakness. "Once I drop the boys off, I'd be glad to come back and give you a hand."

Good heavens, the man could say more with those dark eyes of his than most people could say in a whole paragraph of words. She could feel their power, coaxing, flirting, practically seducing her. Shutting her own eyes for a moment, she inhaled a fortifying a breath. "No, thank you. As I told Brandon, I can handle it."

He shot her a perplexed frown. "It's no trouble—"

"Mr. McBride," she interrupted, allowing her exasperation to vibrate in her voice, "is it the *N* or the *O* you don't understand?"

The wretched man laughed. "The name's Zack, and I get the concept of the word *no* fine and dandy. I just don't hear it very often."

I'll bet you don't. Especially from women. Sighing, Lori decided she would have to be brutally direct with Zack. Otherwise, he would continually come back, expecting that eventually, she would change her mind.

"Listen, I don't mean to be rude," she said. "But I'll only be here a few weeks and I have a young, impressionable son to raise. Flattered as I am by your interest, I hope you can understand why I'd prefer to avoid any involvements with men."

"I guess when you put it that way, I can see how you might make a decision like that." One of the boys honked the Blazer's horn. Indicating with a wave that he'd heard, Zack kept his gaze trained on Lori. And though his voice sounded perfectly serious, his darn gorgeous eyes glinted with wicked amusement. "But I didn't ask you to have an affair with me, darlin'. I only asked if you could use some help with your horses."

While Lori was still sputtering, he walked back to his vehicle and drove away. Of all the nerve. He had *too* been flirting with her. She knew when a man was flirting with her, for heaven's sake. And he *had* been. Maybe he hadn't said it in so many words, but a woman would have to be facing the opposite direction to miss those come-and-get-me eyes of his.

She shook her head in outrage, then suddenly started to laugh. Well, she supposed she *had* been a bit hasty in rejecting Zack's advances because her own attraction to him scared her witless. And, maybe she'd overreacted just a *little* because he was a cop. So, perhaps she'd deserved that jab to her ego. Should she apologize to him? Good grief, no. That would only make the whole thing worse.

Whenever she thought about it, she chuckled and winced

at the same time. The girlish, fluttery feelings reminded her of high school. Or the first time she'd met Hugh.

That last thought brought her up short and ended any silly romantic fantasies she might have entertained about any man alive. She'd been absolutely right to warn Zack off. If she thought it was necessary, she would do it again without a second's hesitation. She had too much at stake to do otherwise.

But when Brandon came back to the trailer for dinner, raving that the Flying M was the coolest place in the whole world, that all of the McBrides were super nice and that he wished they could stay here forever, Lori felt a lot of empathy for him. The Flying M really seemed to be a wonderful place. If only her circumstances were normal, she would flirt right back with Zack McBride and enjoy every moment of it.

Unfortunately the two most futile words in the English language had to be *if only*.

Chapter Three

In response to a call for help from his brother Jake, Zack walked into the main house at ten o'clock the next morning, swiped one of Grace's fresh cinnamon rolls from the kitchen and stuffed a huge bite into his mouth on his way through the house to Jake's office. As always, the warm sugar and cinnamon melted on his tongue with a pleasure so intense it was darn near sexual. If Grace ever decided to open a bakery, Zack intended to be first in line to invest in it.

Pausing at the open office door, he saw Jake shove one hand through his hair as if he might be thinking about tearing out a few chunks and heard him mutter a string of cuss words that would have made their mother run for a bar of soap. Zack rapped his knuckles on the casing. Jake looked up from a fat stack of papers on his desk, then waved Zack inside. Noting his brother's gaze zeroing in on the rest of the cinnamon roll, Zack crammed the whole thing into his mouth and gave the most taunting smile he could manage.

With his cheeks packed tight, he probably looked like a

crazed chipmunk, but he wasn't about to share a crumb of
his pilfered treat. According to the sibling rule book, it was
his job to harass Jake, and the empty plate and crumpled
napkin beside the phone provided all the evidence he needed
to know that Jake had already swiped one for himself.

"You are one gross and disgusting pig," Jake said.

Zack would have laughed at his brother's disgruntled expression, but with his mouth so full, he was afraid he might
choke. Instead, he shrugged one shoulder, parked his behind
on a corner of the desk and raised his eyebrows at Jake. Jake
leaned back in his leather swivel chair and laced his fingers
together on top of his belt buckle.

"Why did I call you?" Jake asked.

Chewing vigorously, Zack nodded.

"I need you to clean out the ditches in the south pasture."

Zack groaned and shook his head. Cleaning out irrigation
ditches was boring, filthy, miserable work, especially in the
spring. Besides, he already had plans to take another shot at
getting acquainted with Lori Jones. He swallowed the re-
mains of the roll in one hard gulp.

"No way. I've got other things to do today. The ditches'll
keep and it's Dillon's job, anyway."

"Dillon's got his hands full," Jake said.

"Oh, right. Poor cousin Dillon is just workin' his butt
off." Zack snorted. "Pardon me, but traipsin' around with a
gorgeous actress doesn't strike me as any big hardship."

"Come on, Zack, be fair. Dillon feels damn uncomfortable
bein' around her with his face so scarred up. And he's not
just traipsing around with Blair. He's got to teach her how
to do all kinds of stuff before they start filming, and we
promised we'd fill in for him with the ranch chores."

"I didn't promise anything," Zack said. "You and Marsh
did. So you and Marsh go out there and clean those damn
ditches. I'm not doin' it."

Jake inhaled a deep breath, then blew it out, leaned forward and started thumping his index finger on the desktop.
"Marsh won't be in until afternoon, and I'm tied up here

coordinating this big fat mess that's getting bigger and fatter with every truck that pulls in the driveway. This ranch is yours too, little brother, and you stand to profit from this movie as much as the rest of us. Everybody else is busy up to their necks right now, and I damn well need your help."

Zack lunged to his feet and pivoted to face Jake. He'd learned early on in life that the only way to deal with his bullheaded, bossy brother was to meet him head-on. Even that didn't always help, but it was his best hope. "Well, what's the big rush? It's not even June. We don't have to start irrigatin' just yet, do we?"

"No, we don't have to irrigate just yet," Jake replied, his tone patiently condescending. "But the longer we wait, the more chance we have of running into problems with these production folks. They're building infrastructure right now. If we wait until they're all done, we may not be able to get to those ditches without fouling up their power lines and equipment. For all I know, they may choose that area to film part of the movie, and then they won't want us to do anything that might change the way the background looks."

Zack knew he'd already lost this argument, but he grumbled anyway. "Aw, hell, Jake. It'll take forever."

"Yeah, tell me all about it," Jake grumbled back. "I'm just trying to keep the big picture in mind. These folks will be gone by the end of July, but we're still going to need hay next winter. If we don't irrigate this summer, we won't have any."

"Oh, all right. I'll do it. But why don't you make out a list of the stuff that needs to get done, and I'll work 'em into my schedule."

Jake grinned. "Or delegate it to one of the others?"

"If they're slow and I'm lucky," Zack said with a laugh.

"Thanks, I knew I could count on you." Jake leaned back in his chair again. "So what else did you have planned for today?"

"Nothin' that big." Zack sidled toward the doorway. The last thing he wanted was for Jake to get a whiff of his attraction to Lori Jones. Not that he feared competition; Jake hadn't seriously looked at a woman since Ellen had died. No, it was the relentless sibling teasing Zack wanted to avoid. "Just thought I'd hang out with the wranglers for a while and see if I could learn anything."

Jake's gaze focused intently on Zack's face, which suddenly felt ten degrees hotter. Thank God for his beard.

"Uh-huh," Jake said. "There's something about horses you don't already know?"

"Well, ya just never know," Zack said, willing his guilty flush away. "Can't hurt to try, can it?"

"Probably not. But which wrangler were you hoping to hang out with, Zackie? That pretty little lady?"

Oh, damn. Jake could sniff out a potentially embarrassing secret with his nose pinched shut. Zack struggled to slap on a neutral expression. If Jake succeeded in riling him, there'd be no end to the razzing. "You got a problem with that?"

Jake chuckled and shook his head. "Hell, no. She seems nice enough. Her boy is too. He was over here for a while yesterday."

"Yeah, he's a great kid, but he's awful damn quiet," Zack said. "Did you notice that?"

"Now that you mention it, I guess he is," Jake agreed. "But he's got better manners than Riley and Steven. Not that *that* would take much." Frowning, Jake fell silent for a moment. "Well, maybe *quiet* isn't really the right word. It's more like he's...watchful or maybe the word I'm looking for is *wary.*"

Though his cop's radar made the hair on the back of his neck tingle, Zack shrugged. "These days a kid should be a little wary of strangers, Jake. Especially one who lives around a big city like L.A."

"I suppose you're right," Jake said, without much conviction in his voice. "Maybe he's just shy around adults."

"Yeah, that's probably it," Zack said, though he really didn't believe it, either. "Well, if I'm gonna clean those ditches, I'd best get started."

Zack left then, barely hearing Jake call, "Later, Bro," after him. As much as he and Jake enjoyed picking at each other, Zack considered Jake to be his best friend, as well as the most intelligent and observant guy he'd ever known. Knowing that Jake had sensed something a little "off" with Brandon strongly reinforced Zack's own impression of the boy and his mother. They were nice people, but they were more wary than the situation called for.

Hell, they were more than just wary. They were *afraid*. Sooner or later, he intended to find out why.

Brandon eyed the backpack in Lori's hands with obvious distaste. "Aw, Mom, I don't want to do that today."

Lori ignored his whining, opened the bag and set his books and papers out on the picnic table. "You need to do it anyway. I know you'd rather go to a real school, but lots of kids are homeschooled now. There's no need for you to fall behind your grade level."

Brandon rolled his eyes, reminding her that he'd heard that argument too many times.

"Can I go riding with Riley and Steven again if I'm done when they get home from school?"

"Oh, Brandon, I don't think that's wise."

"I don't care if it's wise. They're really neat guys, Mom. I had *fun* yesterday."

"I know you did, sweetie, but—"

"Don't call me that!" Glaring, he crossed his arms over his chest and stuck out his chin. "I'm not a little kid anymore. I want to have some friends, dammit."

Lori counted to fifteen, then quietly said, "I understand all of that, but you may *not* curse at me."

Brandon dropped his hands to his sides and curled his fingers into fists. "Well, maybe I *feel* like cursing."

He looked so much like Hugh in that moment, Lori's breath caught in her chest and she had to fight an instinctive urge to back away from him. It was ridiculous. Of course it was ridiculous. Brandon was smaller and weaker than she was, and he would never hurt her. She simply needed more time to get over the trauma Hugh had inflicted.

"Stop it, Brandon," she said. "Fighting with me won't change anything. Now please, sit down and do your schoolwork."

"Can I go riding?"

Desperately wanting to give him something to look forward to, Lori hesitated a moment before her good sense returned. Sadly, she shook her head. "No. You may not go riding, and you know why. We can't afford to let down our guard."

He opened his mouth as if he would protest, then clamped his lips together and ducked his head. His narrow shoulders slumped in defeat and Lori heard him gulp. Her heart ached, but she didn't know what else she could do for him. She could only hope and pray that someday they would feel safe enough to live like other people.

Until that day arrived, however, she would do whatever she had to do to protect him. Even if he ended up hating her. Judging by the ferocious scowl he gave her before settling down with his books, that was a distinct possibility.

The thought ripped open a fresh wound in her heart. Had it been a physical wound rather than an emotional one, she undoubtedly would have bled to death. Choking back a sob, she went back to work, feeling drained and haunted by a past that simply would not go away.

The horses greeted her with playful nips and whinnies, touching her battered soul with the balm of their acceptance and affection. Her relationship with the big animals always had been wonderfully uncomplicated; she loved and took care of them, and they loved her back and allowed her to ride them. She wished humans could be half as easygoing and predictable.

Now that their equine stars had been checked for injuries and exercised after their long trip, Wade had asked Lori to spend the afternoon running the horses through their individual tricks. She brought the first small group into the corral.

With the appropriate hand signals, Lulu counted and did simple arithmetic problems with her hoof. Blackie reared up onto his hind legs on command and pawed the air with his front hooves, then bowed low. Socks pranced and swished her golden, high-flying tail like a streetwalker.

This was the work Lori truly loved. It was easy to be patient when her charges willingly gave their best effort in return for soft praise, gentle pats and an occasional chunk of carrot or apple. Time passed so quickly and pleasantly, she completely lost track of it. She lined up Blackie, Rebel and Barney and signaled them to rear one at a time like a troop of equine Rockettes.

"Wow. Wouldja get a load of that?"

The sound of Riley Kramer's voice startled her from her reverie. She glanced over her right shoulder and spotted him hanging over the top fence rail with Steven on one side of him and Brandon on the other. Good grief, she hadn't even heard the Kramer boys arrive.

"Yeah," Steven agreed, his eyes wide with amazement. "Outside of that circus Mom took us to in Billings, I've never seen anything like that before."

Brandon puffed out his chest. "My mom's the best trainer in the business. She can get any horse to do anything she wants."

While she enjoyed being a source of pride for her son, Lori suspected his smug tone would be perceived by the Kramer boys as some sort of male challenge.

"Oh, huh," Steven said, proving her more right than she really wanted to be. "Maybe she can get these *movie* horses to do tricks, but I bet she can't do it with Uncle Zack's."

"Yeah," Riley agreed. "He doesn't raise wussy horses."

"Wussy?" Brandon yelped. "These aren't wussy horses. They're really smart, but they're as tough as any of *yours*. Some of them can even fall down from a gallop. On cue."

"Big deal," Riley said. "Bet they can't cut off a runaway steer or face down a riled-up cow."

"Can too," Brandon said.

"Cannot." Steven waved one arm toward the pasture to the west. "And I'll bet your mom couldn't even catch ol' Satan, much less ride him."

"Yeah," Riley said. "Nobody can ride him. Not even Uncle Dillon, and he used to be a rodeo bronc rider."

"My mom can," Brandon insisted. "She can ride any horse alive."

"Not Satan," Steven insisted. "He's such a renegade, Uncle Zack might even have to put him down."

Sighing, Lori walked toward the fence. Males of the human species would always jockey for position in their weird world of hierarchies, and she'd better intervene before this turned into a full-fledged argument. With a little luck she could distract them with food and send the Kramer boys home.

"Hi there," she said, smiling when all three of the boys whipped their heads around to face her. "Is anyone besides me ready for a snack?"

Riley straightened up and stepped back from the fence. "No, thank you, ma'am. We had one at home before we came over here."

Steven elbowed him in the ribs and beamed a hopeful smile at Lori. "But then, we could always eat again. What've you got?"

"Juice, granola bars and apples," Lori said. "Interested?"

"Yeah," Steven said. "Mom just had some dumb old cinnamon rolls."

The boys followed her to the pickup and helped her lift out the cooler, then settled in at the picnic table to munch their treats. Lori tried to blend into the scenery as much as she could, yet still keep one ear on the conversation. She hated feeling that she had to spy on her son and his friends, but she was still free only because of constant vigilance. If Brandon slipped and said something he shouldn't, she needed to know about it.

Unfortunately, the food only distracted the boys while they were still chewing. The minute the last bite of granola bar vanished, they were right back to the subject of Satan and Lori's ability to ride him. Before the discussion could become heated, she broke in.

"There's no point in bickering, boys. I might love to see what I could do with Satan, but I would never work with someone else's horse without permission. Brandon, did you finish your schoolwork?"

Brandon shot her an irritated glance. "Yeah."

"In that case, you should start your chores."

"Aw, Mom—"

"Brandon, it's not open for negotiation." She turned to Riley and Steven. "I'm sorry, boys, but I'm afraid Brandon will be tied up for the rest of the afternoon."

"Well, shoot, ma'am," Steven said, "we'll be glad to help him. We do chores all the time."

Lori gazed down into those oh-so-innocent brown eyes and had to bite her lip to keep from smiling at the little devil. By the time he was grown, she suspected he would positively reek with charm. She also suspected he knew it and would use it to his advantage at every opportunity. In fact, he reminded her more than a little of his uncle Zack.

"That's very nice of you," she said, "but don't you need to do your own chores before dinnertime?"

They exchanged sheepish grins, then looked back at her. Riley shrugged. "We can always do 'em later."

"Well, I'm afraid Brandon can't, and I really prefer that he does his own work. Perhaps you boys can get together later."

Steven nodded in acquiescence, but asked, "If we can get Uncle Zack's permission, would you really try to ride Satan?"

Brandon's eyes implored her not to refuse. She had to give him this much. "Yes, I would. I wouldn't just jump on his back, of course. I'd want to work with him for a while first."

"How long of a while?" Steven asked.

"That all depends on Satan and how afraid he is. Was he abused?"

"We don't know for sure," Riley said, "but Uncle Zack thinks he was."

"It might take a long time then. And some horses never get over that kind of treatment."

"We'll still ask Uncle Zack," Steven promised.

The Kramer boys turned away then and headed for their dirt bikes. Brandon watched them leave, disappointment plainly etched onto his face. Lori shoved back the automatic twinge of guilt, sighed, then gathered up the debris from their snack and stowed it away. She glanced at her watch and hissed at the time.

Where in the world was Wade? Surely he knew that one person could hardly care for twenty-four horses who demanded as much attention as these beauties did. Before Manny had his heart attack, Wade was mainly involved with shoeing the animals. Maybe he didn't realize she needed help. She missed having Manny around to organize the work details and keep Wade in line.

Now that she thought about it, she hadn't seen Zack McBride all day, either. She should be grateful for that, of course, but she couldn't help being curious about him. Maybe he was off chasing criminals…or reading Wanted posters. The thought sent an uneasy shiver dancing the length of her spine.

Sighing again, she decided to groom as many horses as she could before dark. Since the weather was mild and the pastures had decent grass, she wouldn't have to feed them tonight. Just as she was about to turn away, however, she saw the telltale plume of dust announcing an approaching vehicle. Shading her eyes with one hand, she recognized Zack's Blazer and felt her pulse rev up a notch.

He parked in front of his garage, climbed out, and after looking around for a moment, he ambled across the barnyard in her direction. He was covered with dust from his hat to his boots; his face and neck had muddy tracks where drops of sweat must have mixed with the dust. A pair of dark leather gloves dangled from his back pocket. One of his knees poked through the worn material of his jeans, and the front of his shirt sported a jagged tear below the right shoulder seam.

Oh mercy. He looked like a man who had put in a hard day's work, who didn't mind getting dirty and sweating, who would use his own hands and muscles to get the job done. Compared to Hugh, who had always looked carefully groomed and perfectly dressed, Zack looked strong and rumpled and...sexy. His easygoing smile only added to his appeal, and when he took off his hat to brush his hair back out of his eyes, the lighter skin of his forehead made him look touchingly vulnerable.

"Hi, there," he called, banging his hat against the side of his leg, sending up a small dust cloud. "You folks need anything?"

"We're fine, thank you." Lori swept one hand in an arc, including the barn, the corral and the pastures. "You have a wonderful facility here. Everything is extremely organized and convenient."

"That's the way I like it," he said. "How're you doin', Brandon?"

Brandon looked down and dug the toe of his sneaker into the dirt. "Okay."

Zack's eyes narrowed as he studied the boy more closely. "Is something wrong?"

Brandon shook his head and dug at the dirt some more. "I just have to do my chores."

Zack grinned at Lori before addressing Brandon again. "I know how you feel, pard. I've spent the whole day cleaning out irrigation ditches. Not my idea of a good time, and I'll have to do it again tomorrow. But, it's gotta be done."

Brandon glanced up at him with a wry smile. "Yeah. I guess I'd better get mine started." He turned to Lori and the smile vanished. "What do you want me to do first?"

"You can groom Lulu for me. We need to get as many of them done as we can, and since Wade's disappeared, we're on our own."

"Oh, he's up at the main house," Zack drawled, his eyes glinting with amusement. "Seems to be real interested in Grace."

With considerable effort Lori resisted the urge to curse her boss. If this wasn't the worst possible time for him to go cross-eyed over a woman, it was in the top five. She could only pray that he would hire some extra help this week.

"I see," she said. "In that case, I need to get back to work. I'll, um, see you later."

She turned away, and to her dismay, Zack walked along beside her. Intending to protest, she looked up at him and found herself gazing directly into his eyes. Words died in her throat and her tongue suddenly clung to the roof of her mouth. Though she sensed he liked what he saw, he was studying her with an unnerving intensity.

"I'll give you a hand," he said easily. "With three of us working, it won't take long."

"But this isn't your job," she croaked. "I mean, you've obviously put in a full day's work."

He shrugged one shoulder and flashed a lazy smile. "Shoot, it was hot and dirty, but not all that hard. Besides, I don't consider grooming horses work. To me it's just plain fun."

Unable to think of a way to discourage him without getting nasty about it, Lori swallowed her objections. Sometimes discretion was the better part of valor and this felt like one of those times. She certainly didn't want to make him suspicious enough to run a background check on her.

Brandon took off as soon as he finished grooming Lulu. Lori decided to let him go rather than risk another argument with him today. Surprisingly, she found herself sharing a companionable silence with Zack as they worked on the other four horses in the corral. She couldn't help admiring his calm and efficient handling of Blackie and Socks. She held open the pasture gate while Zack shooed the animals out of the corral.

Lulu led the way with Blackie and the others hot on her

heels. Like children released from a strict schoolroom, the horses romped and played, relishing the freedom of a bigger space. Lori closed the gate and turned to watch them.

"That's the most beautiful sight in the whole wide world."

The sound of Zack's voice drew her attention. The unabashed pleasure and affection in his eyes as well as his voice touched her more deeply than his obvious attempts to charm her ever would. Surely a man who loved horses this much would also have a lot of patience and gentleness in his personality. Wouldn't he?

She'd never seen Hugh abuse his horses—they were far too valuable to him for that. She had occasionally seen him hurt dogs and cats on the farm, however, simply because he felt like inflicting pain on some living creature. Lori had hated him for it, but always felt guiltily relieved that he'd vented his wrath on something other than herself.

But Zack wasn't like that. Though she constantly looked for it in every man she encountered, she couldn't see that streak of cruelty in Zack at all. At the moment, she couldn't even imagine him willingly hurting anyone or anything. The realization scared her. As if he felt her gaze, he glanced down at her, and she found herself looking directly into his eyes. They were so beautiful. Too gorgeous for a man. If only he wasn't a cop...

The air practically sizzled with the sense of attraction, of the powerful connection between them. Lori saw his pupils widen and his nostrils flare, and she couldn't repress a soft gasp of dismay at the strength of the pull she felt toward him. This simply could not happen.

She had to remember that he *was* a cop. She had to remember that if she was caught, Brandon undoubtedly would end up in the hands of the man she most hated and feared. God only knew what Hugh would do to him.

Zack's eyes narrowed and his forehead wrinkled in a frown. She turned away, instinctively trying to hide her fear and confusion. When his hand touched her shoulder, she started violently, jerked herself out of his grasp and whirled back to face him.

"I'm sorry." He held up his hands, palms-out, as if showing her he was unarmed. "I didn't mean to scare you."

"I know," she said. "I…just don't like to be touched."

"I could tell that." His smile was reassuring rather than mocking as she might have expected, his voice low and husky. "And I'm real sorry to hear it."

Unable to trust her own voice, she gave him a halfhearted shrug. He waited a moment, but when she didn't speak, he continued.

"My little brother Cal owns a bar and a pretty decent restaurant in town. Everybody at the main house is plannin' to go there tonight for supper and a little dancin' afterwards. I was hopin' you might join me."

"Oh, I couldn't possibly—"

"If it's Brandon you're worryin' about, don't," he said. "He can come along with us for supper and then come back here with the other kids. Grace or somebody will look after them. I'll be the designated driver, so you don't have to worry about ridin' with a drunk."

"No," she said, firmly shaking her head while she mentally smashed the part of her that ached to accept his invitation. "I really can't go out with you, and I believe I've already explained why."

He frowned. "Hey, I told you before I'm not expectin' you to have a flaming affair with me in front of your kid. But I don't see how one little date could hurt anything."

"No."

"But—"

"No," she repeated.

His frown deepened and he heaved a frustrated sigh. "Are you always this stubborn?"

"No. Sometimes I'm even more stubborn. The answer is still no. Now if you'll please excuse me, I have more work to do."

He gave her one last long, considering look, then shoved

his hands into his front pockets. "All right. When a lady says no, that's that. I guess I'd better go do my own chores." He started to move away, then paused and said over his shoulder, "But if you should change your mind—"

"I won't," she said. "Thanks for your help."

He waved one hand as if waving off her thanks and headed toward the pasture that held his horses. She told herself she'd only wounded his massive ego, but deep inside she didn't believe it. Oh, he'd tried to hide it, but she'd seen the flash of pain in his eyes at her rejection. She felt awful about it.

Zack McBride had never been anything but helpful and polite to her and to Brandon. He didn't deserve to have his feelings stomped on by her or anyone else. She could only hope he would give up on her now. And yet, the thought of him ignoring her hurt.

Men weren't the only ones who could be perverse.

Chapter Four

Cal's Place was packed with bodies that night. There were almost enough McBrides to fill the bar, and when the movie crew, cast members and rubbernecking locals were added, the waitresses and barmaids could barely do their jobs. Zack usually enjoyed being part of a crowd like this, even when he couldn't drink because it was his turn to be the designated driver. Next to horses, people were the most interesting creatures God ever invented, and Zack always got a kick out of watching his relatives and neighbors interacting with each other.

Tonight, however, he just couldn't get into the swing of things. His mind kept going back to his confrontation with Lori Jones, and he didn't know why he couldn't just let go of it. Okay, so she'd shut him down. He'd been rejected by women, especially his ex-wife. It hurt, but he'd lived through it before and he'd do it again this time. Because of the movie, there were plenty of other new and attractive women coming into town every day. So why didn't he forget about Lori and move on?

The question nagged at him through dinner and followed him into the bar. He looked at a stack of photographs their parents had sent back from Australia with his sister Alex. He broke up a potential fight over one of the few empty tables. He laughed himself silly when he saw his brother Jake dancing with a gal from California who had blue hair, a Western-style getup that looked as if it had come from the wardrobe of some old country singer, and long, blue metallic fingernails—hell, they were more like talons. To put it mildly, she was *not* Jake's usual type. Then he had to make sure Alex didn't try to drive home when she got into a snit with Dillon and stomped out of the bar.

But even with all of that and more going on around him, Zack still felt…disappointed that Lori wasn't here to share it with him. It was disconcerting, to say the least. He wouldn't deny feeling attracted to her, but he knew he wasn't in love with her, either. He didn't know her well enough for that. Furthermore, he didn't want to be in love with her or with anyone else. He just wanted to have some fun with her.

But the dang unreasonable woman would hardly even talk to him, much less go out with him. And it wasn't as if she didn't like him. Dammit, he knew she felt the same tug of attraction that he did, and it wasn't just his dented ego talking. He could see it in her eyes as plain as that big *E* on the eye doctor's chart.

So why was a pretty young woman like her refusing to explore those feelings? Better yet, how could he convince her to change her mind?

"Careful there, Zack. You keep thinkin' that hard and you'll sprain your poor little brain."

Zack jumped at the sound of his cousin Grace's voice coming from his right. He glanced over at her and felt an immediate twinge of envy. Flushed and smiling, she had one arm wrapped around Wade Kirby's waist and Wade had one of his wrapped around her shoulders. They'd obviously been dancing and enjoying each other's company a lot. Without waiting for an invitation, they sat at his table, and while Wade ordered a round of drinks, Grace tipped her head to one side and studied Zack intently.

"What's wrong?" she said.

"Oh, nothin', really," he said. "You look good tonight, Gracie. It's nice to see you having some fun for a change."

"Yeah, well, it's nice to actually *have* some fun for a change," she replied.

It was hard to tell in the dim, smoky atmosphere of the bar, but Zack thought she might have actually blushed. Interesting. Like Jake, Grace hadn't shown any interest in the opposite sex since her husband had died. Zack didn't know if Wade Kirby was the right man for his cousin to get serious about, but he was grateful to anyone who could shake her out of her rut of grief for that SOB she'd married. Of course, she didn't know what an SOB Johnny Kramer had been, and Zack had no intention of telling her. If it looked like Grace might be getting in too deep with Kirby, Zack would check him out. It was enough for now, just to see her acting like a woman again.

Was that what was going on with Lori? Was she grieving a dead husband or lover? Was she still aching with the horrendous sense of failure that had dogged Zack since his divorce? Maybe her rejection had nothing to do with him personally.

A barmaid delivered two bottles of beer for Grace and Wade, and a fresh soda for Zack. Zack lifted his glass in a salute of thanks and took a long drink. Wade and Grace did the same.

"If nothing's wrong, what were you thinking so hard about?" she asked, grinning at Zack.

Zack glanced around, and after making himself reasonably certain that nobody was listening in on their conversation, he decided to take Grace and Wade into his confidence. For one thing, he knew Grace would keep her mouth shut around the other siblings. For another, Wade might know more about

Lori than he'd previously let on. With a few beers pumping through his system and a pretty woman beside him, he might have a looser tongue.

As briefly as possible, Zack related what had happened with Lori that afternoon, then grimaced in frustration. "I don't know why she's so standoffish, and it bugs the hell out of me that she won't even let me try to get to know her."

"Don't take it personally," Wade said. "She's like that with everybody."

"But why?" Zack asked. "Is it possible she's still married?"

"Like I told you before, I don't know diddly about her background," Wade said. "And I don't think it's really anyone's business but Lori's."

Grace pursed her lips for a moment. "That's probably true, Wade, but I noticed something a little odd that first day you all came to the ranch."

"What was that, Gracie?" Zack said.

"Remember when I came out to tell you about Warren Fisher drinkin' himself stupid that afternoon?"

"Yeah, and I had to come into town and dry him out before he went home," Zack said. "What's that got to do with Lori?"

"Nothing, except that after you left, she asked me what was going on. When I told her you were a deputy, she turned white as a sheet. She tried to hide it, but I could tell she was really upset. I remember thinking she must have had some lousy experiences with cops to react that way."

After taking another gulp of beer, Wade laughed and arched his eyebrows dramatically. "Maybe she's wanted for something. She does have that…criminal look about her."

Grace playfully punched him on the arm. "Oh, stop, she does not. I'm sure she's really a nice person. That was just a fleeting impression I had. It probably doesn't mean a thing."

Zack wanted to believe Grace's last statement, but once the seed of suspicion had been planted, he couldn't dismiss it that easily. "Are you sure that's even her real name, Wade? Jones is such a common name…"

"I'm not sure of anything, Zack, but I seriously doubt she's got a record. I'd appreciate it if you'd just leave her alone."

Zack nodded, but he wasn't at all sure he could do that. The woman would be working at his place for a couple of months, so he could hardly avoid her. He glanced around the room and realized there were other people in this crowd who might have worked with Lori before. Maybe one of them knew more about her than Wade did.

Feeling better at having something to do other than stew about it, Zack excused himself and started working his way around the room. Over and over he introduced himself, chatted for a few minutes and finally asked a few discreet questions. Sooner or later, he was going to find out about Lori and her son. It was either that or go nuts wondering.

The day after the Memorial Day weekend Lori was delighted to find the commissary tent operational. She didn't mind cooking under normal circumstances, but a little trailer with a miniature kitchen hardly qualified as normal. Besides, eating in the tent saved her time and money, and gave her and Brandon more choices of nutritious foods than she would have been able to provide. Everything else about a movie location might be primitive, but the food was usually quite good.

When their trays were filled, she led Brandon to a table at the rear of the tent. While she always tried to stay as inconspicuous as possible, she couldn't completely avoid the rest of the cast and crew. The community of Hollywood professionals was a rather small group, and it was inevitable that she would become acquainted with some of her co-workers and repeatedly run into them on other movie sets.

Lori knew all of that logically, but it still was a bit shocking to hear her name yelled in delight and find herself in the middle of a hug sandwich between two young women she'd met on her last job. Gina DiCicco was a wardrobe assistant with dreams of becoming a designer; Mary Spencer was a lowly production assistant who wanted to be a director.

Laughing and chattering they each embarrassed Brandon half to death by kissing his cheeks, then hurried off to fill their own trays. When they returned, Brandon fled. Gina braced her elbows on the table and gave Lori a wicked grin.

"Met any interesting men lately?" she asked.

"Yes, tell us everything," Mary said with an equally wicked grin. "You can start with that gorgeous man with the beard who's been asking everyone about you."

"What?" Lori demanded, praying she'd misunderstood.

"Well that's how we knew you were here," Mary said. "What was his name, Gina?"

Gina heaved a dreamy sigh. "Who cared about his name? I just wanted his body. Lord, but he's fine." She sent Lori a mock glare. "Unfortunately, some horse-training wench got to him first. Smart girl to be so coy about her background."

Lori looked from Gina to Mary and back to Gina, desperate to get a straight answer. "What are you talking about?"

"Like you don't know this guy?" Mary let out a distinctly unladylike snort of disbelief. "Uh-huh. He's only one of the owners here. I think his name is Jack."

"No, not Jack," Gina said, "but it's sounds like Jack."

"You mean Zack?" Lori said, her voice croaking from her suddenly dry throat and mouth. "Zack McBride?"

"Oh, so you *do* remember him," Mary said.

Lori nodded. "But I barely know the man. Nothing is going on between us."

"Well, he'd *like* for something to be going on between you," Gina teased. "And he certainly is curious about you."

Fearing she might vomit, Lori inhaled a shaky breath. "What did he want to know?" she asked faintly.

"Just general background stuff, like where you're from originally and whether you're widowed or divorced." Mary frowned thoughtfully. "Which is it, by the way? Since you never talk about Brandon's dad, I always assumed you were divorced, but—''

''Yes, I'm divorced,'' Lori said, shoving back her chair with a strength born from panic. ''Not that it's anyone else's business. I've got to go now.''

Three minutes later she knocked long and hard on the door of Wade Kirby's trailer. She heard him cursing and banging around inside before he wrenched the door open and stuck his head outside. His eyes were still bleary with sleep and his sandy hair stuck up in patches. Squinting into the sunlight, he took a moment to recognize her.

''Lori?'' He wiped one hand down over his face and squinted at her again. ''What's going on?''

She had to gulp before she could speak. ''I'm sorry to have to do this to you, Wade.''

''Do what? Wake me up at this ungodly hour? No prob—''

Lori shook her head and took a deep breath. ''No, it's not that. I just have to quit my job, and I can't give you more than a few days' notice.''

Zack held his coffee cup out for a refill, winking his thanks at Grace because his mouth was full of pancakes. The back door banged open, and a moment later Wade Kirby stomped into the kitchen wearing a pair of jeans, a shirt that looked as if he'd grabbed it out of the laundry hamper and a scowl fierce enough to make any sane person nervous. To Zack's surprise, Kirby took one look at him and bellowed with outrage.

''Damn you, McBride, I hope you're happy.''

''Wade, what on earth is the matter with you?'' Grace demanded.

Zack climbed to his feet and nudged Grace behind him. ''Happy about what?''

''Running Lori Jones off. She just gave me her resignation.''

Stunned, Zack rocked back on his heels. ''And you think I'm responsible?''

"No, I damn well *know* you're responsible," Kirby retorted. "She said you've been asking everyone questions about her and prying into her background. Strangely enough, she resents having her privacy invaded. Did you learn anything that's worth the best damn trainer I've ever had?"

"I haven't learned a blessed thing," Zack admitted. "It seems that *nobody* knows anything about her. Doesn't that strike you as being a little odd?"

"No. Some people just like to keep their private lives to themselves. That's a rare, but highly commendable trait in my book. Who gave you the right to harass that poor woman?"

"I didn't harass her," Zack said indignantly. "I only asked a few questions about her."

"Well, I think you *are* harassing her, and I think it's because she shut you down. Now, that's an abuse of police power."

Pushing her way out from behind Zack, Grace propped both hands on her hips. "Oh, for pity's sake, Wade, don't be ridiculous. Zack wouldn't do any such thing. He was just curious—"

"It went beyond that, Grace, and I can't afford to lose her. There's no way I can take care of all those horses by myself."

"I'm trying to find you some extra help," Zack said, "but everybody I've asked is tied up with one thing or another until school lets out at the end of the week."

"I appreciate that," Wade conceded, raking one hand through his hair. "But I'll still need Lori. I'm a damn good businessman and a decent farrier, but I'm no horse trainer. Not like my dad was or my partner and Lori are now. If I hadn't thought I could count on Lori, I'd have canceled this gig when Manny had his heart attack."

"Why come to me?" Zack asked. "What do you think I can do about any of this?"

"Apologize to her," Wade said. "Convince her you're no

threat. Promise you won't ask any more questions that are none of your damn business.''

"Do you think that'll do any good?''

Wade shrugged helplessly. "Damned if I know, but anything's worth a try. It'll hold up the whole production if she leaves. My partner's not well enough to come back to work yet, the rest of my crew won't be here for another ten days and they'll never find another company with enough horses and props in time to meet the shooting schedule.''

Though it went against his most basic instincts, Zack could hardly refuse Wade's request. It didn't make sense to risk costing the production company thousands of dollars because of a hunch. He *hadn't* found any solid evidence to suggest that Lori Jones was anything other than a hardworking single mother. He sure as hell didn't want to violate her constitutional rights.

Zack heaved a disgruntled sigh, then slowly nodded his head. "All right, I'll talk to her. Any idea where she is now?''

"She was headed for your place when she left me,'' Wade said.

"I'll find her then.'' Zack brushed past him and hurried out the back door. Dang woman. No matter what he did around her, he was wrong, and he would be more than happy from here on out, to leave her the hell alone.

"Mom, somebody's coming,'' Brandon called, pointing toward the corral.

Lori turned her head in the direction indicated, and felt her breath hitch when she recognized Zack McBride loping toward her on a bay gelding. A combination of fear and anger made her chest feel tight and she had to fight an instinctive urge to flee. Instead, she sent Brandon off on Lulu to exercise the first group of horses by chasing them around the pasture and turned to face the man she was rapidly coming to regard as her nemesis.

Judging by the thunderous frown on his face, he felt exactly the same way about her, though why that should be, she couldn't begin to guess. She hadn't done any prying into his past. Of course, the McBrides were all so blasted perfect, he probably had no dirty little secrets to hide. Whoop-de-do for him.

The thought boosted her anger past her fear, and she raised her chin in defiance when he reined his horse to a stop three feet from her own mount, Blackie. "What do you want, Mr. McBride?"

"Hello to you, too, Ms. Jones." Zack dismounted and walked even closer to her. "Mind if we have a little chat?"

Lori stayed in the saddle. He could be the one to get a crick in his neck from looking up at her for once. "I'd rather not. I don't believe we have anything to discuss, and I have work to do."

He tipped his hat back and gazed off toward the horizon, a muscle ticking along the side of his jaw that suggested he might well be counting to ten. Or twenty. Then he looked back at her, and when he spoke, his voice had taken on a softer, almost placating tone. "It won't take long. I just want to apologize."

"For what?"

"For bein' so damn nosy. I just wanted…well, I wanted to get to know you a little, even if it had to be secondhand. I'm really sorry I've upset you. I didn't mean to invade your privacy or make you so uncomfortable you'd quit your job."

"Oh, I see," Lori said. "Wade yelled at you."

One side of Zack's mouth quirked into a guilty grin. "Yeah, he sure did. To hear him talk, the whole production will have to shut down without you. Says he's not much of a trainer."

Lori hadn't considered the situation from that angle before, but after a moment's thought, she realized there was truth in Wade's statement. "I suppose he's more like a…manager than a trainer. He loves his horses and he's great at fitting their shoes, but when it comes to actually getting them to do what he wants, he doesn't have quite the right temperament."

"Then don't give up your job," Zack said. "Those horses need you, and I promise I won't bother you anymore."

Lori sincerely doubted that. He'd bothered her from her first glimpse of him, though not in a way she could willingly admit to him. He was simply too…appealing for her peace of mind. Hugh had done far worse and never even thought about apologizing to her. Not once.

While it was clear that Zack hadn't particularly enjoyed apologizing, he hadn't flinched from it or even tried to spread the blame around. He'd accepted responsibility for his own actions, seemingly without a qualm. She'd never known a man to do that before.

"Please, Lori. I know I came on pretty strong when you got here, but if you're really not interested, I can handle it, and I understand why you just want to be friends. You can tolerate me that much, can't you?"

Her throat felt tight as she gazed into his dark, sincere eyes. "Why should I trust you?"

"Because I'm one of the good guys," he said, flashing a charming smile. "Listen, if my bein' a deputy worries you for some reason, don't let it. Sunshine Gap doesn't need much law enforcement, which is good, because I'm really not much of a cop. I catch a few speeders, dry out drunks and stop family spats when I can, but I don't go lookin' for work, and you don't exactly strike me as bein' real dangerous. You're not, are ya?"

Did he think she would tell him if she was? The question seemed so ridiculous, Lori sputtered with laughter. "No, I'm not dangerous to anyone in Sunshine Gap."

"Well, there you go then. We've got no problem. So you'll stay and I'll be your assistant until we can find you some permanent help."

"Wait a minute. *You're* going to be *my* assistant?" She shook her head in confusion, then raised a doubtful eyebrow at him. "When did that happen?"

"Just now." He smiled again, looking quite pleased with

himself. "Wade's been on me to find some folks to work with you, but I haven't had any luck yet."

"We're managing," she said stiffly.

"Yeah, from what I've seen, you're pretty darn good at coming up with creative solutions, but…" He waved a hand toward the far end of the pasture, where Brandon was still chasing his group of horses around. "This is way too much for one grown-up and a kid. I can't promise to give you the whole day, but I'll put in as many hours as I can."

"These aren't ranch horses," she said. "They require special care and special handling."

"Of course they do," he agreed easily. "I'll pay real close attention and do things your way. Shoot, I'm hopin' I can learn some things from you that'll work with my own stock."

The skepticism she felt must have shown plainly on her face. Zack burst out laughing, then said, "What? You think I'm lyin'?"

"I don't know," she admitted. "Most of the horsemen I've worked with have expected me to be incompetent until I proved them wrong. I didn't expect a Wyoming cowboy to be quite as…enlightened as you seem to be."

He laughed again, the sound rich and infectious. "Some wouldn't be, but women in Wyoming have always worked right alongside their men. McBride men have learned to respect a woman's abilities more than most. This ranch never would have survived without the women. That's what this movie's all about. You knew that, right?"

"Not really," she said. "I haven't had a chance to see the script. I just have a brief description of scenes that include horses and what they'll need to do."

"My cousin Marsh wrote that script." Zack's voice carried a wealth of pride. "You can borrow my copy, if you want."

"That would be great. It always helps to know the whole story, but the studios are protective of their scripts. They usually operate on a need-to-know basis."

Zack shrugged. "I think you need to know this stuff." Pausing, he looked up into her eyes, his expression suddenly serious. "So, what do you think? If I keep my nose out of your business, will you stay and let me be your assistant?"

She wanted to believe he was for real, but it was difficult. "On one condition. I want to work with your horses, too."

His brow wrinkled in a frown. "These are ranch horses, not movie horses. You'll have to use my methods with them."

"I will. As long as I don't have to abuse them—"

"You know I don't work that way."

She nodded. After a moment of consideration, he gave her a nod in return. "All right. We'll try it. Deal?"

She reached out and took the hand he held up in offer of a handshake. His fingers closed around hers in a firm grip, and the warmth of his palm against hers felt...right. Absolutely right. His eyes met hers in a heart-stopping gaze that seemed to see through all of her masks and insecurities to the real woman deep inside her. Her sexual awareness of him returned, and with it came a thousand new doubts about the wisdom of spending time with this man.

It was too late for doubts, however. She could no more turn away from Zack at this moment than she could have turned away from Brandon. Besides, her efforts to push him away had only made him more curious about her. It might be wiser to keep him close enough to allow her to keep an eye on him. And there was something here she really had to explore. Taking a deep breath for courage, she pumped his hand twice.

"Deal."

Chapter Five

During the next three days of working with Lori and Brandon, Zack felt as if he was watching two butterflies emerge from their cocoons. At first, every time he joined them, neither mother nor son had much to say that didn't involve the task at hand. But with every passing hour they grew more used to his presence, the tension gradually eased and the three of them became something that resembled a team.

While he thought Lori's horses were incredibly pampered, Zack had few problems adopting her methods. For one thing, her horses were also incredibly well-mannered, which, in his book, said a lot for their training. For another, her philosophy of nonviolence and noncoercion toward the animals was real close to his own.

He knew lots of guys who weren't kidding when they bragged about "breaking" their horses. All you had to do was look at one of their cowed, droopy animals to know just how brutal their "breaking" had been. Zack wanted his

horses to have a little fire and zip, and he didn't mind making
an occasional adjustment to a particular horse's personality.

He didn't let them get away with any damn thing they
wanted, of course. A horse wouldn't be of much use to him
or to his customers if it acted like a knothead, but he really
thought of his horses as young children. A good parent didn't
crush a child's feelings; a good rider didn't crush his horse's
spirit.

The longer he watched Lori interacting with her animals,
the more he admired her skills. It almost seemed as if she
could hear their thoughts and figure out exactly what they
needed to be comfortable and happy. The horses clearly
adored her for it, and Zack didn't blame them.

He'd never met anyone who came as close to sharing his
own passionate fascination with the big animals as Lori did.
Unlike his ex-wife, his daughter and most of his other relatives and friends, she didn't appear to think he was obsessive
about them. Not that she'd have a speck of room to talk. If
he was dotty about them, she was just as bad, if not worse.

Damn, but he liked that. He liked a lot of other things
about her, too—her seldom seen, but impish sense of humor,
her unabashed joy in simple things like sunshine and wildflowers, her sweet smiles that sometimes held a touch of wist-
fulness, as if she expected her happiness to be fleeting. He
wanted to ask her about that last one, but he didn't quite
dare.

He liked her body, too, but he tried not to think much
about that sort of liking. He suspected she felt the same
strong physical attraction he did, but he figured it was probably just as well she was so determined to fight it. She really
wasn't the kind of woman a guy could just have a fling with,
and that was all he had to offer a woman these days.

But even while he told himself all of that made sense, he
still wanted to kiss her at least once, just to know what she
tasted like. Unfortunately, if he so much as accidentally
touched her, she flinched like he'd jabbed her with a hat pin.
Made him wonder if somebody hadn't done just as big a

number on her as Satan's former master had done on him. Well, he would bide his time and hope she'd come to trust him enough to allow him to be a real friend.

Maybe it would help the process along if he kept his part of the bargain. After they finished with Kirby's horses that afternoon, Brandon took off somewhere with Riley and Steven. Zack took Lori to meet his babies. As he'd expected, it was love at first sight for Lori and for the horses. They clustered around her, curiously sniffing her and shamelessly soaking up her attention and affection.

Zack watched the birth of their friendship, feeling distinctly left out. An indignant scream from the adjacent pen told him he wasn't the only one. He looked over at Satan and sadly shook his head.

A big, showy chestnut with four white socks and a star on his forehead, Satan stood sixteen hands high. Zack had fenced off an acre for him, hoping that a little time and space of his own might settle the gelding down. Instead, he had become extremely territorial and increasingly hostile.

The poor horse was absolutely unpredictable in every way but his fear and hatred of human beings. If Zack didn't find a solution to Satan's potentially violent behavior soon, he would have to put the horse down. Zack sure as hell didn't want to do that, but he was running out of ideas and options.

Lori stepped out of the big pasture and headed for Satan's pen. Zack ran to catch up with her. The boys had told him about their conversation with Lori regarding Satan. Even thinking about her getting close to that big renegade had made him nervous then. It made him even more nervous now.

"Hold on, Lori," he said. "You don't want to get too close to that one."

She shot him an irritated glance. "Are you *sure* I don't, McBride? Thank you so much for telling me."

"Aw, don't get all huffy on me." He grabbed her arm, pulling her to a stop. "That's Satan. I know the boys told you about him and he's dangerous as hell."

Satan neighed a loud challenge. She tilted her head toward

his pen. "I think I could have figured that out for myself. There's just something about a horse with his teeth bared and his ears pinned back that makes me feel a need for caution."

Zack grinned at her caustic tone. Man, if she were a porcupine, he'd be wearing quills everywhere. He released her arm, then swept his own arm in front of himself like a snooty hotel doorman. "After you, Ms. Jones."

She gave him a baleful stare, then slowly approached Satan's pen. The closer she came to the fence, the more agitated the horse became. He ran the perimeter of his acre, turned around and ran it again from the other direction. Then he paced like a caged tiger, ears still pinned back and eyes continually locked on Lori as if he intended to run like hell at the first sign of attack.

Lori studied him intently but silently, reminding Zack of one of those infuriating doctors who makes a scared, sick patient wait forever before delivering a diagnosis he'd probably formed in the first two minutes of the examination. Zack forced himself to keep quiet until she reached out and grasped his arm, using her free hand to turn his body at a forty-five-degree angle to the fence. She angled her own body the same way, keeping her gaze on Satan.

"Why are we doing this?" Zack murmured.

"To see how much he'll relax if we're not facing him head on. Horses tend to interpret that as a challenge or even an act of aggression."

"I know," Zack said. "But it doesn't help with him. I've tried just about everything, and nothing works."

She looked over her shoulder at him. "Well, you've got to do something. You can't just leave him alone all the time. He needs a herd."

"I know that, too," Zack said, letting his frustration come through in his voice. "But I can't even get close enough to rope him now without tranquilizing him, and I don't exactly trust him to act like a gentleman if I put him in with the others. Would you put him in with your horses?"

Without a second's hesitation, she shook her head. "No, I wouldn't. Why did you buy him?"

"I didn't," Zack admitted. "One of Dillon's old buddies from the rodeo circuit did. Thought he'd make a good roping horse, because he's so big and fast."

"Didn't he notice anything wrong with Satan's behavior?"

"Yeah, but he didn't pay much attention to that because he thought he was getting a great deal, and he figured he'd be able to straighten out Satan's attitude problem."

"But he couldn't."

Zack shook his head. "He figured the seller already had Satan tranquilized when they were making the deal. By the time he got up the next morning, Dillon's friend had a renegade on his hands and the previous owner had ridden off into the sunset."

"Why did he buy a horse so quickly?" Lori asked.

"That's how it is on the rodeo circuit sometimes. Your horse gets hurt or sick, you've gotta replace him in a hurry. Sometimes you can borrow one, but it's not the same as having your own."

She nodded her understanding. "So, how did you get stuck with him?"

Zack gave her a rueful smile. "Dillon's friend called us from Casper and begged for help. He didn't want ol' Satan anymore, but he's not the kind of a guy who could live with abandoning him or putting him down without doing what he could for him."

"And you just had to try to help him?"

"Yeah, that about covers it. As you can see, I haven't had much success."

"You're not thinking of putting him down, are you?"

"I may have to, Lori. Having a horse like Satan is an invitation to disaster. We've got two boys—no, make that three counting Brandon—who know just enough about horses to be dangerous. What if one of them decides to prove his manhood by climbing onto Satan's back?"

Lori paled, then slowly shook her head. "Oh, they wouldn't—"

"Don't you count on it. When I think of some of the risks the seven of us took when we were kids, it's a wonder any of us survived beyond grade school. I can't chance keeping him around much longer, and I can't in good conscience pass him on to anyone else. You have any bright ideas?"

Her forehead crinkled with worry, she studied Satan again. The gelding was still pacing nervously, baring his teeth, laying back his ears and making threatening noises whenever they looked in his direction. "Have you tried using a round pen?"

"You bet. I've tried every method I've ever heard of, read up on all the new methods and never laid a hand on him in anger, but he just plain hates me."

Lori gave him a sympathetic smile. "No, he's afraid of you. There's a difference, Zack."

"What good's that gonna do if the result is still the same?"

"Let me think about it, okay? Somebody out there somewhere can help Satan. Wade's partner, Manny Rodriguez, should have some good ideas, and if he doesn't, he knows the most successful trainers in the business."

"You think he'd be willing to help?"

"Manny? Of course he would. When it comes to horses, he's the ultimate marshmallow." She wrinkled her nose at him. "Well, now that I've met you, he's probably just a close second."

Her teasing made Zack laugh, and any offer of help lightened the burden of responsibility he felt every time he saw Satan. He pulled himself up as tall as he could and gave her a mock glare. "You makin' fun of me, woman?"

Lori's smile vanished. She retreated a step and shoved an errant strand of hair behind her right ear before turning back toward the barnyard. There was a nervous edge to her voice when she spoke. "Well, I suppose we should go."

"Hey, wait a minute," Zack protested. "I didn't mean to scare you, Lori. I was just teasing you like you teased me."

She studied him warily, as if she didn't know whether she could believe him. Then, biting her lower lip, she gave a jerky nod and looked down at her feet. "Okay. But I still have to go now."

"Fine." Heaving a silent sigh of frustration, Zack turned and followed her, wondering why she had overreacted to his teasing. There were a couple of hard cases in Sunshine Gap who had good reason to fear him, but most folks regarded him as a source of help and protection. So why had Lori's first reaction to his glare been fright?

Something just wasn't right here, and knowing that he couldn't find out what was wrong because he'd promised to stop digging into her past bugged him worse than a bed full of chiggers. Someone had taught her to seriously fear an angry man, just as someone had taught Satan to fear human beings. Dammit, she sure didn't deserve that. Nobody did.

And somehow, he wanted to find a way to convince her that he was her friend, not an enemy.

Wishing she hadn't acted like such a nincompoop when Zack had glared at her, Lori hurried away from him. She'd thought she had finally gotten over these stupid, knee-jerk reactions every time a man shouted or frowned at her. With most men, she had.

But Zack McBride wasn't most men. He was so big physically, he could snap her, or even Hugh in half with one hand. His dark eyes, swarthy skin and black hair and beard made him look even more intimidating. And his personality was so forceful and unpredictable, she couldn't pinpoint what kind of a man he really was.

Honestly, he had more sides to his psyche than a geodesic dome. One day he drove her insane fussing over a misplaced item in his tack room. When she asked him if anyone had ever told him he was compulsively neat, he gave her a proud smile and said, "Having a place for everything and everything in its place is a virtue."

The next day he was as laid back as any hippie ever had

been, playing with his horses, riding them bareback, draping himself over them like an overgrown kid and making her laugh until her sides ached.

When he broke out his video camera to record film clips of horses he wanted to sell on his Internet website, he was a worse perfectionist than any Hollywood director. But when Brandon expressed an interest in trying out the camera, Zack turned it over to him with only a mild warning to be careful. At the same time, Lori was hyperventilating over how she would ever be able to pay for the thing if Brandon accidentally dropped it.

By far the most disconcerting thing he did, however, was the simple act of bathing and grooming a horse. It was a ridiculous thing to get her hormones all…stimulated over a routine chore; grooming a horse was hardly an attractive affair, much less an erotic one. The groomer usually ended up covered with horse hair, mud, water and shampoo, as well as a number of other substances too bizarre to mention. Zack was hardly immune to any of that, and it wasn't as if he used any exotic methods she'd never seen before.

At first, she was so busy grooming her own charges, she paid little attention to Zack. But as she settled into her own rhythm, she was able to spare an occasional glance in his direction, and soon found herself watching him for longer and longer periods of time. The animals stood so quietly for him, she couldn't help feeling impressed. And it wasn't just a grudging acceptance on the animals' parts. It was more as if they really enjoyed everything he did to them.

The longer she watched, the more she understood why the animals reacted that way. Zack worked at a smooth, steady pace, taking time to let the horse examine each piece of equipment he was going to use. If a horse did fidget, he stopped the whole process until he discovered what was bothering the animal.

He also kept up a running commentary in a low, soothing voice that helped the horse remain calm. Lori liked the deep, husky tones of Zack's voice, but they didn't exactly calm her. In truth, she found the sound of his voice incredibly sexy. To hear him wooing an animal was the next best thing to hearing him woo her. Not that he seemed interested in doing that anymore. Which was exactly what she'd wanted all along. Of course it was.

If listening to his voice disturbed her mind, watching his big, strong hands caressing a mare's glossy hide assaulted her libido. He curried and brushed, scrubbed and rinsed, scraped and clipped with firm, but gentle strokes, moving with the assurance of an expert. She could almost feel the horse's pleasure when he rubbed circles over her sides and flanks and deeply massaged tight muscles with his fingertips.

When he carefully worked the tangles out of a mane or a tail, she imagined what it would feel like if he ran his long fingers through her hair. He smiled and patted a horse's neck or cheek, and she imagined him doing the same thing to her. He puckered his mouth and played kissy face, and she imagined the feel of his lips against hers, his beard whiskers brushing her skin, the taste and feel of his tongue exploring her mouth....

Oh, God, make me be a horse. Make me be that horse.

He looked over at her then, and gave her such a sexy wink, she nearly whimpered. With her face feeling as if it had caught fire, she ducked her head and stared at Lulu's black coat without actually seeing it. Had she lost her mind? Was it possible she'd said those words out loud? If she had, she would have to die of embarrassment. She couldn't possibly face him again if he knew what she'd been thinking.

She heard him toss several items into his plastic box of grooming tools, then discerned footsteps crossing the concrete floor, coming in her direction. She gulped down confusion and panic, and still had to turn off the clippers for fear of leaving Lulu with an unsightly bald spot. The toes of his boots appeared in her line of sight, but she couldn't bring herself to look up.

Zack reached out and tucked a finger under her chin, silently urging her to lift it. She resisted for a moment, then slowly gave in and forced herself to meet his gaze. His eyes were absolutely unreadable. Though she desperately wanted to, she couldn't look away.

"What's goin' on, Lori?" he asked.

"Nothing, really." Her voice sounded soft and breathless in her own ears. What on earth did it sound like to him?

"Didn't look like nothing," he said. "You looked real…intense."

"I did?" He was standing so close she could smell the wet horse hairs clinging to his clothes, feel the warm puffs of his breath against her skin and the heat radiating from his big, solid body. She wanted to touch him. Locking her fingers together, she rubbed her sweaty palms against each other. "Well, I suppose I was, um, daydreaming or something."

One corner of his mouth curved into a half grin. "Must've been some daydream. Looked like a mighty nice one, too."

Her whole face felt hot again. She cleared her throat. "I guess it was. I really don't remember it anymore."

"Uh-huh," he said, though his eyes said he really didn't believe her.

He lowered his gaze to her mouth and ran the tip of his tongue across his bottom lip. She barely resisted the urge to mimic him, but he was watching her reactions so closely, she didn't dare. Finally he gave her a slow, knowing grin and ambled back to the mare he'd been working on.

Focusing her attention on Lulu, Lori did her best to ignore Zack for the rest of the day. He was not an easy man to ignore, however. No matter what he did, some part of her was constantly tracking his movements, evaluating his motives, guessing at his thoughts.

She lectured herself every time her concentration strayed from her horse of the moment to the man on the other side of the grooming room. Of course it didn't help. It had been so long since she'd felt any attraction to a man, she didn't have enough experience to turn it off at will. Besides, she really liked feeling the tingles and anticipation that came with it. It made her feel…alive. Young. Pretty. So many things she'd lost because of Hugh.

Most of the time Zack seemed completely different from Hugh. If only she could believe that he would never change. But that was impossible. No one could guarantee such a thing, and she needed to remember that. No matter how many wonderful qualities Zack McBride had, she couldn't let temptation and hormones get in the way of protecting herself and Brandon.

After breakfast the next morning, Lori left the dining tent in search of Brandon. She'd given up any hope of keeping him away from Riley and Steven—especially Steven, the charming little scamp—and settled for frequent private reminders to be careful about what he said. The Kramer boys had unofficially adopted Brandon into their family, and he was having so much fun with them, she couldn't bring herself to deny him the opportunity to be a kid.

The adult McBrides were so warm and welcoming, she couldn't forbid him to play with the other boys without raising more questions than she wanted to answer. Still, there had to be a limit as to how much Grace was willing to tolerate having an extra child underfoot. Assuming that Brandon was already over at the main house with his buddies, Lori hoped to discuss the situation with Grace and set some ground rules.

Grace greeted her at the backdoor, waved her inside and hurried into the kitchen. Lori followed, and found herself the object of interest from the large group seated around a huge table. Along with the usual variety of McBrides and Kramers, the group contained Blair DuMaine, the female star of *Against the Wind;* her cousin, Hope DuMaine, whose short, spiky hair was a startling shade of blue; Wade Kirby and Lori's missing son. Zack was not among the McBride contingent, and Lori felt oddly relieved and disappointed at the same time.

She took the chair Grace produced and gratefully sipped

the mug of strong coffee that appeared as if by magic, then took a moment to catch her breath and assess the situation before asking Grace for a few minutes of her time. That turned out to be a wise decision, as Grace was flitting between the table and the stove, delivering platters of pancakes, fried eggs and bacon and retrieving empty platters in order to fill them up again.

Lori admired her efficiency and stamina, and it only took a few moments to understand why Wade was eating breakfast here rather than at the tent. Grace blushed every time she came close to him, and he barely took his gaze off her long enough to spear bites of food from his plate with his fork. Well, well, well. This was starting to look serious.

Ten minutes later the kids took off and the rest of the adults hustled away in a variety of directions. Grace sighed, then rolled her eyes at the mess, gathered up a load of dirty dishes and carried them to the sink. Lori gathered another load and followed her.

"Oh, put those down," Grace protested. "I can handle this."

Lori grinned. "Hey, after watching you this morning, I think you can handle anything. Unless you despise the idea of another woman in your kitchen, I'd really enjoy helping you while we talk."

"Well, if you put it that way, have at it, hon," Grace said with a laugh. "It's just sort of a foreign concept for me. If I want help in the kitchen, I usually have to drag somebody in here, kicking and screaming all the way."

"I promise, this is strictly voluntary. Besides, I owe you for putting up with Brandon."

"Aw, phooey," Grace said. "We always have so much commotion goin' on around here, one more kid is nothin'."

Lori made another trip to the table, unable to resist pausing to study the collage of photographs, school papers and art-work stuck on the refrigerator with magnets. There was an especially cute one of a younger Zack, with an adorable toddler sitting on his shoulders. They were both laughing, and the little girl definitely carried the McBride bloodline.

Grace stopped beside Lori and looked over her shoulder as if to see what she'd found that was so interesting. "That's Zack and Melissa," Grace said.

Though she was dying to know more, Lori tried to sound casually interested. "His daughter?"

"Yup. She lives in Portland with her mom. We haven't seen her now for five years." Grace reached around Lori and tapped another photograph. "She probably looks a lot like my cousin Alex's daughter Tasha now. Melissa's just a couple of years older."

Lori studied the photograph. "Oh, she's a pretty girl."

"She sure is," Grace agreed. "Nice kid, too. She gives Alex fits sometimes, but she's got a good heart."

Grace returned to the table for another load. Lori reluctantly followed. While she knew she could never have a romantic relationship with Zack, she couldn't help being a little bit curious about him.

Well, all right, she was a *lot* curious about him. Why hadn't his family seen his daughter for five years? Did that mean he hadn't seen her for five years, either? Didn't he care about her? Or didn't he even have visitation rights? If not, why not? It was a disturbing possibility; the courts rarely denied a father visitation rights, unless it could be proved that he might endanger the child. Lori couldn't imagine Zack was capable of any such thing, but she hadn't thought Hugh was capable of it either.

She'd been wrong.

"Was there something special you wanted to talk about?" Grace asked.

Deep in thought, Lori started at the sound of Grace's voice. Then she smiled sheepishly. "Sorry, I was thinking about something else. Actually, I wanted to talk about Brandon's being here all the time. I appreciate your generosity, Grace, but I really can't impose on you so much. I thought perhaps we could agree on a certain number of hours the boys can play together, or I could trade you some baby-sitting or even pay you—''

"Pay me?" Grace gave an indignant huff. "Absolutely not. And I really don't need baby-sitters that much, because I've always got a cousin or a brother around who's willing to keep an eye on the boys. Just don't worry about it. Brandon's polite and well-behaved, and since he's been here, I haven't had to listen to my varmints whine about how bored they are. Do you have any idea how much that's worth?"

Lori laughed at Grace's eye-bulging, melodramatic expression. "Of course, I do. But it just doesn't seem fair."

"People out here take their kids everywhere with them," Grace said. "We don't think of them as being in the way or inconvenient. As long as Brandon obeys the rules and acts like one of the family, he's no trouble at all."

"Do you promise to let me know if he does cause you any trouble? Or if you have other plans, or if there's anything I can do for you?"

"You bet," Grace said. "Zack told me you've got a real nice touch with horses. I just might have you work with a couple of mine."

Lori nodded, but before she could say anything, Wade, an assistant director named Cecil Dixon and Jake McBride entered the kitchen. Wade's eyes lit up when he saw Lori.

"I'm glad you're still here," he said. "Cecil wants us to go to Cody with him today and block out our part of the action."

Lori frowned at Wade. "Today? A little more warning would be appreciated, boss."

"Why? Zack's here to help out, and this is your job, Lori."

"I know it's my job, but I do have a child, and—"

The child in question and his cohorts banged into the house, cutting her off with their excited chatter. Zack sauntered in after them, and his slow, easygoing smile put flutters in the pit of Lori's stomach. Uh-oh. She shouldn't be this glad to see him.

"What's goin' on?" he asked.

Wade gave him a quick explanation. Brandon scrunched up his face and whined his opinion.

"Aw, Mo-o-o-m. I don't have to go, do I?"

Lori scowled at him. "That's enough, Brandon."

"But that's always so-o-o boring. Can't I stay here?"

"I don't mind," Grace said with a smile. "As long as I don't have to hear that B word again."

"B word?" Brandon asked.

Steven elbowed him in the ribs. "Boring. Mom hates that word."

Brandon quickly shook his head and made a criss-cross motion over his chest. "I won't say it again, Mrs. Kramer, I promise."

Zack laughed, then ruffled Brandon's hair. "Don't make promises you can't keep. But I was kind of hopin' you boys could go fishin' with me today after we're done with the chores. Would you like that?"

"Fishing? No sh—I mean, no kidding?" Brandon said, shooting his mother a pleading look.

Lori sighed inwardly. The McBrides simply didn't give a person a chance to be reserved. Under any other circumstances, she would have loved it, but how on earth would she ever be able to control Brandon at all after they left the Flying M?

"What do you say, Lori?" Zack asked. "He's too young to need a license, and we've got plenty of gear."

"Brandon doesn't swim very well yet."

"We're just goin' to the creek, and I'll keep a real close eye on him."

"Ple-a-s-e, Mom," Brandon begged. "I'll be really good, I promise."

"You'll be careful? Especially around the water?" Lori asked. "And you'll wear your sunscreen?"

Brandon's head bobbed up and down so vigorously, he looked like a candidate for whiplash. "Yes, yes, yes."

"All right," Lori said, as if she had any real choice in the matter. "I'll see you at dinner, then."

"Okay, fellas, beat it before she changes her mind and do your chores so we can go," Zack said, flashing Lori a broad grin.

Whooping and hollering, the boys obeyed, banging back out of the house as loudly as they'd come in. The adults all chuckled in the sudden silence. Grace and Jake went into a private huddle over by the stove. Wade and Cecil Dixon left after arranging to meet Lori in fifteen minutes. She turned to Zack, not sure whether she wanted to thank him or strangle him for putting her on the spot.

"I don't want to seem ungrateful, but I'm not used to just turning him loose like this," she said.

"Most places, you probably shouldn't turn him loose," Zack replied. "But it's okay here, honest. Everyone on the place will look out for him. Let him enjoy being a ranch kid while he's got the chance."

She winced at the buckets of guilt raining down on her head at the thought of how few childhood pleasures her son had enjoyed. "I'll try."

He leaned down and dropped a playful kiss on the tip of her nose. "Do that."

Zack sauntered back out the door then, leaving Lori with warm cheeks and what felt like a goofy smile on her face. She glanced over her shoulder and had her suspicions confirmed by the amused and extremely interested smiles she received from Grace and Jake. Zack would have to pay for this moment of embarrassment someday.

But now she might get a glimpse of what Zack would be like as a father. Spending a whole day with three active and energetic boys should bring out the real man. If his good humor survived the day, he might be one of the good guys after all.

Chapter Six

His chest filled with a tangle of emotions, Zack watched Lori climb into a big pickup between Wade and Cecil Dixon from the shadows of the barn door. He didn't like seeing her leave without him. He *really* didn't like seeing her leave with two big, halfway good-lookin' men.

Oh, he knew this was purely a work situation, and Lori didn't have anything going on with either one of those guys. But there was still a twinge of jealousy inside him he couldn't deny. It was strictly a primitive, territorial sort of feeling, with a dash of protectiveness thrown in for good measure. He had no right to feel that way toward Lori, but knowing that didn't stop him from feeling it.

His ex-wife would have laughed at him. Billie had often accused him of being hopelessly old-fashioned in his attitudes toward women. She'd called him bossy and controlling when that hadn't been his intention at all. He'd just wanted to take care of her the best way he knew how.

It worried him to realize he was feeling all of the same

things for Lori that had caused him so damn much trouble with Billie. Hadn't he learned anything from the divorce? And why feel such things for Lori when he still had so many unanswered questions about her? Or was he just feeling attracted to her because he missed being needed, and she so obviously needed someone to be her friend?

Realizing he was standing around and analyzing his feelings, he cursed softly and crossed the barnyard to the storage shed that held all of the camping and fishing equipment. As far as he was concerned, coming this close to his so-called "feminine side"—whatever the hell *that* was—could only mean that he really needed to spend a day with some guys doing guy stuff. He'd show the boys a good time or die tryin'.

If he was lucky, Brandon would turn out to be as big a blabbermouth as Steven usually was, and spill a few tidbits about his mom and dad. Zack wouldn't grill him, of course, but it wouldn't be his fault if Brandon volunteered the information in casual conversation. Grabbing enough fishing gear for all of them, Zack went to hurry the boys along with their chores.

After letting them catch their limits, he gave them a swimming lesson in the frigid creek. When they were dressed and barely shivering, he spread out the picnic lunch Grace had packed for them. The boys fell on the food like starving coyotes. Then he took them back to the big house, where he gave them all a roping lesson.

While the boys took turns throwing their ropes at Jethro, a plastic steer head embedded in one end of a hay bale at the side of the yard, Zack stretched out on the grass for a nap, pulling his hat down over his face to block out the sun. Before long he heard furtive giggles and stealthy footsteps approaching, and braced himself for the inevitable wrestling match.

"Gotcha, Uncle Zack," Steven crowed, pouncing on Zack's chest and pinning his arms down with bony knees.

Riley grabbed Zack's legs and shouted for Brandon to sit

on his belly. Zack turned his face to one side, flipping his hat out of harm's way, then looked up into Steven's face.

Zack returned the boy's wicked grin. "Think you've got me?"

"Yup," Steven said. "Piece of cake."

"How about you, Riley?" Zack asked. "Think you've got me?"

Riley tightened his arms around Zack's knees. "Damn right. You're toast, Uncle Zack."

"What about Brandon?" Zack said. "Isn't he gonna help you little wimps?"

"Wimps?" Steven bounced his rear end hard on Zack's chest and gripped Zack's shoulders with surprising strength for such a young boy. "We're not wimps."

Riley twisted his head around toward the plastic steer head. "Hey, Brandon, come on. We do this all the time."

"N-n-no," Brandon said in a hoarse voice that made Zack wonder if something was wrong.

Rolling onto his left side as if the boys weighed no more than a pair of mosquitoes, Zack scanned the yard for Brandon. Even in the bright sunshine, he looked deathly pale, his eyes were huge and his rigid posture reminded Zack of Satan quivering on the edge of flight. Poor kid was scared to death.

Before Zack could go to him, however, Steven and Riley launched a more vigorous attack, tickling him, pounding on him and struggling to roll him onto his back again. Laughing, Zack fended them off as best he could, freeing one arm and then the other. Tucking Steven under one arm, he reached down and tickled Riley in the ribs, and managed to free one leg.

"Come on, Brandon," Steven shouted. "He's gettin' away from us."

Zack looked at Brandon again and nodded. "It's okay, Brandon. We're just havin' fun."

His gaze locked on Zack's face, Brandon took one hesitant step forward, then another, then another. Zack nodded again and held his free arm out to him. "Come on, kid, let's see how tough you are. Only rule is you can't intentionally hurt anybody.''

That was all the invitation the boy needed to throw himself into the melee. Zack suddenly had his hands full with panting, writhing boys trying to pin him back down. He could have dumped all of them any time he wanted, but he enjoyed letting them pit their strength against his. Young male animals of most species needed this kind of rough play to learn how to defend themselves.

They rolled and tumbled around on the grass like puppies, laughing, yelling and cursing until an elbow collided so hard with Zack's nose, blood spurted out onto his shirt. Cupping one hand around it, Zack called a halt to the wrestling and struggled to his feet. The boys turned worried eyes in his direction.

"Is it bad?" Steven asked.

"Nah," Zack replied. "I just need to get some ice for it."

Grace took one look at him when he entered the kitchen, grabbed a dishtowel and hurried to the refrigerator. Opening the freezer compartment, she scooped some ice cubes from the bin, wrapped the towel around them and brought the makeshift ice bag to Zack. The boys gathered around him while she alternately lectured and fussed over his injury.

"Oh, you're gonna have a shiner for sure. Maybe two.'' Plunking the towel into his hand, she said, "Honestly, Zack, don't you think you're gettin' just a little old for this?"

Cautiously pressing the ice against his nose, Zack glared at her. "Old? Hell, no, I'm not old. The day I can't handle three scrawny little dudes like these yahoos is the day they plant me in the ground."

The boys laughed, but abruptly fell silent when Grace turned her wrath on them. "Just look at you. Your clothes are all filthy and grass-stained, and there's a stinking bucket of fish on the back porch that need to be cleaned. You catch 'em, you clean 'em.''

"Yeah, Mom, we know," Riley said, rolling his eyes for

Zack's benefit when she turned her back for a moment. "Could we have something to eat first?"

She hesitated, opened her mouth as if she would refuse, then sighed and headed for the cookie jar. Carrying a full plate, she snagged a stack of plastic glasses from the cupboard, returned to the refrigerator for the milk and shooed the boys outside with their snack. Then she pried the ice away from Zack's nose and studied it with a grim expression.

"That bad, huh?" Zack asked.

"Oh, you'll live. You just won't be very pretty for a couple of weeks."

She replaced the compress and started to turn from him. Zack grasped her wrist and held her there. "What's wrong?"

"Nothing," she grumbled, not quite meeting his eyes.

"Come on, bumps on the nose and dirty clothes don't usually make you so cranky. What happened?"

She gave him a grudging smile and lowered herself into the chair adjacent to his. "Nothing really happened, Zack. I'm just feeling a little...confused."

"About what?"

"About Wade. I really like him."

"I don't see any problem with that. He seems like a pretty decent guy to me."

"He is." She linked her fingers together and rested them on the table, studying them as if she might have to pass a test on them later. "It's just...well, I guess I feel a little guilty about enjoying a man's company again. Somehow, it seems disloyal to Johnny's memory."

Anger surged inside Zack at the pain in Grace's eyes. She didn't deserve to torture herself like this, but it wasn't his place to tell her why. Instead, he reached over, laid one hand over the top of hers and said in the mildest tone he could manage, "Last time I heard the wedding vows, they were only supposed to last until death parted the couple. That happened a long time ago for you."

"I know that logically," she said with a sad smile. "I

guess my heart hasn't caught up to my head, yet. It's just really hard for me to let him go.''

"I can see that.'' He squeezed her hands, then released them. "But you were a good and faithful wife to Johnny. If he loved you so much, he wouldn't want you to mourn for the rest of your life. He'd want you to be happy. I really think it's time for you to move on now.''

She studied him for a moment, then tipped her head slightly to one side. "All right. I will if you will.''

"If I will? I'm not a widower.''

"No, but you're still mourning over losing Billie and Melissa. And there's a real nice little gal workin' right here on the ranch who'd be perfect for you.''

Catching the distinct stench of a matchmaker close by, Zack eyed her warily. He planned to pursue Lori, but he sure didn't want any "help" from his siblings and cousins. "Oh, yeah?''

"Yeah. She's interested in you, too.''

"What makes you say that?''

"Oh, she was in here this morning, staring at the picture of you and Melissa on the fridge with this sweet, wistful sort of smile on her face. And then, when you kissed her on the nose and left, Jake and I both saw that look again.''

Unable to resist in spite of his better judgment, Zack leaned closer. "Are you sure about that? She always acts real skittish around me.''

"Well, she probably still needs some wooing, but she's interested all right. If you don't believe me, ask Jake.''

Zack noted the wicked twinkle in her eyes, laughed, then climbed to his feet. "No, I believe you, but if you tell anybody else about this conversation, I'll deny it.''

Grace dragged an imaginary zipper across her lips. "I'll take it to my grave.''

"Do that.'' He leaned down, gave her a brotherly peck on the cheek and went looking for Brandon. They had some serious work to do.

* * *

At five o'clock that afternoon, Lori gratefully climbed out of Wade's pickup and made a beeline for her trailer. She was hot, thirsty and hungry, not to mention being covered with grit and dust from walking around Old Trail Town's unpaved streets all day. She gulped down a glass of water at the tiny kitchen sink before hurrying into the bathroom, where she washed her face, neck and hands. A shower would be lovely, but the trailer's water supply was minimal, and she needed to find Brandon.

When he wasn't at the main house, she drove out to Zack's place. She'd barely opened her door when Brandon crashed out of the house, yelling his lungs out. "Mom, mom, mom! Jeez, I thought you'd never get here."

Smiling at his excitement, she held her arms out to him, faltering only a little when she got a better look at him. Good Lord, he wasn't just dirty after a regular day of playing, he was absolutely filthy. Barreling right into her, he hugged her long and hard. When he finally pulled away from her, his mouth motored into high gear before she could even draw a breath.

"Mom, I had the best day in the whole world. You wouldn't believe all the stuff we did. I caught ten fish. Ten! And Riley and Zack taught me how to clean 'em, and everything."

Lori sniffed, then wrinkled her nose. "I see." Grinning, she tweaked the front of his T-shirt. "Then that must be fish entrails I smell."

"Entrails? No, they were *guts,* Mom. Fish guts. They're real cool and we've got some right out back. You wanna see 'em?"

"Maybe later," she said. "So what else did you do?"

"Zack taught me how to rope on the funny steer head, you know? I'm not as good as the other guys, but Zack said I did real well for my first time."

"That's wonderful, sweetie."

Brandon didn't even notice her lapse with the hated endearment. "And then, you know what? Zack laid down on the ground to take a nap, and Steven and Riley just jumped right on top of him, and he didn't get mad or hit 'em or nothin'. And he let me do it too. And we wrestled for a long, long time, and he didn't even get mad when one of us accidentally gave him a bloody nose. And he's gettin' a black eye, too.''

"Goodness," Lori said, trying not to laugh at the mental image Brandon's description provoked. "Is he all right now?"

"Oh, yeah. He's tougher'n hell, Mom."

"Brandon, you know better than to curse."

"Well, the other guys here do, Mom. Even Zack says 'hell.' ''

Obviously, whatever Zack McBride did had become absolutely okay to her son. The excitement trembling through Brandon's body and total hero worship in his eyes prompted her to silently count to ten before answering. Only by the time she reached four, Brandon continued his breathless recount.

"I heard him say it right in front of Mrs. Kramer when she put ice on his nose. And she scolded us a little bit, but then she gave us these really great chocolate chip cookies and milk. And when we were done with that, Zack brought me out here and we've been makin' a really cool surprise for you."

"That sounds nice," Lori said, allowing him to pull her up to Zack's front door. When Brandon would have dragged her inside, however, she balked. "Wait a minute, wait a minute. Don't you think we should knock?"

Zack's voice boomed from somewhere inside. "No need for that, Lori. Come on in."

"Yeah, Mom, come *on*," Brandon insisted.

Rather than let him yank her arm out of its socket, she followed him across the threshold, pausing to allow her eyes to adjust from the sunshine outside to the dimness of Zack's living room. It had plenty of windows and a thick, grayish carpet on the floor. The furniture was big enough to suit a man Zack's size; the upholstery was all soft, burgundy leather. With Brandon still urging her toward an open doorway at the far end of the room, she didn't see much else, other than a glimpse of some framed photographs on one wall and an entertainment center.

Approaching the doorway, she heard the distinctive sizzling of food frying and smelled enticing aromas coming from what must be the kitchen. She pulled back on Brandon's hand.

"Honey, if Zack's getting ready to eat, we should go," she said softly.

"No, Mom, we can't leave," Brandon argued.

Zack appeared in the doorway carrying a spatula in one hand and a cast iron skillet in the other. "That's right, you can't leave. We're cookin' this boy's first mess of fish, and you're darn well gonna help us eat 'em."

His tone was so commanding, it was all she could do to stop herself from saluting. But when she stepped into the kitchen and got a better look at him, all she could do was murmur, "Oh, my."

The poor man looked as if he'd gone to war that day, and lost. His black eye was approaching magnificent, his nose looked swollen and his shirt was every bit as filthy as Brandon's, and had blood on it, too. He gave her a crooked grin, glanced down at his shirt and shrugged one shoulder.

"It's been a busy day," he said.

"So I hear. Is there anything I can do to help? With dinner I mean?"

He carried the frying pan back to the gas stove and turned the contents over with the spatula. "It's pretty well under control. Brandon made us a salad and set the table, and the fish and fried spuds are almost done. I don't have any wine on hand, but if you'd like a beer, it's in the fridge."

A cold beer sounded wonderful. Lori helped herself to one and after taking a glass out of the cupboard Zack indicated, she looked around the room. Other than the usual number of dishes it took to cook a meal, the kitchen looked clean and tidy. Brandon waved her over to a round wooden table sitting beside a large bay window that looked out on acres of green pastures with a backdrop of jagged, snow-capped mountains in the distance.

"Mom, look what I did," Brandon said, drawing her attention away from the stunning scenery.

The table held three settings, each lined up with military precision on a red-checked place mat. Since Brandon didn't know the difference between a dinner fork and a salad fork, she could only assume that Zack had supervised his work. He must be as particular about doing things the right way in his house as he was in his barn and with his horses. But in the center of the table stood a mayonnaise jar stuffed with wildflowers that had to be Brandon's handiwork.

"Did you pick those flowers for me?" she asked.

"Yeah. Do you like 'em?"

"No, I *love* them. Almost as much as I love you." She hugged him and kissed his cheek. He shot an appalled glance over his shoulder toward Zack and wiggled out of her embrace, his neck and ears a fiery red.

Zack served the food then, and as the meal progressed, Brandon chattered happily and without any apparent fear. Zack was attentive to Brandon and charming to Lori. The trout and fried potatoes tasted wonderful, the view was spectacular, the atmosphere cozy and relaxed.

Everything was so nearly perfect, Lori soon found herself wanting to weep. *This* was what a family was supposed to be like. *This* was what she'd thought her life would be like when she married Hugh. *This* was what she'd always wanted for Brandon and what she still longed for when she awoke alone in the middle of the night—a sense of safety and sharing and finding joy in life's simplest pleasures.

When she thought of those years with Hugh...no, she couldn't allow herself to do that. The mansion, the designer clothes and the jet-set vacations were all behind her now, and good riddance. None of that had ever been important to her. She would have sacrificed her own life to make certain her son wouldn't have to grow up in a continual state of danger and fear.

She'd never seen Brandon act so full of life before. Seeing it now made everything she had endured during the past four years seem insignificant. She owed Zack a huge debt for whatever he had done to bring Brandon out of his shell. How could she ever repay his kindness? She'd never even seen the kind of life Zack and all the other McBrides took for granted.

She studied his battered eye and nose, listened to his low, husky laugh, watched genuine enjoyment cross his face while he interacted with Brandon, and realized he truly *was* one of the good guys. In spite of everything standing between them, she was very much afraid that she could learn to love him. Oh, God, what on earth was she supposed to do now?

As if in answer to her silent prayer, Zack and Brandon chose that moment to clear the table and serve dessert. The most elegant Baked Alaska couldn't hope to compete with the chocolate sundaes and Twinkies snack cakes Brandon proudly carried to the table. Zack met her gaze over the top of Brandon's head and winked at her with his good eye. The moment of shared delight and amusement made her heart flutter, and she turned her head away in the hope that he wouldn't see the effect his simple gesture had had on her.

Since Zack and Brandon had cooked the meal, she insisted on doing the dishes. Brandon asked if he could watch TV and happily trotted off to the living room when he received permission. Suddenly finding herself alone with Zack, Lori immediately felt as awkward and bashful as any fourteen-year-old girl unexpectedly encountering her first big crush in the school hallway. Zack, however, seeming oblivious to her tension, wiped down the stove, the counter tops and the table.

By the time they finished restoring the kitchen to order and went into the living room, Brandon was sprawled on the sofa in the deep, boneless sleep of an exhausted child. Lori brushed his hair off his forehead, feeling a wave of such tenderness for him, her whole chest ached with it. Zack uttered a soft chuckle and turned off the TV, then tipped his head toward the front door and swept his hand to one side.

She nodded in agreement, and preceded him to his front porch. He indicated a pair of weathered wooden rocking chairs and folded himself into one with a weary-sounding sigh. She took the other one and settled into it, smiling at the way it creaked when she rocked.

The glaring sunshine had softened into twilight, and the air had cooled to a comfortable temperature. The stillness of the country gradually seeped into her soul, releasing her from the roller coaster waves of emotions she had been riding since arriving at Zack's house. If she could only bottle this sense of well-being....

"That's quite a boy you've got," Zack said quietly. "You've done a good job with him."

"Thank you." She met his gaze and offered a shaky smile. "And thank you for giving him such a wonderful day. I know he'll never forget it."

Zack's eyebrows rose in surprise. "We just hung out and did some guy stuff. It wasn't any big deal."

"Oh, but it was. For Brandon, it was an enormous deal. He doesn't get to do much guy stuff, and his father never did anything like that with him before the divorce."

"Well, his father must be a damn fool. I'd give anything to be able to spend time with my daughter again."

"Why don't you?"

"Portland's a long way from here and that's where she lives now." Zack grimaced and then gazed off into the distance. "But, the real reason I quit exercising my visitation rights is that she doesn't want to spend time with me anymore. Truth is, she can hardly stand the sight of me."

"Oh, Zack, I don't see how that can be true," Lori protested. "You're so wonderful with children—"

He interrupted her with a bitter laugh and shook his head. "Well, my ex-wife doesn't agree with you. It wasn't what you'd call an amicable divorce, you know? And I think Billie's been poisoning Melissa's attitude toward me. I sure never did anything mean to that kid.''

"How old is she?"

"Fifteen, but the trouble started when she was about Brandon's age, so I don't really think it's just teenage rebellion at work here. About all I can do is pay my child support, send her Christmas and birthday presents and hope like hell that someday she'll stop believing her mother's lies and decide she wants to see me again.''

"Even if you and your ex don't get along, I can't believe any responsible mother would intentionally harm a child's relationship with her father unless there was a good reason to do so. Surely you don't mean to blame the entire problem on her."

He shot her a chagrined look, then shrugged as if he knew he should agree with her, but couldn't quite bring himself to do it. She rushed on before he could refute her statement.

"A father is as important to a daughter as he is to a son, Zack.''

"I know that, and I worry about Melissa all the time," he said. "But Billie considers herself to be quite the liberated woman, and she thinks I'm too bossy and hardheaded to be a good father. Personally, I don't see that in myself. Do you?''

Lori thought about the precise place settings at dinnertime, his perfectly—make that rigidly—organized tack room, his bodily tossing Bob Grant off the trailer ramp and threatening him. Bossy and hardheaded? Undoubtedly. And, he definitely was a man who didn't hesitate to take charge of a situation and bend it to his will.

Within limits, those were not necessarily bad qualities. Anyone working in law enforcement would need to be able to do all of that. But if he brought the same attitude home all the time, Lori could easily see how that might become annoying. The longer she remained silent, the deeper his frown became.

"Aw, hell, Lori. *Do* you see that in me?''

"Not exactly, but—"

"But what?"

He looked so pained at the idea, she wasn't certain how honest she should be. She settled for the truth with as much tact as she could muster. "Well, um, you certainly have a forceful personality, Zack. And you do hold strong opinions about lots of things. I mean, you seem to see most issues in black-and-white rather than in shades of gray."

"You're right about that," he conceded with a shrug. "I do see things as either right or wrong, and I never did see much point in bein' wishy-washy or beatin' around the bush. You either have standards or you don't. Does that make me a bad father?"

"Of course not," Lori said. "But sometimes dealing with children requires a bit of flexibility. Is it possible that Melissa simply finds you too rigid?"

"Well, I guess I've probably mellowed out some over the years. The last time she came for a visit, maybe I *was* a little strict. It's different when it's your own kid, you know? You always feel sort of...responsible for their behavior, so you expect more from 'em than you do other kids."

"That's certainly true," Lori said, hoping he would stay with this train of thought.

After a moment's silence, however, Zack's expression hardened and he gave his head one emphatic shake. "No, dammit, even back then I was right. Billie was lettin' Melissa grow up way too fast."

"What do you mean?"

"Aw, she had her ears pierced and she was wearin' makeup, and her clothes looked like something you'd see on a streetwalker. I even caught her smokin' cigarettes, for God's sake, and she was only ten years old."

"The smoking was bad for her, of course, but most kids do experiment with that sort of thing, Zack. As for the other things, ten does seem a bit young, but some girls are more precocious than others. She's bound to have different peer pressures in a city the size of Portland than she would in Sunshine Gap.''

"Yeah? So what? Just because other kids do something that doesn't mean she should.''

"Lighten up, Dad," Lori said with a teasing grin. "The local girls I've seen here and in Cody would seem awfully young compared to the girls in California, or in Portland. If her ears are the only parts of her body she's pierced by now, consider yourself lucky. And makeup, hairdos and clothes tend to be temporary fads she'll grow out of. I wouldn't get into a power struggle with a kid over something like that.''

"You wouldn't?"

"No way. If I had a daughter, I'd save my energy for battling out the biggies like drugs, sex, eating disorders, curfews, abusive boyfriends—the things that could potentially ruin her life or even kill her.''

Zack's swarthy complexion paled visibly and his fingers gripped the arms of his rocker so hard the tendons in his hands stood up in sharp relief. "Wow, Ms. Jones." He uttered a weak laugh. "You sure know how to comfort a guy.''

She gave him a rueful smile. "Sorry, pal, but that's the ugly truth about raising kids today. My personal theory is that you can't keep them too close, you can't sweat the small stuff and ninety-five percent of the things most parents fight with their kids about is small stuff. They need unconditional love and acceptance more than anything else we can give them.''

"That's how you've been raisin' Brandon?"

"As much as possible. I don't always do it perfectly, but that's my goal.''

"Where's his dad, Lori?"

Dead and in Hades if I'm lucky. The response was so true and so automatic, for a second she feared she had said those words out loud. Zack was simply looking at her with interest, however, and she concluded with relief that she'd merely thought those words. She cleared her throat and took her own turn at gazing into the distance.

"We're divorced. I haven't seen him for four years now."

"Did he just take off?"

"No. I was the one who insisted on it. It wasn't a good marriage."

"Yeah, I sort of figured that. What kind of custody agreement do you have?"

"I have complete custody of Brandon. He was, um, denied visitation rights."

Zack's eyebrows shot up in surprise. "Completely?"

"Yes. He hurt me and he hurt Brandon."

"How bad?"

"Bad enough to lose all parental rights. Believe me, he got exactly what he deserved."

Zack cursed softly and shook his head in disgust. "I'm real sorry you went through that, but I'm glad you had the backbone to divorce the SOB. Some women can't seem to get themselves out of a situation like that."

"I didn't have any choice. He was so violent at the end, if we had stayed with him, sooner or later, he would have killed one or both of us."

"Well, I guess now I understand why you and Brandon have acted so skittish around me." He angled his chair to face hers and took one of her hands between his palms. "Like I said before, he's a fool. Most men don't hurt their wives and kids."

Lori gulped, then nodded. "My head knows that, Zack. My gut's not convinced yet. When you've made such a huge mistake once, it's awfully hard to trust anyone again."

Leaning closer, he smiled into her eyes. Ever so gently, he stroked her cheek with the backs of his knuckles, then tucked a strand of hair behind her right ear. "I hear ya. But you know, one of these days you're gonna have to take the plunge and fall in love again."

His words and his gentleness kindled a warm, sweet glow in the center of her chest. Unable to look away from him, she leaned closer, too. "Oh, yeah?"

"Yeah. How long's it been since you've even kissed a man?"

"A long time."

"You could...practice on me, if you wanted to."

If she wanted to? What a master of understatement. She shouldn't. Everything she'd told him about her past was true. It simply wasn't the *whole* truth. If he ever discovered the rest of her story, he would be livid. But, God help her, she could feel his warm breath on her face, hear his quiet breathing, see a deep, aching hunger in the depths of his dark eyes that more than matched her own.

"All right." Wrapping one hand around the back of his neck, she pulled him the last fraction of an inch closer, murmuring, "I'll practice on you, but just this once."

His lips brushed over hers once, twice, then settled into a firmer contact that sent her heart skipping erratically and made her want to melt against him. His whiskers tickled her upper lip until she chuckled and pulled away for a moment.

"What?" he said hoarsely, reaching for her again.

"Your beard tickles."

"Want me to go shave it off?"

She stroked the wiry hairs with an index finger and smiled at him. "Oh, please don't do that. I really like it. I've just never kissed a man who had one before."

He licked the tip of her finger, and when she gasped, he gently caught it between his teeth and licked it again. The simple, but highly suggestive action provoked a startling variety of sensations all over her body. His eyes gleamed with wicked amusement, as if he knew exactly how her nipples were tingling, how her toes were curling, and she didn't want to think about the rest of it. Fortunately, two could play this game.

She retrieved her finger, clasped both hands around the sides of his head and teased his firm upper lip with her own tongue. She'd forgotten that he was a take-charge kind of guy, however, and the next thing she knew, she was draped across his lap with his hands buried in her hair and his clever tongue exploring the inside of her mouth. Mercy, but he was one fantastic kisser, and she never wanted him to stop.

God only knew how far the kiss would have gone if Brandon hadn't suddenly appeared at the screen door and said, "Hey, what are you guys doing?"

Chapter Seven

The rest of Wade's crew arrived the next day, freeing Lori from the daily maintenance chores of feeding, grooming and exercising the horses. Zack made it a point to hang around and watch the newcomers working with the animals, and found them to be a congenial, thoroughly professional group. Satisfied there wouldn't be any repeat performances of Rob Grant's brutality, Zack went in search of Lori.

She was not easy to find, however, and he suspected that was by design rather than by accident. After Brandon had interrupted their lip-blistering kiss last night, Lori had gotten all flustered and upset, dragged the kid into her truck and peeled rubber getting out of his driveway. Damn, if she wasn't the most confusing woman he'd ever met, she was right up there in the top three.

On a scale of one to ten, that kiss had been headed straight for a twelve, and he ached to do it again. It wasn't as if he'd pounced on her out of the blue; she'd had plenty of warning and participated with enough enthusiasm to leave him hard and hurting half the night. She'd enjoyed it, too, he *knew* she had. He'd heard her making soft little moans deep in her throat and he'd seen the hardened tips of her nipples pressing against her shirt when she'd jerked herself out of his arms. So what the hell was her problem?

An ambulance run to Cody, followed by a reported burglary and a car wreck to clean up prevented him from tracking Lori down and having it out with her. By the following morning, his irritation had cooled, and he decided yelling at her probably wouldn't get him very far. What he really needed to do was talk to her. Unfortunately Wade had most of his crew trailer half of their horses up to Cody's Old Trail Town, so Lori could start training them to do the specific actions the director wanted. Since Zack's services were no longer needed, he wasn't invited to go along.

Disappointed but resigned to waiting until she came back, he spent the day catching up on the endless list of jobs Jake kept giving him to do around the ranch. He repaired three headgates for the irrigation system, restrung a section of fence and patched a hole in the barn's roof.

During the afternoon, he saw his cousin Dillon and Blair DuMaine walk out of some bushes with their arms around each other's waists. They looked happy, but rumpled, as if maybe they'd been necking. Then they jumped into Blair's little red rental car and sped off toward Sunshine Gap. Though he felt a pang of envy at the couple's obvious closeness, Zack smiled to himself.

He didn't begrudge Dillon a relationship with a woman, even one as beautiful as Blair DuMaine. Dillon had been in the accident that had killed Grace's husband. He'd suffered so much and withdrawn so much since Johnny Kramer's death, Zack was glad to finally see him coming out of his self-imposed exile. He just wanted to feel that closeness with a woman again, too. That shouldn't be too much to ask.

When he finished the barn roof, Zack put away his tools and drove back to his house. Telling himself he might have more luck with Lori if he didn't smell like a polecat, he showered, shaved and put on fresh clothes. The swelling in his nose had gone down, but his eye was still black and blue and starting to get an ugly yellowish tinge around the edges. Well, there was nothing he could do about that.

He drove back to the main house then, intending to greet Lori the instant she got back from Cody. He'd no sooner climbed out of his Blazer, when Dillon and Blair roared up beside him. Then his niece Tasha and her pal Rick Larson piled out of the back seat, babbling about Alex becoming a movie star and the upcoming cattle drive. Grace, Jake and the boys rushed out of the house to see what the commotion was all about.

Eventually it all made sense. Zack's sister, Alex, was going to play a jaded saloon girl in *Against the Wind*. In the morning Tasha and Rick were going to help Grace and her boys drive the Flying M's cattle up to their summer pasture in the mountains. Everyone but Brandon seemed happy enough with the whole arrangement.

Shoving his hands into his front pockets, Brandon hunched his shoulders, lowered his head and trudged off toward the trailer he shared with Lori. When Zack called out to him, he just shook his head and trudged faster. Guessing that the boy was fighting to hide tears, Zack decided he'd better follow.

He caught up with Brandon twenty feet from the trailer and discovered he'd been right. There were tracks of clean skin streaked down each side of Brandon's grubby face, and his eyes were filled with misery. Zack put an arm around him and waited until they entered the trailer before he asked what was wrong.

Brandon sniffed, swiped a fist under his nose, then started to cry again. "It's nothing," he mumbled, dashing the new tears away with the backs of his knuckles.

"Hey, buddy, this is *me* you're talkin' to," Zack said, "and you look like you just lost your last friend."

"I did," Brandon muttered.

"What? You have a fight with Riley and Steven?"

Brandon shot him an impatient scowl. "No, but they're

going to go off and leave me behind. What am I supposed to do all day when Mom's working in Cody?''

"What makes you think the boys will leave you behind?"

"Nobody said I could go on the cattle drive. And when Mom's gone all day, I'll be bored to death without the guys.''

"Hold on a second," Zack said. "Nobody said you *couldn't* go on the cattle drive, did they?''

"Well…no,'' Brandon admitted.

"You boys have been thicker'n thieves for days now and you're a good rider. I'll bet everybody just assumed you were gonna come along.''

"You think so?''

"You bet. They can always use an extra hand.''

"But I don't know how to drive cattle.''

"You don't have to. The horses do, and they do most of the work. If you can stay in the saddle, you can drive cattle.''

The joy in the boy's eyes wrenched Zack's heart. Driving cattle was far from a glamorous job. This kid sure didn't need much to make him happy. Dammit, he needed a father.

"Oh, man, that would be soooo cool,'' Brandon crowed. An instant later, however, the excitement faded from his eyes and his bony little shoulders slumped. "Who am I kidding? Mom won't let me go. I know she won't.''

"Why not?''

Brandon suddenly found the toes of his sneakers of great interest. "That's just the way she is. She's always afraid I'll get hurt or lost or something stupid like that. She hardly ever lets me out of her sight.''

"She's let you hang out with Riley and Steven all day lately. Maybe she's ready to ease up on you.''

Brandon blew out a disgusted snort and rolled his eyes toward heaven. "No way! She'll still treat me like a baby when I'm forty.''

"Yeah, moms are like that sometimes.'' Zack chuckled and ruffled the boy's hair. "But I still think you should ask her. What've you got to lose?''

Brandon shrugged. "Not much. Will you help me convince her, Zack?"

"I can't promise anything, but I could try."

Crossing his arms over his chest, Brandon pinched the sides of his lower lip together and scrutinized Zack's face. "Are you in love with my mom?"

The blunt question nearly made Zack swallow his tongue. After what Brandon had seen the other night, though, Zack figured he deserved an honest answer. After a little consideration, he said, "I don't know yet. I really like her a lot, Brandon, but it takes a while longer to know if it's love. Would you mind if I did fall in love with her?"

Still pinching his lower lip, Brandon took a moment before answering. "I don't know. I mean, I like you a lot, Zack, but..." A faraway, haunted look came into his eyes, giving Zack's heart another wrench. "If you didn't...hurt her, maybe it would be okay."

"I've never hurt a woman in my life, and I sure don't intend to start with your mother. I don't hurt kids, either."

Brandon's eyes focused on Zack again, and his cheeks flushed, giving Zack the impression that he hadn't meant to reveal so much. "You know?"

"That your dad hurt you and your mom? Yeah. She told me a little about it."

That awful, haunted expression returned to the boy's eyes. "I tried to help her, but I just...couldn't."

"Of course, you couldn't. You're a brave kid, Brandon, but you're still just a kid. He's a grown man. He's the one who's responsible for what happened, not you. And not your mom, either."

Brandon's throat muscles squeezed down a hard, dry-sounding gulp. "You really think so?"

"I know so. I've seen this problem before. Men like that usually blame other people for their own lack of control, but they're the ones who make the decision to hurt somebody."

The kid smiled at Zack as if an incredible burden had just been lifted from his conscience. Before he could say anything, however, the door opened and Lori stepped into the trailer. She froze in her tracks the instant she saw him with Brandon. Raising his eyebrows at her, he waited for her to speak.

Brandon wasn't that patient. "Mom, guess what."

Lori started at his loud demand. "What, Brandon?"

"Remember that cattle drive I told you about the other day? They're going to start it tomorrow, and Zack says I can go if it's okay with you."

"Oh." She shot Zack an angry glance before turning back to Brandon. "Well, um, gee, honey, I'm going to have to think about that."

The kid cranked himself into a full, ear-grating whine. "Aw, Mom, don't. Just say yes, okay? Please, please, please?"

Lori held up one palm like a traffic cop. "Stop it, Brandon. I said I'll think about it, and I will."

"But there's no time for that. I'll have to pack, and—"

Someone hammered on the door, cutting off the rest of what he would have said. Steven's voice filled the sudden silence.

"Hey, Brandon. Come on out. Mom says we gotta get ready for the drive."

Brandon pushed past his mother and opened the door enough to poke his head outside. "Just a sec, Steven. I'm tryin' to get my mom to let me go."

"What? Ya *gotta* come, man. We'll have a blast."

Lori looked more harried with every sentence the boys exchanged. Zack guessed the situation would only get worse if Brandon came back to hassle her again.

"Brandon, why don't you go on outside with Steven and let me talk to your mom about this in private?" he suggested.

Brandon shot a questioning look over his shoulder. Zack scowled and made a shooing motion with one hand. The kid gave him a pleading smile, then hurried through the door, banging it shut behind him.

When the boys' voices faded into the distance, Lori turned on Zack in fury. "*Did* you tell him he could go?"

"Calm down, Lori. He was standin' right there when the plans were announced. He came over here in tears 'cause he thought he hadn't been invited."

"So you invited him?"

"Well, sort of. I mean, you heard Steven out there. Everybody just assumed that he'd tag along with Riley and Steven. Is there a reason you don't want him to go?"

"Does it matter now if there is?"

"Sure it does. Why wouldn't it?"

"If I say no, he'll hate me, that's why. You've left me no choice."

"You always have a choice, Lori. But you're gonna be so busy for the next few weeks, you won't be able to spend much time with him. Why not let him go out and have a little adventure?"

"He's never done anything like this before."

"He can learn. He's already a good enough rider to help out, and you know darn well Grace'll take good care of him."

She looked down at her feet and said softly, "I don't want him to be off somewhere that I can't reach him if I need to."

"They'll be home on Monday, which is less than a week, and he'll never be more than a day's ride from the ranch."

"But he could get hurt."

"He could get hurt right here," Zack said. "If they run into trouble, Grace knows first aid, and any one of those kids can come back for help in a flash."

"But—"

"Jeez, Louise, Lori, give the kid a break and let him grow up. You can't keep him tied to your apron strings forever. It's time to start letting him go."

"Letting him go?" Her face paled. "Are you crazy? He's only ten years old."

"Which is halfway to twenty, and only three years away from bein' a teenager. Remember what you said to me about

Melissa? It applies here, too. It's real easy to dish out the advice when it's not your own kid, isn't it?''

"This is a completely different situation."

"Melissa wanted to dress like her friends. Brandon wants to be like his. How is that different?"

"It just *is*."

Moving closer to her, Zack put his hands around her upper arms. "Come on, Lori, you know it's not any different at all, and I know you're honest enough to admit it."

She glared up at him for a moment, then sighed in resignation and turned toward the doorway. Opening it, she stuck her head outside and called Brandon. After telling him he could go, she turned back to Zack.

"He'll be fine, I promise," he said.

"I hope you're right, McBride. I truly do. Because if he's not..."

"If he's not, what? Are you gonna have to hurt me?"

"As if I could." She gave him a withering look that reminded him so much of Billie, it hurt him a hell of a lot more than Lori would ever know. "I just really wish you would have given me a better chance to think this over."

"There's nothing to think about," he protested.

"From your point of view." Turning away from him, she crossed her arms over her breasts. "Darn it, Zack, you always think you know what's right for everybody, but sometimes you really don't have a clue."

He studied the stiff line of her spine and the rigid set to her shoulders, and decided to leave before he said something he might later regret. Honest to God, sometimes that woman drove him batty with her melodramatic reactions to everything. It wasn't his fault if he didn't have a clue. If she wanted him to have clue, maybe she should tell the truth about herself and Brandon. The whole truth, no matter how unpleasant it was.

Brandon was so excited that night, it was all Lori could do to get him into bed. By the time he finally fell asleep, she felt so stressed and claustrophobic, she had to step outside and get some fresh air or explode in a tantrum of frustration. The air was pleasantly cool and scented with a hint of pine and dust and animals nearby. Twilight had vanished with the earth's rotation into darkness, and the stars overhead filled her with a sense of her own insignificance. Compared to the vastness of the universe, her troubles were minuscule.

That didn't stop her from worrying about them, of course. And nothing would ever make her stop worrying about Brandon's safety and well-being. *Was* letting him go on this cattle drive the right thing for him? Or was she abdicating her parental responsibility in favor of making herself more popular with everyone at the Flying M? She honestly didn't know.

"Well, then, try to be logical," she muttered.

Grace *would* take good care of him, and he *would* have a blast. They were headed into the mountains; it was highly unlikely that they would see anyone else, much less one of the few people on the planet who might recognize Brandon. Brandon was not reckless by nature, and he *was* an excellent rider. There was no reason to assume disaster was inevitable or imminent.

And yet, she couldn't shake the feeling that letting Brandon go on the cattle drive might be the worst decision she had made since the day she agreed to marry Hugh. Fear put an acrid taste in her mouth and made her heart lurch painfully inside her chest. Anger surged up behind the fear.

Closing her hands into fists at her sides, she glared up at the heavens, as if the glittering stars could somehow give her the answers she so desperately needed to find. "Dammit, did I kill him? Or is that monster still alive?"

Grace and the kids left for the mountains at six o'clock the following morning. Lori, Wade, two helpers and the assistant director left for Cody at eight. Zack hurried through his list of chores, cleaned himself up and left for Cody at two.

Named after Buffalo Bill and home of the eastern entrance

to Yellowstone National Park, Cody was a small, but thriving community whose population doubled with tourists during the summer months. The arrival of the production company had made the traffic even more obnoxious than usual. Zack stuck to the back roads to get to Old Trail Town, which was located a few miles west of the city limits.

Old Trail Town's parking lot was crowded with Wade's pickups and stock trailers, the production company's electricians, carpenters, sound technicians and media vans representing TV stations from all over the northwest, as well as a few of the gossipy entertainment programs from Hollywood. Zack found himself a space, however, and went in search of Lori. Finding her turned out to be a much harder task than he'd expected.

The whole complex was clogged with people, equipment and electrical cables, turning each street and alley into an obstacle course. The din of shouted orders mixed with the regular drone of conversation made it impossible to pick out any one voice at a time. He couldn't even see the horses or their temporary corral until he'd battled his way through to the last row of vintage cabins.

Even then he almost didn't recognize Lori when she rode past him, perched on the seat of a huge freight wagon, pulled by a matching team of bays. She had her hair all stuffed up under a sweat-stained cowboy hat and a big pair of sunglasses covered half her face. Leather gloves camouflaged the daintiness of her hands, while an oversize windbreaker hid the feminine curves of her body. To a casual observer, she could have been a young, skinny boy instead of a grown woman.

He recognized her battered boots, however, and when she stopped to avoid mowing down a camera crew crossing the street, he jumped up onto the wagon's running board and climbed onto the wooden seat beside her. She gave him a startled look that made him laugh. Her face turned pale when she recognized him. "Zack! What are you doing here? Is Brandon okay?"

"He's fine, Lori. Honest. I just came to watch you work."

Her shoulders slumped a little, no doubt with relief. Then her cheeks turned pink, as if she'd realized how much she had overreacted to the situation. "Sorry. I'm not used to being away from him. Do you suppose we could start this conversation over?"

Zack suspected her fear came from something more than separation anxiety, but he didn't want to hassle her about it yet. For now, he just wanted to enjoy her company. Tipping his hat to her, he drawled like a cowboy from one of those old, black-and-white movies he'd loved as a kid. "Howdy, ma'am. Mind if I hitch a ride?"

She grinned, then drawled right back at him. "No, I reckon that'll be all right, pardner."

Delighted to see a little playfulness in her for a change, he settled himself more comfortably on the wagon seat. "Thank you kindly. My feet are plumb wore out."

"Set up here on this hard ol' wagon seat all day, you'll have another part of ya that's plumb wore out."

He cast an appreciative glance toward her bottom and laughed again. "Other than that, how's it goin'?"

"All right." She inclined her head toward the horses. "I'm putting them through their moves and letting them get used to all the activity they'll have to cope with next week, but these guys are old hands at this."

She made a left turn, then another one and drove the team back in the opposite direction. Glancing off to his left, Zack spotted the camera crew who had given him the opportunity to join Lori and gave them a friendly wave. When one of the guys waved back and then pointed at the wagon while he said something over his shoulder to the man carrying the camera, Lori let out a muffled groan and tugged the brim of her hat lower.

"Please, don't do that, Zack."

"Do what?"

"Attract attention from those creeps."

Zack craned his neck around, wanting another look at the camera crew. "Who are they?"

"They're tabloid-TV gossipmongers."

"Those guys?"

She nodded. "They're all over the place, and if you give them any encouragement, they'll hang around all the time trying to get you to tell them some dirt about the actors."

"Sounds nasty."

"That's exactly what they are. Nasty. They really don't care whether your information is true or not. They just want a juicy story that will titillate the public."

"All right. I'll be surly as hell the next time I see 'em."

She smiled a little, but shook her head at him. "No, don't do that, either. Then they'll be after you to find out why you're so surly. Ignoring them is the safest option."

Safest? She was always looking for the safest way to handle everything. It bothered him to realize that because what he was hoping to convince her to do with him could hardly be classified as "safe."

"Sure looks busy around here, today," he said.

"It's actually fairly quiet. Wait until we've got the whole cast here and all of the extras, the wardrobe trailers and the caterers. It's a study in barely controlled chaos."

"You sound like you enjoy it, though," Zack said.

"Oh, I do. It's a fascinating process, and these people are so creative and funny sometimes, I can always find something entertaining to watch."

She made another left turn at the next corner, then another left to complete the circuit she'd already covered at least once before. Zack figured she'd probably been driving or riding around in this circle for most of the day.

"How late do you have to work tonight?"

She arched an eyebrow at him. "Why?"

"Well, since Brandon's gone, I was hopin' you'd have supper with me tonight. At my brother Cal's place in Sunshine Gap."

She glanced down at her clothes and grimaced. "I'm not really dressed for a restaurant."

Zack laughed. "Cal's Place is not what you'd call an elegant restaurant. There'll be lots of folks in there who've been working hard all day and didn't bother to change. Believe me, you'll fit right in."

"Oh, Zack, I don't know. I'll have to get up early again tomorrow morning, and—"

"I know you will, Lori. I promise I'll get you home early."

Though he couldn't see her eyes through the dark lenses of her sunglasses, he could feel her studying him. Her front teeth worried her bottom lip. Tension radiated off her body like July heat waves shimmering off the highway.

"Aw, come on, sweetheart. I won't pounce on you. It'll do you good to get out for an evening before they start filming and you'll have to work late all the time."

After another agonizing moment, she slowly nodded her head. "All right. But I rode over here with Wade this morning."

"I'll pick you up whenever and wherever you want."

"Five-thirty." She pointed to a small grove of aspens at the far end of the grounds. "We've got our corral and equipment set up just beyond those trees."

"I'll be there."

When she slowed the team to negotiate the next left turn, he jumped down, walked around in front of the horses and climbed onto the running board on the driver's side. Snatching her hat off with one hand, he tipped her sunglasses on top of her head, then slid his other hand into the cloud of hair that tumbled to her shoulders and swooped in for a thoroughly satisfying kiss. Then he plunked her hat back down on her head and jumped to the ground. She stared at him, shook her head as if to clear it, then stared at him again.

"You said you weren't going to pounce on me."

"Pounce? That wasn't a pounce." He clapped one hand on his chest and gave her the most wide-eyed, innocent smile he could manage. "Shoot, honey, that was just a friendly little smooch. When I decide to pounce, you'll know it."

Her laugh sounded reluctant, even grudging. "You're a terrible man, McBride. Really terrible."

"Yeah, but I'm a hell of a good kisser."

She snorted, then clucked to the team and drove away. Zack cupped his hands around his mouth and called after her. "See you later?"

She waved one hand in acknowledgment and continued on down the dusty street. Chuckling to himself, Zack turned toward the parking lot, intending to go back into Cody and do a little shopping as long as he was already here. Instead, he found himself on the receiving end of another one of those camera crews Lori despised. The guys all gave him a thumbs-up sign, and the one with the camera pointed to it, indicating that he'd caught Zack's "friendly little smooch" on tape.

Uh-oh. If Lori ever found out, she'd skin him alive and then nail his sorry hide to the barn door. Aw, well, what the little lady didn't know couldn't make her mad.

Lori spent the rest of the afternoon trying to forget Zack's "friendly little smooch." She failed miserably. Her lips actually tingled with remembered sensations, all of them building a sense of pleasant, even eager anticipation for the evening ahead. Dratted man. He was just so darn...cute. Well, all *right*, she'd admit that he was far more than cute.

The truth was, that she found him nearly irresistible in every way that mattered—sexually, mentally and emotionally. The timing couldn't have been worse. Without Brandon there to remind her of everything she had at stake....

No. She didn't need a ten-year-old boy to remind her to be careful, and she wasn't going to second-guess herself. Darn it, she hadn't had any free time to feel and act like a woman in four years, and she *would* benefit from a night out.

Didn't she deserve a little happiness? Just this once? Yes, she did.

She felt a fierce attraction to Zack, but she wasn't some giggly teenager drowning with hormones. She could and would control herself. Even if Zack decided to pounce, after all.

Chapter Eight

Cal's Place was a rustic, smoky little restaurant where beef was king and nobody believed in fat or cholesterol. Since it was only Thursday night, business was slow. The staff and the few customers present enjoyed a jovial atmosphere, however, and Lori quickly discovered that showing up as Zack McBride's date was enough to buy her automatic acceptance as "one of them." His brother Cal sported a thick black mustache instead of a full beard, but otherwise, he could have passed for Zack's twin.

After harassing Zack as only a little brother can for a good five minutes, Cal escorted them to the most private table in the restaurant and left them alone. From that moment on, Lori felt as if she'd stepped into a dream world. The conversations around them provided a mellow backdrop of sound. Having no need to hurry for once was a gift in and of itself. Zack was attentive and good-humored. The prime rib practically melted in her mouth and the house wine slid down her throat like liquid sunshine, warming her from the inside out.

When Zack suggested they move into the bar next door to take advantage of the jukebox and the dance floor, she didn't even consider refusing. He loaded the machine with quarters and punched in his selections, then opened his arms to her in invitation. Heart fluttering, she stepped into them, and when they closed gently around her, she wrapped her own arms around his waist and snuggled against him with a soft, satisfied sigh.

A pair of silver-haired cowboys sat at the bar, visiting with the bartender and chain-smoking, and a younger pair of men had taken over the pool table. Zack and Lori had the dance floor to themselves and they circled it again and again without speaking. He tugged out the clip holding her hair up in an untidy knot, smiled at her, then hummed along in a low, pleasant baritone. Holding her securely against him, he kept one hand at the back of her waist and the other hand folded around one of hers.

His lead was so easy to follow, she let go of her natural inhibitions, allowing him to carry her into the rhythm of the song. His chest was hard and his heart thumped a strong, steady beat beneath her cheek. He smelled of shaving lotion and soap and a hint of leather, and for the first time in months and months, she felt safe and relaxed.

She also enjoyed the pleasant tingles of arousal she felt whenever their chests and hips bumped together. She had forgotten, or perhaps never even known that a man's embrace could feel so delightful. Executing a dizzying turn, he smiled down at her, then slowly lowered his head and kissed her.

Letting her head fall back, she simply closed her eyes and surrendered, incapable of caring whether anyone saw them. With only his lips and tongue, he filled her with pleasure— glorious, energizing pleasure that stripped away her weariness and her worries. Never before in the history of the universe had there been a more delicious, tempting, heart-thumping, mind-bending, toe-curling kiss. She was sure of it.

Her only possible response was to kiss him back until he felt the same sensations, the same riot of needs and desires, the same greedy passion that was stealing her breath and the strength from her knees. The kiss went on and on while their dance slowed to a dreamy shuffling of feet. She curved one hand behind his neck and cupped her other palm over the side of his beard. His hands shifted smoothly, shaping themselves to the curve of her waist and hips, holding her closer and closer still, showing her with his body exactly how much he wanted her.

Had it come from any other man, she would have found such a graphic display of arousal frightening. That it came from Zack thrilled her. She could no longer deny or rationalize away the feelings she had for him. He was strong and, without a doubt, all man, but he was also caring and gentle, and not afraid to show it occasionally.

The truth was, she was already three-fourths of the way in love with him. And yes, she *wanted* him to want her. She *wanted* to feel his passion, to experience it and, yes, to revel in it. She *wanted* to know what it was like to make love with a man who really wanted her, a man she didn't fear.

When he finally lifted his mouth from hers, she felt dazed. She stood there in the middle of the dance floor, gazing up at him and wondering why he'd stopped kissing her. Slowly, she realized the jukebox had quit playing and everyone, including the bartender, had left. For some unfathomable reason, the knowledge made her laugh.

One side of his mouth curved into a crooked grin and he raised a not-quite-steady hand to stroke the side of her face. When he spoke, his voice sounded huskier than usual. "What's so funny?"

She glanced pointedly around the room, then smiled at him. "Do you do this often?"

"Kiss a pretty lady in public?" He grinned. "Not since I was about fifteen. And I sure never cleared out a bar this way before."

"Why did they all leave?"

"Could be we fogged up their glasses."

She laughed softly. He joined in, rubbing his chin against

the side of her head, as if he enjoyed the feel of her hair against his beard. Lord, if he kept doing that, she would start purring like a stray cat. If he kissed her again, she suspected she would melt into a little puddle on the floor.

He looked down at her again, then rested his forehead against hers. "Hey, Lori?"

"What, Zack?"

"If we don't get out of here in the next thirty seconds, I'm gonna have to pounce on you after all."

Visions of all sorts of erotic love play flashed through her mind. Goodness, where had *those* ideas come from? She cleared her throat. "That, um, sounds rather...serious."

"Yeah, I guess it is. Could be one heck of a lot of fun, though. What do you think?"

"I think...oh, Zack, I don't know what I think. It's not that I don't want you to...pounce. I'm just not certain I can make a rational decision right—"

"I want you like hell on fire, woman. Think about this on the way back to the ranch, and when we get there, you can make your rational decision."

Sliding his hands down into her back pockets, he pulled her flush against him and kissed her senseless. Then he slung one arm around her waist and half walked, half carried her out to his Blazer. She hadn't known a four-wheel-drive vehicle could fly.

Riding along in the dark, with desire simmering between them like a living thing and a heady sense of anticipation building with every fence post that whipped by her window, Lori struggled to regain at least a semblance of perspective. She knew there were a thousand reasons she should say no when they arrived at the ranch. Possibly a hundred thousand reasons.

Right this minute, however, she couldn't think of one. Not even a little one. She simply couldn't focus on anything but that scorching kiss, and the empty, aching chasm in the middle of her being she knew he could fill.

Her past didn't matter. His job didn't matter. Even her son

didn't matter half as much as she knew he should. But Brandon didn't need her attention right now. In truth, he was probably having the time of his life playing cowboy.

No, this was *her* moment, *her* time to feel like a woman again. Quite possibly, this could be her one chance to experience an hour or two of happiness with a special man who made her feel worthy. After all she'd been through, didn't she deserve that much? Just this once? She'd thought so before, but now she didn't know. She couldn't think. Didn't want to think.

All too soon Zack pulled into the ranch yard and stopped midway between the path to her trailer and the dirt road to his house. He remained quiet, leaving the decision completely up to her. Darn him, it would be so much easier if he would just kiss her senseless again and carry her off to his bedroom.

But that wasn't his way. He was an extremely sexy and sensual man, but he obviously wasn't into seduction. He would want a partner who willingly gave him everything, with no regrets the morning after. She respected him for that, even while she wanted to hit him for being noble enough to make sure she knew exactly what she was doing.

The silence stretched out and gained mass like a billowing thunderhead, making her painfully aware of her own heartbeat and the pulsing of the engine. Should she? Shouldn't she? She *had* to make a decision, damn it. It shouldn't be this hard to make it. But it *was.*

The last time she'd made love— No. That hadn't been making love. It hadn't even been having sex. The real word to describe her last sexual encounter with Hugh was too ugly to repeat or even to think. Zack wouldn't hurt her that way. Of course, he wouldn't. And yet…he was so big, if she had misjudged him, she would be utterly powerless against his greater strength.

He turned to her then, and caressed her cheek with the backs of his knuckles. The flashback rolled over her with the speed and strength of a tornado. Her lungs locked up, her heart slammed against her sternum, and black spots danced before her eyes until she thought she would faint.

The pain was as real and as physical as it had been that awful night so long ago. The humiliation and degradation burned like acid in her throat, in her gut, in her soul. And yet, sheer terror paralyzed her. If she didn't submit, Hugh would destroy her by destroying Brandon.

She had no reason to doubt his ability and willingness to carry out the threat. He'd already destroyed her favorite horse, her dog and everyone and everything else she'd ever loved; Brandon was simply the next logical step in a long progression of atrocities. Worse yet, Hugh would do it without any outward evidence of anger, just as he had all those other times.

Zack's voice came to her, wavering as if it had traveled a great distance. "Lori? Sweetheart? Are you all right?"

She started, blinked hard, then violently shook her head in an attempt to clear it.

Zack's face slowly came into focus, replacing the hideous visions of Hugh in her mind. Her palms were damp, her muscles ached, her stomach roiled. Fumbling with the door handle, she scrambled out of the Blazer just in time before her dinner spewed onto the ground.

Choking with embarrassment, she frantically waved Zack away when he tried to come to her aid. When the vomiting finally ended, tears of rage and humiliation gushed down her cheeks, and she used the backs of her hands to wipe them away. Zack reached for her again, but she jumped back out of his reach.

"Don't touch me," she shouted. "For God's sake, just don't touch me."

"Lori, what's wrong?" he asked. "What did I do?"

She held out both palms, as if they could provide her with some sort of defense, a silly illusion given his size and strength. Her breath shuddered going in and going out, while the adrenaline pumping through her bloodstream gradually dissipated and her brain began to function normally again.

His forehead knotted up in a worried frown, Zack stared at her in stunned silence. After the way she'd behaved on the dance floor, she could hardly blame him. Talk about giving mixed signals!

Oh, Lord, how on earth could she ever explain this?

He held up his own palms as if to show her he was harmless. "I won't touch you, Lori," he said softly. "Everything's all right now. You're safe."

"I'm s-s-sorry, Zack."

"Don't worry about it on my account. I just want to know you're okay."

"I'm, uh…I'm fine now," she whispered.

"What happened?"

She couldn't tell him the truth, but she didn't want to lie to him, either. She lied anyway. "I…I'm not really sure."

He raised an eyebrow at her. "It looked like some kind of a panic attack. Maybe a little post-traumatic stress?"

His perception made her skin prickle with uneasiness. "I don't know. I don't want to talk about it."

"All right, we'll leave it alone for now."

At his calm, easygoing tone, her stomach clenched painfully. Nobody—no *man*—was that laid back when disappointed, especially when the disappointment aborted all hope of having sex. Zack really should be angry at her. Oh, she wished he *would* get angry, so she'd know what he would do then. Was he like Hugh after all? Would he pretend everything was okay and then turn on her when she least expected it?

He waved a hand toward the Blazer. "Come on. I'll take you home."

Without waiting for a reply, he returned to the driver's side and climbed in. She eyed him warily for a moment, then told herself she was acting more than a little paranoid. Zack had never done anything to earn her distrust. Damn Hugh for making it so impossible for her to trust anyone.

Muttering to herself, she hurried to the vehicle and climbed in beside Zack. He waited until she fastened her seat belt, then drove onto the lane that led to his house. She stiffened automatically.

"I thought you were going to take me home," she said.

He shot her a surprised glance. "I am. To my house. I'm not leavin' you alone when you're this upset."

"I'm fine. Really."

"You don't look fine," he said quietly. "You look like you've seen a real nasty ghost."

She scowled at him, crossed her arms over her breasts and pointedly turned her gaze toward the window. Inwardly, she cringed at such accurate perception on his part. Other people complained about not being able to read her, but Zack seemed to see everything no matter how hard she tried to hide her thoughts and feelings.

Well, he could poke, prod and pry all he wanted. She wasn't going to answer his questions. Eventually he would get bored with her refusal to cooperate and take her back to her trailer. Then she could fall apart in private.

Concerned about Lori's mental state, Zack cast repeated glances at her the rest of the way home. She sat so close to her door, she probably had a permanent impression of the armrest imprinted on her side. He couldn't see her face, but she was hugging herself as if she were literally trying to hold herself together.

He wasn't even sure if he could help her, much less how to start; he only knew that he had to try. He also knew she was lying through her pretty white teeth when she said she didn't know what had happened. He'd seen enough post-traumatic stress reactions to recognize a flashback when he saw one. Whatever she'd experienced back there at the turn-off had been damn ugly.

What exactly had her blasted ex-husband done to her, anyway? He'd give a lot to know. He had his suspicions, of course, but he hoped like hell he was wrong.

When he parked in front of his house, Lori opened her door and jumped out of the Blazer before he even turned off the engine. Zack followed more slowly, giving her a little time and space to calm down in. Once inside, he walked through the house to the kitchen. Lori visited the bathroom, then returned to the living room.

By the time he carried in two mugs, one with ginger tea to settle her stomach and one with coffee for himself, she appeared to have regained her composure. She accepted the tea with an appreciative sniff and settled back on the sofa as if they'd never shared those kisses on the dance floor or even considered making love tonight. The thought irritated him, but he clamped down the emotion.

This wasn't about him. At this point, it was all about her. One way or another, he intended to learn the truth. After giving her time to finish her tea, he set his cup beside hers on the coffee table and turned to face her.

"What really happened tonight?" he asked.

"Nothing."

"Nothing?" His laugh had a harsh edge, even to his own ears. "Shoot, I've had women turn me down before, but none of them ever vomited over it. All you had to do was say no."

She looked down at her tightly clasped hands, but he could still see one side of her face flush a vivid red. She exhaled a shaky sigh, then lifted her gaze to meet his again. "I know. And I'm really sorry I...overreacted that—"

"I don't want an apology. I want to know *why* you had that flashback. Was it something I said? Something I did?"

"I don't know what you're talking about."

"Bull. We've got a couple of Vietnam vets in town who still have them once in a while. And my cousin Dillon's had them ever since the accident that tore his face all up. I know what I saw tonight, and I want to know why you have flashbacks."

She crossed her arms over her breasts again. "It's none of your business."

"Wrong. You made it my business when you kissed me the way you did tonight."

"I know I led you on," she said stiffly. "And I really am sorry you were disappointed."

He dismissed her apology with a wave. "Forget it. That's not the issue."

"Oh? Then what is?"

"If we hadn't been in a public place, we would've ripped each other's clothes off and made love right then and there. It's gonna happen again. Real soon."

"It most certainly is *not.*"

"Yes, it is, darlin'. You know it and I know it, and I need to understand what's going on with you so I don't scare the hell out of you or accidentally hurt you when it does."

"Your ego is showing, Mr. McBride."

He couldn't help laughing at that. Of course his laughter ticked her off. Which, unfortunately, only tickled his stupid funny bone even more. She got up and headed for the front door. He barely managed to get in front of her in time to block her way with an arm across the doorway.

"Aw, come on," he said. "Be fair and be honest with yourself. You wanted me as much as I wanted you. Since we're both single, consenting adults, what's so bad about that?"

She lowered her gaze to his arm, and he saw her throat muscles contract. "Nothing's wrong with it," she whispered. "But isn't it obvious that I'm not capable of following through? I suppose I'm actually rather…frigid."

"You? Frigid?" He shook his head at such a ridiculous notion. "No way. You're about the warmest, sexiest, most vibrant women I've ever met."

"But, I've never been any good in bed."

"If that's even halfway true, you've had damn poor lovers."

"I've only had one."

"Yeah? Was he the one who decided you weren't any good in bed?" When she gave a jerky little nod, Zack snorted in disgust. "Well, he was just blaming his own shortcomings on you."

She looked up at him, and he thought he spotted a flicker of hope in her eyes. "How can you be so certain of that?"

"Frigid woman are made, not born. Young women aren't much different from young horses. Given enough patience and gentle treatment, almost all of them will respond positively. Know what I mean?"

A small, but definitely wry smile tugged at the corners of her mouth. "I'm not sure I like the comparison, but I do know what you mean."

"So, are you gonna let one inadequate, inept idiot with a big mouth wreck one of life's very best pleasures for you?"

"You think you can make it…better?" she asked.

"Hell, I *know* I can make it better. My ex complained about a lot of things I didn't do well enough to suit her, but never that one." Moving cautiously so as not to frighten her, he tenderly cupped his hands around her face. "Besides which, I care about you, Lori, and I'm not some horny teenager who can't wait for his lady to find satisfaction."

"Oh, really?"

"Damn straight. I've got all the patience and gentleness you'll ever need. If you'll just tell me—"

"Zack?"

"What?"

"Will you shut up and kiss me?"

"It won't stop with a kiss. Are you sure this is what you really want?"

"Yes. Please, Zack, just…do it."

The instant those words came out of her mouth, Lori wanted to recall them. At the same time, she really didn't. Didn't she deserve a shot at being with a man who would treat her with the warmth and tenderness she deserved? Hadn't she already let Hugh destroy too much of the good in her life without allowing him to take this away from her, too?

Yes. Yes, she had. If there was any hope at all that she could find pleasure in Zack's arms, she wanted—no, she *needed* to know it. Just this once. Just this once, damn it, she

needed to take the chance. She raised her mouth and closed
her eyes in preparation for his kiss.

It seemed as if she waited forever, but finally, he said, "All
right, darlin'."

A chuckle rumbled out of him, and when he pressed his
lips against hers, she could feel his smile. The hard knot in
the pit of her stomach slowly relaxed. Sighing, she opened
her mouth to admit his tongue, but he merely traced her upper
lip and the ridge of her front teeth. He repeated the teasing
motions on her lower lip and teeth in a tag-you're-it sort of
gesture.

She crossed her wrists behind his neck and deepened the
kiss herself. He smiled again and crossed his own wrists at
the back of her waist, holding her in a loose embrace. But
now, she didn't want a loose embrace; she wanted to feel his
strength and his warmth. Raising up on her tiptoes, she lifted
her arms higher, wrapped them around his neck and pressed
closer to him.

He hesitated a moment, as if giving her an opportunity to
reconsider. When she didn't, he slid his own arms farther
around her waist, bringing her flush against him. They both
groaned softly and moved even closer, intensifying the pleasure of touching each other this way.

Their kisses deepened. She slid her fingers into his thick,
glossy hair, moved them down the sides of his head, tracing
his ears, then moved them lower still, into the springy softness of his beard. An odd sense of restlessness seized her.
She wanted more, but she wasn't sure what more was. The
wretched man seemed determined to make her take the lead,
only she didn't know how to initiate something new or even
what that something new might be.

Even if she had known what she wanted, she didn't know
how to ask for it, much less take it. She only knew how to
submit, not how to participate. Her ignorance was frustrating,
infuriating, mortifying. She was so close to something she'd
wanted forever, she knew she was. But any second now,
Zack would turn away from her in disgust. Yes, of course he

would. He must think she was some kind of freak. She moaned at the thought of losing this…whatever it was she was close to.

As if he could read her frantic thoughts, he eased her away from the door and shuffled back across the living room with her. Keeping his mouth fastened to hers, he lowered himself to the sofa and settled her onto his lap. An impressive bulge behind the zipper of his jeans pressed against her hip. Before she could start worrying about it, however, he cradled the back of her neck against his arm and kissed her deeply.

He hadn't exaggerated when he'd said he had all the patience she would ever need. Again and again he kissed her, holding her close with one arm while using his free hand to stroke her hair, her face, her neck and shoulders. His hands were big, scarred and otherwise banged up, but his touch was as tender and gentle as if he were caressing a newborn baby. Despite his warning that he wouldn't stop with a kiss, he seemed perfectly content to kiss her for the rest of the night.

She felt drugged with delight in his strong arms, tasting his unique, salty-sweet taste, feeling his warmth and his passion, breathing in the distinctive woodsy scent of his aftershave. She felt devoured, but cherished, desirable, but cared for, aroused, but eager. And still, he kissed her.

Her bones warmed and softened. Her breasts swelled and tingled. Her lower body grew damp in preparation for his penetration.

It was the most wonderful, liberating set of sensations she'd ever experienced. How could she have been married for all those years and never known this joy? This exquisite sense of flying without a plane? This…oh, Lord, she didn't have any names for what was happening to her.

Her earlier restlessness returned. She cautiously raised one hand to his chest and tested the hard padding of muscle beneath her fingertips. He stiffened slightly, then sighed, closed his eyes and let his head fall back against the sofa. Fearing she'd done something wrong, she yanked her hand away.

"I'm sorry," she said. "I didn't mean—"

Uttering one of his deep, rumbly chuckles, he raised his head and met her gaze. "Sweetheart, I liked it." Gently grasping her hand, he placed it on his chest and laid his own hand on top, trapping it there. "You can touch me anytime, anywhere you want, and I'll love every second of it."

Then he went back to kissing her. She turned toward him, the better to exercise her new freedom. With each tentative pat she grew bolder and more aroused, and if the sighs and moans he emitted were anything to judge by, she would have to say he enjoyed her touch as much as she enjoyed his. As if to agree with her thought, he reached between them, gave one hard, quick jerk with his hand and popped open the snaps on his shirt from his collarbones to his belt buckle.

She simply looked at him for a long moment, noting the wedge of curly dark hair between his nipples and the tapering lower edge until it formed a thin line just above his navel. Beneath the hair lay an inviting expanse of smooth, swarthy skin stretched over ridges of muscle. Her fingers literally itched to explore all the bumps and indentations and textures.

"Do it, darlin'," he murmured. "Touch me. Please."

His breathing roughened and he arched toward her when she complied. Feeling as if she were seducing him, she herself was seduced. Knowing she was giving him pleasure made her feel powerful, which she found incredibly erotic. Since he was basically bare to the waist, it only seemed right and natural when he unfastened her blouse and her bra.

As she had done earlier, he simply looked at her breasts for a breathless moment, and the admiration in his eyes dispensed with any sense of modesty or shame she might otherwise have felt. Her nipples contracted into hard peaks, whether from exposure to the night air or from the nearly physical touch of his gaze, she didn't know. At the moment, she only knew that she desperately wanted him to touch her there.

His callused hands whispered over her skin, and it was her turn to arch forward in search of more satisfying contact. Placing one hand at the center of her spine, he increased the

curve of her arch, covered her neck and shoulders with
kisses, then moved down and across her chest so slowly she
felt insane with impatience before he finally reached her aching breasts. By the time he cupped them between his hands
and took one nipple into his warm, wet mouth, she could
have wept with the pleasure of it.

Liquid heat raced from her nipples to the sensitive spot
between her thighs. She shifted and squirmed on his lap,
trying to ease the aching emptiness inside her. She'd never
felt like this. Never wanted like this. Never *needed* like this.

He slid one arm beneath her knees and surged to his feet,
then carried her into a dark room. His legs banged into something and he muttered a curse that made her laugh. Then he
bent over and she felt the softness of a mattress against her
back, a pillow beneath her head.

She heard a click, and a bedside lamp came on, revealing
a starkly masculine bedroom. The furniture was all big and
solid-looking, the curtains and bedspread on the king-size
bed were a rich navy-red-and-white plaid. She paid no attention to anything beyond that. No woman in her right mind
would care about decor when she had a big, muscular, handsome man slowly stripping off his clothes not five feet away
from her.

He was, in a word, *beautiful.* He undoubtedly would object
to such a description of his manly charms, but it was the
word that truly fit him best. He really did want her, and
though she quailed inwardly at the sheer size of him, she
wasn't afraid of him, either. Besides, she was too aroused
and too curious to entertain any serious thoughts of backing
out now.

Pausing, he gazed down into her eyes and gave her a lazy,
sexy smile that made her crave his touch all over again. She
held out one hand to him. He took it, turned it over and
dropped a gentle love bite in the center of her palm. She
gasped, and he chuckled, and released her long enough to
take a foil packet from the drawer in the nightstand. Then he
lay down beside her and took her into his arms.

From that instant he took charge, leading her into his love-making as confidently as he had led her on the dance floor. Her clothes fell away with a minimum of fuss, and her whole body was attuned to his every movement. She felt like a greedy sponge, soaking up every sensory delight he offered, and thrilling to the sounds of his moans and sighs that told her she had succeeded in returning the favor.

His kisses deepened. His caresses became bolder and firmer. His earthy, guttural suggestions lit fires of anticipation in her nerve endings. He gave her heat and light, color and excitement, and an appreciation of the capabilities of her own body that absolutely astounded her.

When he parted her thighs with his hands and touched her intimately for the first time, she instinctively flinched away from him. Soothing her with his voice, he kissed her again and again, so deeply she forgot everything but the sensual magic he created so effortlessly. By the time he finally worked his way back to her thighs, she had no desire to object.

She gazed up at him while he knelt between her legs and took care of protecting her, then opened her arms to him when he turned back to her. He lowered himself onto her, supporting most of his weight on his forearms. She felt an exquisite sort of pressure as he slowly entered her, but no pain. He held himself still for what seemed like forever, stroking her tousled hair out of her eyes and praising her in soft words and tones that reminded her of his horsey patter.

The thought made her smile, and when he saw it, he smiled back at her and started moving his hips, slowly and carefully at first, and then with growing speed and power. The sensations sent her flying into previously uncharted territories. She arched up to meet his thrusts, and his gusty shouts of encouragement set off charges of excitement along her own nerve pathways.

The pleasure built and built inside her, then folded in on itself, and drew into a tight spiraling need where their bodies were joined. She strained against him, whimpering and reaching for that shining, mystical something that tauntingly eluded her. She sobbed in frustration, and he lowered his mouth to hers, mimicking the thrusts of his arousal with his tongue.

The spiral grew tighter and tighter yet, and she clung to his back with her fingertips, digging her short nails into his flesh. Then he slid his hands under her bottom and lifted, changing the angle of penetration in a way that made her head swim with delight. She wrapped her legs around his hips and held on for dear life.

Then the spiral snapped, and the resulting torrent of sensations tossed her over the edge of sanity into a pure, sweet ecstasy so intense her body throbbed with it. The sudden release left her exhilarated, but exhausted. Smiling at him, she reached up and caressed the side of his face. He froze for an instant, groaned and repeatedly hammered himself into her until his body convulsed and he collapsed on top of her, sweating and panting for air.

She wrapped her arms around him, hid her face in his neck and promptly burst into tears.

Chapter Nine

Wanting to prolong the pleasure for both of them, Zack gritted his teeth and tried to ignore the familiar warning signals in his groin, but there was no holding back. When it was over, he collapsed against Lori, too drained to move.

At first, all he could hear was his own ragged breathing and the roar of his racing heartbeat. But as he finally began to recover, he heard a choked little cry and realized the dampness in the crook of his neck wasn't sweat, but tears. Lori's tears.

He reared up onto his forearms and felt his heart slide right down to the bottoms of his feet when he saw her lying beneath him, her hands covering her face and her shoulders shaking with the force of her sobs. His fingers trembling, he cautiously stroked her hair.

"Lori? Sweetheart? Did I hurt you? I swear I never meant to be so rough."

She made a sound sort of halfway between a snort and a sob, but she didn't answer. Well, damn. He started to pull away from her, but she clamped her legs tighter around his hips, silently refusing to let him go.

What the hell was going on with her? If he'd hurt her bad enough to make her bawl, why wasn't she pushing him away? To have any hope of figuring this out, he needed to see her face.

"Lori, please, look at me. At least tell me why you're crying. What did I do wrong?"

Sniffling, she took her hands away from her face and looked up at him with a tremulous smile. "You didn't do anything wrong. And you didn't hurt me. Not at all. I'm crying because it was so…wonderful."

A lump clogged his throat and he felt humbled. He hadn't done anything to deserve the blatant adoration in her eyes. Well, he'd tried his best to make it good for her, but any man worthy of the name would've done exactly the same thing. Good Lord, a guy could look at her face and think she'd never experienced ultimate pleasure before. But she'd been married for five or six years, maybe, and she had a ten-year-old kid. Surely, her ex wasn't *that* much of an idiot, was he?

Since she still wouldn't let him go, he rolled over onto his side, bringing her with him, allowing him to see her face and continue to cuddle her. She burrowed in like a little animal seeking shelter, and it yanked at his heartstrings to know she was willing to turn to him like this. He offered his shoulder for a pillow, then slowly stroked his fingers through her hair after she accepted.

The sex had been pure dynamite, no doubt about that. But this was all right, too. In fact, for the first time in a long time he felt at peace. Yeah, lying here with Lori like this felt damn good. Better than good, it felt…right.

"Sure you're okay?" he asked.

She looked up at him and gave him the sweetest smile he'd ever laid eyes on. "If I was any more okay, you'd probably have to scrape me off the ceiling."

"Yeah, me too."

"Really?"

He leaned down and kissed her forehead. "Really."

Rubbing her cheek against his chest, she smiled again, draped one arm across his middle and gave him a quick hug. The hug had a cautious quality about it, as if she halfway expected him to push her away. Not likely. It was the first spontaneous gesture of affection she'd ever given him, and in a funny sort of way, it touched him as deeply as having sex with her had done.

A smart man would probably question all these tender, protective emotions he felt at the moment. He knew damn well it wasn't a good idea to fall in love with her. But he was just too...content to worry about anything.

He must have dozed off for a while, and maybe she had too. The next thing he became aware of, he was flat on his back, the arm and shoulder she was using as a pillow had gone numb and there was a small hand tentatively combing through his chest hair, tracing the ridges of his collarbones, stroking his belly. He yawned and stretched, then chuckled when she snatched her hand away as if she'd touched a hot stove.

"Not so fast." Grabbing her wrist, he brought her hand back to his belly and trapped it with his own. "That feels real nice."

Her startled gaze flew up to meet his. The questions in her eyes bothered him, but the fear he saw there finished off what was left of his patience. They'd already been just about as intimate with each other as it was possible for a man and a woman to be. Her return to shyness didn't make any sense.

"Why are you so afraid to touch me?" he asked.

She lowered her gaze to his chest. After a long moment she said, "My ex didn't like it."

"Why not?"

"I don't know. He just...didn't."

Zack couldn't hide his astonishment. "But you still made love?"

She gave him a stiff nod, then grimaced as if at a particularly unpleasant memory. "Well, there really wasn't any love involved. It was more like a...bodily function."

Aw, jeez, this guy must be a total loser. No wonder she'd flipped out in the Blazer. No wonder she'd acted like a timid virgin when they'd started making love. And no wonder she'd wept in his arms when she found satisfaction. For her to be treated like that...well, Brandon's conception must have been a miracle. Zack wanted to find the jerk and beat him senseless.

He tucked one finger under her chin and gently raised it until her eyes met his again. "Well, I'm not him. I'm not anything like him. I love it when you touch me."

"Are you sure? I mean, do you like it...all the time?"

"Damn straight, and I intend to touch you every chance I get. But I really want you to tell me if I do anything that makes you feel uncomfortable. This is supposed to be fun for both of us."

"Fun?"

Her incredulous laugh told him the idea of sex being anything other than a burden was a new one for her. Why in the world had she allowed him to make love to her? She must have really had to dig deep to find the courage to go through with it. He wished he'd been more sensitive to her fears.

"Yeah," he said with a grin. "Fun. Didn't you have fun tonight?"

She frowned thoughtfully before answering. "No. It was too intense to be fun." As if she'd just realized what she'd said, she shot him a worried glance and hastened to add, "But it was wonderful, Zack. Really quite wonderful."

He stroked her hair in reassurance. "I'm glad, darlin'. The best thing about sex, though, is that it comes in a lot of different varieties."

"What do you mean?"

"I can show you better than I can tell you." Wrapping both arms around her, he rolled her onto her back and settled himself to one side. "There's super-duper, intense, blow-the-top-of-your-head-off sex, which is what we've already had tonight.''

"Okay…" she said, arching a doubtful eyebrow at him.

Using only the tips of his fingers, he leisurely traced every curve and indentation between her chin and her navel. Her cheeks flushed a lovely shade of pink and her nipples perked right up. "Then there's slow and lazy sex," he drawled. "You're usually about half-asleep and you just sort of start feelin' each other up, you know? You do a lot of pettin' and sighin' and kissin', and there's no big hurry to get to the finish line. It feels real good, but you don't get yourself all worked up until the very end."

She cleared her throat, but her voice still came out sounding a little scratchy. "I see. What other kinds are there?"

"Well, there's the romantic kind." He kissed her luscious mouth thoroughly, then dropped quicker kisses all over her neck and shoulders while continuing his lecture. Her breathing made funny little hitching noises with every kiss.

"This kind usually happens on anniversaries and Valentine's Day, or if the woman orchestrates it. You have a fantastic dinner and use the best china and crystal and all that kind of stuff. You also have candles and soft music and a good wine. Maybe you go dancin'. It's real nice and relaxed, and you both know exactly what the expectations are."

A smile tugged at her mouth and she gave him a knowing look that made him want to forget the lecture and go for the gold. He restrained himself, however. It would just be that much more fun when they finally got where he wanted to take her.

"There's also what I call comforting sex, which is what happens when somebody needs to be held, and things escalate from there." He put his free hand at the back of her waist and hugged her against him for a moment. "There's more tenderness than passion with this kind. It's not exactly thrilling, but it makes you feel real close to each other."

Her eyes took on a misty cast. Oh, damn, the last thing he wanted to do right now was make her cry. Desperate to head off another round of tears, he sped on to the next variety. "One of my favorites is down-and-dirty, behind-the-barn-or-a-bush, quickie sex."

She sputtered with laughter. "What?"

He kissed her for that laugh. Then he pretended to suck a hickey on her neck and slid his hand between her thighs, stroking her sweet spots. "It's exactly what it sounds like. Somebody gives off teasing vibes, the other person decides to pounce, and the fun is on."

She gasped, then arched against his fingers. Her breasts looked full and ripe, and it was all he could do to maintain his train of thought. Bravely, he battled on.

"This kind is real physical and real fast, and you get an extra kick from knowing somebody else might come along and catch you in the act, so to speak. Guys usually like it more than women, but as long as they get the other kinds on a fairly regular basis, most women are willing to oblige."

"Oh my," she said, her eyes a little glazed. "Are there any...other kinds?"

"You bet. There's kinky sex, hot-and-sweaty sex, shoot, there's a kind for every mood you can imagine. As long as you remember it's supposed to be *mutual* pleasure, anything goes. There's even goofy sex."

She snorted at that. "Goofy sex?"

"Yeah. Which is what we're gonna have right now."

With no more warning than that, he lowered his head and blew loud, sloppy raspberries on her belly. She shrieked, tried to push his head away and collapsed in helpless laughter. Just for the fun of it, he ran a line of big, smacking kisses down her legs, nibbled on her toes, rolled her over and nipped her little behind. She shrieked again, then rolled back over, grabbed his hands and wrestled with him the same way the boys always did.

They were both laughing their fool heads off and rolling all over the bed, covers and pillows flying every which way. Once she got into the spirit of things, she fought dirty, pulling his chest hair, tickling him under his armpits and grabbing him where a man is most likely to obey any command he receives. Damn, but it felt good. And it was wonderful to see her blue eyes shining with the joy of playing.

He let her end up on top of him. She straddled his hips like a jockey perched on top of a Thoroughbred's back. Grinning wickedly, she grasped his shoulders and leaned forward, using all of her weight and strength to pin him to the mattress.

"I've got you now, McBride. Say uncle."

Pretending not to see her, he looked all around the room and asked, "Who said that? A mosquito?"

She gripped him harder with her hands and thighs. "A mosquito? You're going to pay for that."

He gave her his cockiest grin. "Think so?"

"I know so." She leaned down, clicking her teeth as if she planned to bite his nose.

He slid his hands up the insides of her thighs until his thumbs met in the middle. It only took a couple of deft strokes before her eyes dilated, and she got this funny expression on her face that made her look as if her brain had short-circuited. He slid one finger deep inside her and her inner muscles clamped around it in a way that short-circuited his own brain.

That was it. He'd had enough play and now he was ready to move on. Cupping his hands under her buttocks, he lifted her just enough to poke the tip of his manhood into her tight, moist opening. She moaned, and then her head fell back against her shoulders and she settled onto him with a gusty sigh of pleasure.

He reached up to suckle her nipples, and her inner muscles clamped down on him so hard, he damn near lost control. He buried his forehead between her breasts, grabbed handfuls of bedspread on either side of his hips and inhaled deep, ragged breaths. She smelled wonderful—like sunshine and wildflowers and womanly secrets.

She squirmed and whimpered. "What—what should I do?"

"Whatever you want to do, sweetheart. Just follow your instincts and do anything that feels good to you."

Breath bated, he waited in an agony of suspense to see what would happen next. She slowly rocked her hips back and forth, pulling a groan of pleasure from his lips. She paused. Shot him a worried glance.

"It's all right. You're doing great."

She gave him a Mona Lisa smile, then went back to her experimentation, moving this way and that, caressing him with every bit of friction she generated. He gritted his teeth and endured the erotic torment. Using her knees and thighs, she raised herself up, then lowered herself back down on him, discovering the exact motion he'd been praying for.

"Oooh," she murmured, immediately repeating the motion. "Yes. Oh, yes."

He groaned again, but she made no indication of hearing him. She suddenly was too busy creating those luscious, gut-wrenching sensations, over and over. God bless women who rode horses and had strong thighs. That was his last coherent thought while she rode him through one climax, and then another.

Finally, her breathing became erratic, and her strokes lost the smooth, driving rhythm that had driven him to the very edge of paradise. Grabbing her hips, he held her still while he surged up hard against her, triggering a release that felt as if it had come all the way up from his toenails. She swayed, then flopped forward onto him like a rag doll.

He held her close, stroking her hair and her back, murmuring praise for her efforts and kissing her forehead while his heart settled back into his chest and his head stopped whirling.

"Wow," she said without raising her head.

"Yeah," he said. "Wow is right."

A few minutes later, she raised up and braced her forearm across his sternum. "I like goofy sex. Can we do it again some time?"

* * *

Lori headed back to Cody the next morning, driving her own truck so she wouldn't have to wait around for Wade to stop talking to everyone in sight when the chores were done. The rising sun bathed the valley in a brilliant golden light that made the grass look greener and sharpened the craggy edges of the mountains in the distance. The sky was the most beautiful shade of blue she'd ever seen. The air was crisp and sweet. She was incredibly glad to be alive on such a gorgeous morning.

In fact, she felt bubbly and airy enough to fly. As long as she lived, she would never forget the thrill of seeing such approval in Zack's eyes when she asked if they could have goofy sex again. She didn't even mind his hoot of laughter at her question.

In one brief bout of lovemaking—well, all right, several bouts of lovemaking—he'd completely changed her attitude toward sex. Though it was hard to believe after so many years of hating it, it really *was* fun. With the right man, it was absolutely…stupendous. She would always be grateful to Zack for that, and for so much more.

How had he slipped so completely under her guard? And so quickly? She'd only been in Wyoming about three weeks. In all honesty she was a bit embarrassed to realize how soon she'd gone to bed with him. Not that she could ever regret what had happened last night. Never in a million years.

He had teased, coaxed and even seduced her into doing the things he wanted, but he hadn't forced her to do anything, and he'd been more than generous in sharing the pleasure. Just thinking about it gave her such heart palpitations, that if she wasn't careful, she was liable to daydream herself right off the road. He had made her feel beautiful, sexy, powerful. He had made her feel loved.

The inherent danger in that last thought gave her goose bumps. How on earth would she ever find the strength to leave Zack now? Assuming that he'd want her and Brandon to stay, of course. Which might well be a huge assumption on her part, but she really didn't think so.

Though Zack obviously enjoyed sex, she had seen no evidence that he was a man who thought any woman would do. Last night she had hardly been at her best. She'd been dusty and horsey, and even vomited in front of him for heaven's sake, but he had treated her as if she was incredibly wonderful and, well…precious. He certainly hadn't acted like a man who only wanted one thing from her. When he'd kissed her goodbye this morning, he had held her as if he never wanted to let her go.

And she had felt the same way about him. Even now, the hours until quitting time stretched before her like some weird, interminable punishment. Did she want to drive horses around in big circles all day when she could be back at the Flying M making love with Zack? She laughed and shook her head at the absurdity of the question.

Cody appeared on the western horizon, and any urge to laugh dried up. It didn't matter how wonderful Zack was. It didn't matter if he really cared about her or if he wanted her and Brandon to stay. It didn't matter if she fell in love with him.

This relationship could not last.

As long as there was the slightest possibility that Hugh still might be alive, she couldn't have a long-term relationship with anyone. There was no doubt in her mind that Zack would try to help her if he knew what she was up against. But if she truly cared about Zack, she wouldn't drag him into her problems. Hugh would kill anyone who got in the way of his revenge. She couldn't risk Zack's safety or the safety of the other people he loved so much.

The realization stole the morning's beauty as completely as Hugh had stolen her future. Damn him. Damn whatever or whoever had turned him into a monster. Damn herself for being so blinded by loneliness and romantic yearnings she hadn't seen what he really was until after the wedding.

She sighed, shook her head again and told herself to be grateful for what she did have and stop whining about what she didn't have. She still had Brandon. They were both healthy. She had a decent job doing work she enjoyed and enough money to get by on. Anything was better than living with Hugh or going to prison, even the life of a fugitive.

The best she could hope for now was to enjoy every moment she had with Zack until this job ended. Then she would have to move on and start all over again. At least she'd have good memories to replace some of the bad ones.

That evening Zack paced from his living-room window to the kitchen, checked on the roast and baking potatoes for the hundredth time and paced back to the living-room window, muttering, "Where the hell *is* she?"

This had to be the longest day in the history of Creation. He'd worked his butt off trying to stay busy enough to forget about Lori for just a few minutes, but it hadn't worked. From the moment she'd left for Cody that morning, he'd felt as if someone had ripped a big hole in his chest and taken out a piece of his heart. And dammit, he wanted it back.

He wanted Lori to come back.

It had been a long time since he'd made love to anyone, and he desperately wanted to make love with Lori again as soon as possible. But this pain in his chest went deeper than a desire for sex. It scared the hell out of him to realize just how deep it probably went. At the same time, he felt elated and silly and pathetically eager to hold her again.

The connection he'd felt with her last night had brought back to life a part of him he'd thought had died. She'd made him feel invincible. Maybe even lovable.

"Stop it right there, McBride," he scolded himself. "Don't go building castles in the air. The woman's got a lot of problems, and as soon as this movie's finished, she'll be gone."

God, what a depressing thought. It was gonna hurt like hell when she left. He'd miss Brandon, too. He must have been more lonely than he'd realized.

He stomped back to the kitchen. If she didn't get here soon, the roast was gonna look and taste like a ratty old piece of leather. Aw, *jeez,* now he was starting to think like a whiny wife who only lived for her husband to walk in the door.

Stomping back into the living room, he told himself to settle down, to grow up, to get his act together. He wasn't impulsive; he was cautious, logical, rational. He couldn't be in love with her on such short acquaintance, when he didn't even know where she was from or anything about her family.

There it was. The dust cloud behind her truck, which was tearing up his road. The truck screeched to a halt in the driveway. When Lori jumped out and started toward the house, his logical, rational lectures to himself evaporated in a millisecond. To hell with acting cool.

He ran to the door and charged down the front steps to meet her. Her face lit up with a radiant smile when she saw him, as if she'd missed him every bit as much as he'd missed her during the endless hours she'd been away. Grabbing her in a bear hug, he swung her around twice and kissed the daylights out of her before setting her back on the ground.

She wrapped her arms around his waist and leaned against him as if her legs felt rubbery. Tipping her head back, she met his gaze, and the sweet adoration in her eyes gave his heart a fierce wrench. "Hi," she said.

Her voice sounded soft and breathless, just like it had been last night when...well, he'd better not think about that right now. It was one thing to lose your cool in front of a woman. It was something else to be uncouth. No matter how much he wanted to, he couldn't act like a randy stallion and try to jump her bones before she even got inside. He cleared his throat and eased her lower body away from his.

"Hi, yourself," he said, ushering her toward the front steps. "Have a good day?"

"It was all right." She shot him a knowing grin. "A little long perhaps."

"I know exactly what you mean." He followed her across the threshold, then allowed the screen door to bang shut behind him and turned her to face him. "It was a long day for me, too."

"It was?"

"Oh, yeah. It just went on and on forever. It's all better now that you're here, though."

"I'm glad to be back."

"Is it just me, or are we having a dopey conversation?" he asked.

"Beats me. I'm so happy to see you, it doesn't seem to matter what we talk about."

"I've got supper in the oven. You hungry?"

She slowly shook her head. "Not for food."

Well, that did it. He'd tried real hard to act like a gentleman, but he'd just run out of couth. Sliding one arm around her shoulders and the other behind her knees, he swung her up against his chest and carried her into his bedroom.

She came to him eagerly this time, stripping off her jeans, boots and work shirt with the same urgency pulsing through him as he shed his own clothes. Certain he would die if he didn't get inside her in the next thirty seconds, he caught her against him and kissed her until her knees gave out. Somehow they made it to the bed, and when she shouted with pleasure as they came together, he found the missing piece of his heart.

By the time they came up for air, the sun had set, darkness had filled the valley and he could see stars outside the bedroom window. Exhausted, but happier than he'd been in years, he held her against his side and chuckled when her stomach gave a loud rumble. He switched on the lamp and glanced at the clock, grimacing when he saw how long he'd put off feeding her. Good thing he'd finished the chores before she arrived, or his babies would be mighty unhappy by now.

She murmured a sleepy protest when he slid out of the bed. He leaned down and kissed her forehead, promising to come right back. Turning back at the doorway, he studied her for a long moment. She looked so delicate and beautiful and perfect lying in his bed, his chest tightened against the waves of emotion rising up inside of him.

He couldn't deny the truth any longer. Not to himself, anyway. Logic and rationality didn't mean a damn thing. He loved this woman. He loved her boy, too. If she would let him, he'd gladly take care of both of them for the rest of his life.

She wasn't ready to hear that, of course. He figured when she told him about her past, he would know she finally trusted him enough to risk telling her how he felt. He hoped that would happen before they finished this movie. He sure as hell couldn't let her leave without her knowing how he felt about her.

Turning off the oven, he pitched the charred roast and baked potatoes into the sink. Then he made a big skillet of scrambled eggs, toasted a stack of bread, stirred up a pitcher of orange juice and hauled the whole thing back to the bedroom on a cookie sheet. He kissed Lori awake, then laughed at the way her eyes bugged out when she saw how much food he'd cooked.

They had no trouble eating it all, however, and when Lori went into the adjoining bathroom afterward, he dug the remote control out of his nightstand and clicked on the TV, hoping to catch the weather report on the late news. It looked as if he'd just missed it, and he was about to turn the set off and go see if he could talk Lori into taking a shower with him when the scene on the screen changed from the weather map to a picture of Old Trail Town in Cody.

"Preparations are underway for Blair DuMaine's production company to start filming *Against the Wind* here next week," the reporter said. "In addition to the movie's production crew, we saw several other film crews at work catching the action in Old Trail Town."

"Hey, Lori," Zack called. "Come here, you've gotta see this."

She poked her head out of the bathroom door, her eyebrows raised in question. "See what?"

"You might be on national television. One of those tabloid

crews is doing a story on what everyone's been doing to get ready to film the movie. Come here and watch it.''

''What?'' she yelped.

He was so distracted by the sight of her streaking buck naked to the bed, he missed half the story. When he held out an arm in an invitation to cuddle again, she impatiently waved it away and perched on the edge of the mattress as if she didn't plan to stay. Bruised and confused by her rejection, he looked back at the TV just in time to spot her wagon coming around the corner into the camera's sights.

''Well, I'll be a blue-nosed gopher,'' he said with a laugh as he recognized himself sitting on the seat beside her. ''Don't we just look like a fine pair?''

Lori groaned, then clapped her fingers over her mouth while she continued to watch in what appeared to be horrified fascination. Zack frowned. Here it came again. Something wasn't right here, and the hair on the back of his neck was prickling up to prove it. He looked back at the screen.

Oh yeah, he remembered jumping down and walking around to Lori's side of the wagon. Now he was climbing up onto the running board, pulling Lori's hat off and kissing the stuffing out of her. The camera zoomed in for a close-up when she raised one hand to the side of his face and kissed him back. He smiled at the memory of the effects that kiss had had on his equilibrium. Funny, he'd never noticed that little star-shaped scar on her wrist before.

She came off the bed like a rock launched from a slingshot, half sobbing, ''Oh, God. Oh, God. Oh, God, help me, please,'' while she frantically gathered up her clothes. ''Brandon. I've got to find Brandon.''

Zack jumped off the bed and went to her. ''Dammit, Lori, stop freaking out and tell me what's wrong.''

She dodged around him and ran for the living room. When he caught up with her, she was still begging God for help and yanking on her clothes. Her gaze bounced back and forth across the room as if she expected some monster to materialize out of the walls and come after her. Her face had gone deathly pale, and she was desperately trying to button her blouse, even though she'd put it on inside out.

He clasped his hands around her upper arms. "Lori, what is it? Tell me, and whatever it is, I'll help."

Flailing violently, she broke his hold and ran back to the bedroom, grabbing for the pile of socks and boots she'd dropped in the middle of the floor. "You can't help me. Nobody can help me. I can't believe how stupid that was."

"How stupid *what* was? That kiss?"

"That kiss and..." She glanced around the room, as if she could find magical answers to her problems somewhere. Then she jerked a sock over one foot. "And everything else. I *knew* better, but I did it anyway. Damn the media. Why can't they just leave me alone?"

"Hey, it was a great kiss and it was on TV, but it was still just a kiss," Zack said. "What's the big deal?"

"He can find us, dammit. Now he can find us."

"Who? Your ex?" Zack demanded. She didn't answer. Of course, she didn't answer, and Zack was getting real close to having a bellyful of this weird, disjointed conversation. Was she nuts or what? Then a sickening thought hit him. He grabbed her arms again. "Tell me the truth, are you really divorced?"

She struggled against his grip, but he clamped down hard enough to prevent her from shaking him off. She shot him a venomous glare, then let out an irate huff. "Yes, I'm divorced, and I have full custody of Brandon. I have the papers to prove it in my trailer. But some people don't accept the court's decision in these cases."

"Your ex is stalking you?"

"I don't know for sure, but he could be. For God's sake, will you *please* let me go now?"

"Not until I get the whole picture, here."

She struggled to free herself again, but he held on. "Dammit, Zack, *you* talked me into letting Brandon go with Grace, and I have to get to him before his father does."

"Stop it. There's no need to panic. You don't know if he

even saw that film clip, and if he did see it, wouldn't it take a while for him to get here? I mean, where would he be comin' from?''

She opened her mouth as if she would answer, then shot him a wary glance, mashed her lips together and shook her head. "That's irrelevant. But I need to get to Brandon *to-night*."

"That's impossible. He's clear up in the mountains where there aren't any roads. The only way to get there is on foot or horseback. There's no way anyone could find him in the dark."

She bowed her head for a moment and heaved a sigh. When she looked back up at him again, she had clearly made an effort to regain her composure. He reluctantly released her, and she asked, "Will you take me up there in the morning?"

"At first light, if you want. But you know if your ex did come snooping around, Brandon would probably be safer in the mountains with Grace than he would be here at the ranch."

"No, he was so excited about going on a real cattle drive, I'm sure he told everybody on the ranch where he was going. Believe me, his father will find him. I can't let that happen."

Zack frowned. "Well, who the hell is this guy anyway? What kind of resources does he have?"

A shudder wracked her body and her eyes turned bleak with despair. "He has money to burn and political connections to protect him from the law and the media. What more does he need?"

"What's his name?"

"I can't tell you that. The less you know about him, the safer you'll be."

He snorted in disbelief. "Aw come *on*. That sounds like, 'I could tell ya, but then I'd have to kill ya.' Don't you think you're actin' just a tad melodramatic?"

"Believe what you want. Just take me to Brandon. Right now that's all I care about."

"Okay, let's say you've got Brandon back. Then what are you gonna do?"

"We'll disappear again."

Her words, spoken as if she was planning a little weekend trip, carved a deep, painful gouge in his heart. "Oh, really?" he said quietly. "What about us, Lori?"

She had the grace to flush, but she didn't back down. "I'm sorry, Zack, but there can't be any 'us.'"

"There could be. If you'd stand up and fight instead of scurryin' off like a little mouse."

"You don't understand."

"Then make me understand, dammit. I'll protect you and Brandon."

"You can't, Zack. I keep trying and trying to tell you that nobody can, but you just won't listen."

"Nobody's invincible. In case you haven't noticed, the McBrides are not exactly low on resources and political contacts."

"I didn't mean to imply otherwise. You're wonderful and your family is wonderful, but I will not be responsible for dragging anyone else into this mess."

"I don't care who your ex is, he'd be a damn fool to take all of us on."

"Don't even think about underestimating him. He's dangerous. He's not a fool, but he *is* obsessed."

"Obsessed with what?"

"Controlling us. Owning us. Punishing us. Take your pick. He'll do absolutely anything to get us back."

Zack studied her intently. While he wasn't sure how much of her wild story was true, he believed that *she* believed everything she'd told him. Most people just couldn't fake fear that well. Hell, it was more like terror. But had she told him the whole truth? Not likely. She was acting too wary for him to believe she had nothing left to hide. Well, somehow he had to get the rest of it out of her.

He led her over to the sofa, sat down beside her and took both of her hands between his palms. Jeez, her skin felt like

meat straight from the freezer, and she was trembling like a
motor with a rough idle. Gently chafing her fingers with his
own, he gazed deeply into her eyes.

"How long have you been hidin' from this creep?"

"Four years."

"Dear God, Lori, no wonder you're such a ball of nerves.
You can't go on like this. It's not fair to you or to Brandon."

"Zack, please. We've already been over this. Give it up,
will you?"

"No, I won't. I can't, darlin'. You've got to trust me here.
I can help you."

"Just take me to Brandon. That's all the help I need."

Yeah, right. She sure *looked* like that was all the help she
needed. Well, there was no use arguing with a woman when
she got that stubborn, closed-up look on her face. He'd just
have to stick real close to her and see what happened next.
But if her ex ever tried to hurt her or that kid again, he'd
have to go through Zack McBride first.

It'd be mighty damn interesting to see how brave the SOB
was when he had to face a grown man instead of a small
woman and a ten-year-old boy.

Chapter Ten

Knowing there was no way she would ever be able to sleep, Lori spent the rest of the night alternating between bouts of raging panic and long, silent lectures to herself about the importance of remaining calm enough to function. By the time Zack woke up at four o'clock, panic had won out. Relieved to have something useful to do, she cooked breakfast, packed her saddlebags and helped Zack catch and saddle two geldings and a packhorse.

Until the moment Zack loaded the horses into a trailer and they took off on a dirt track, she nearly had to bite her tongue to stop herself from yelling at him to hurry up. He worked with his usual efficiency, but he simply didn't feel the same nerve-shredding sense of urgency that she did. And why should he?

He didn't know she might be wanted for murder. He didn't know what kind of an obsessed freak Hugh had become; he probably couldn't even visualize anyone so awful. He didn't know what it was like to have only one living relative, and a child at that, who was in terrible danger.

Neither of them spoke much during the dusty, bumpy ride through the foothills. At the base of the nearest mountain, Zack parked beside the road. He unloaded the horses, checked their gear and finally took a rifle from the gun rack in the pickup.

Lori hadn't been able to get away from him long enough to retrieve her nine millimeter pistol. She wistfully eyed his rifle, started to ask if he had another one, then reluctantly decided that wouldn't be a good idea. As far as she was concerned, Zack already knew too much about her. Asking for a gun would only make him more suspicious than he already was. He noticed the direction of her gaze, however, and must have thought her frown meant she didn't want him to bring the rifle along.

"Don't worry, I know what I'm doin' with this thing," he said. "I'm only bringing it along in case we run into a cranky sow bear with a cub or a hungry mountain lion."

Lori gave him a stiff nod. "Fine. Are we ready now?"

"Yup," he said with a wry smile. "Let's go."

They mounted the horses, and Zack started up a narrow, winding trail into the woods, holding the packhorse's lead rope. The air smelled fresh and sweet, with a strong touch of pine from the towering trees flanking the trail on both sides. Occasional glimpses of sky revealed a bright, clear blue with no clouds in sight. Disturbed by the sound of the horses' shoes striking rocks, nearby birds and squirrels called out warnings to their neighbors.

As the morning wore on, the sun's heat penetrated the branches overhead. Lori peeled off her warm jacket and gloves when Zack removed his. Her sweatshirt came next, leaving her more comfortable in a pink cotton T-shirt.

Zack called a halt at midmorning. Lori wanted to protest the delay, but knew the horses needed a rest even if she didn't. Zack handed her a canteen. She took a gulp of the

tepid water, grimaced at the metallic taste and handed the
canteen back. He took it without comment.

"Is this the same trail Grace and the kids used?" she
asked, breaking the uncomfortable silence that had settled
over them since their argument the night before.

He shook his head. "There's a better one for the cows
about two miles beyond where we parked. This one's rougher
and steeper, but it's shorter and it intersects with the other
trail real close to where Grace oughtta be by now."

"I see."

Reaching over, he gently squeezed her left shoulder. "It'll
be all right, Lori. We'll find Brandon by tomorrow afternoon
at the latest."

She nearly choked, then pulled herself out of his grasp.
"Tomorrow? Afternoon? Don't you *know* where they are?"

"Sure. I know the general area, anyway." He shrugged.
"But it's not rocket science, you know. Things can get a
little unpredictable up here sometimes."

"Now you tell me?" she said. "Why didn't you mention
this before I agreed to let Brandon go on the drive?"

"Well, it's nothin' Gracie and the kids can't handle," he
said. "Just rock slides, fallen trees blocking the trail, that sort
of thing."

Well, *that* definitely made her feel better. Not. But, it did
explain why he'd insisted on dragging the packhorse along;
they might need all of those supplies. Lori closed her eyes
tightly, struggling to maintain her composure. She should
have realized the mountains wouldn't be like a city park or
the Flying M. The waiting simply was getting to her.

"We'll find him, Lori," Zack said quietly. "I promise you,
we'll find him just as soon as we can."

She nodded, then turned back to her horse so he wouldn't
see the sheen of tears in her eyes. If only she could stop her
mind from imagining hired goons in helicopters locating
Brandon with infrared equipment and then dropping armed
mercenaries into the forest to capture him. Hugh was capable
of pulling off exactly that kind of mission—

Zack sighed heavily. "Let's get going."

She immediately obeyed, and they fell into another silence that lasted until they stopped again for lunch. Halfway through a sandwich, he turned to her, his expression thoughtful.

"Why did you marry this guy?" he asked.

"I've asked myself that question a million times. I suppose the best answer is that I was simply young and stupid." Lori gave a helpless shrug. "My mother had just died and I didn't have anyone else, so I was lonely. I had no money for college, but I'd worked with his horses for several years, and I earned enough to live on. When he started taking an interest in me, I was flattered."

"Because he was rich?"

She nodded. "And he was older and handsome, and very charming and sophisticated. I felt a bit like…Cinderella"

"Were you ever happy with him?"

"Until Brandon was born. That was when he changed. Started…hurting me."

"Why did you stay with him?"

"I had nowhere else to go. No other job skills to make a living. He had so much money and influence, I didn't think I could ever fight him and win."

"But you did."

"Yes, eventually. But every single day for five years, I was terrified that if I tried to get a divorce, he would take Brandon away from me and I would never see my son again."

"He threatened you with that?"

"At every opportunity. There are many ways to force a woman's compliance."

"What finally made you stand up for yourself?"

"Brandon became very…protective of me. When he tried to help me, his father beat him. I couldn't allow that to continue."

"You found a judge who would listen to you?"

"I tried. Believe me, I tried. But I didn't have any success until Brandon suffered a skull fracture." She laughed bitterly.

"Before that, most people saw me as some sort of a demented woman who didn't know how good she had it. Nobody wanted to believe such an important man would treat his wife and son that way."

"A skull fracture? God, what was wrong with those idiots?" Zack muttered. Then he shook his head and sighed. "Aw, sweetheart, that's terrible. Guys like your ex make me sick, and they get away with too damn much because nobody's got the guts to stand up to them until somebody winds up dead. I've seen men beat their wives and kids right here in Sunshine Gap, but I do everything in my power to stop it."

She looked down at the scar on her wrist. Hugh had seared it into her flesh with a cigarette lighter and a star-shaped tie tack. Nausea roiled in her stomach at the memory. Clearing her throat, she continued.

"But when he hurt Brandon so badly, the doctor finally couldn't ignore what was happening any longer, and he convinced the judge to help me."

"So why don't you stand up and fight him again now?"

"Because it won't matter what any court in the world does to him. He'll just keep coming after us, and someone else may get hurt in the process."

Zack studied her for a moment, then finished off his sandwich, brushed his hands off on his jeans and headed into the bushes. Lori watched him leave before throwing the rest of her own sandwich in the opposite direction. She hadn't been very hungry in the first place, and now she had no appetite at all. She should have known better than to try to explain anything to a cop.

Well, it didn't matter whether or not he believed her, because she wouldn't be here that much longer. Once she had Brandon with her again, they would take off at the first opportunity. This time she would be smart enough to avoid having anything to do with horses. It was time to head for a big city where they could disappear into the crowds.

They looked for Grace and the kids until darkness forced them to make camp. Zack had held his peace all afternoon and continued to do so while they ate a quick supper. But when the coffee was done boiling over the campfire and they'd each settled back with a steaming cup, he couldn't keep his mouth shut any longer.

"What you're plannin' to do is wrong, Lori," he said.

She quirked an eyebrow at him. "Gee, that's odd. I don't remember asking for your opinion."

"You didn't. But I'm gonna give it to you anyway. It never pays to run from a bully."

"What do you suggest I do?"

"Stand your ground. If he comes lookin' for you, you and Brandon won't have to face him alone. I'll be right there with you, and he'll have to come through me to get to either one of you."

"Why would you do that, Zack? It doesn't make any sense."

"Beggin' your pardon, but it makes plenty of sense to me." He paused, then took a breath and gazed straight into her eyes. "I want there to be an 'us.'"

She immediately started shaking her head. "No. We've shared some wonderful…moments, but nobody said anything about a long-term relationship."

"Well, I'm sayin' it now. I'm falling in love with you, Lori."

"You can't do that."

"It's too late, I already did. I'm nuts about you, and I'm nuts about that boy of yours. I think we all could be real happy together, don't you?"

She lowered her gaze, but not before he caught a glimpse of raw pain in her eyes. Slowly shaking her head again, she said softly, "You're incredibly sweet, Zack, but I don't want another serious relationship with a man. Not ever."

"Come on, Lori, you know I'm not anything like that SOB—"

She jerked her head up and skewered him with an icy stare. "No, I don't know that. I don't mean to be insulting and I don't want to hurt you, but I will never put myself or my son at any man's mercy again. I'm not capable of trusting or loving anyone but Brandon."

Her words hit his heart with the force of a wrecking ball. Maybe she didn't want to hurt him, but she was doin' a damn good job of it. He poured himself another cup of coffee and sipped it in a brooding silence while he worked out a new line of argument that hopefully would break through her stubbornness.

"I don't believe you're not capable of trusting or loving anyone again," he said. "I think you're just letting your fear of this creep overrule any other consideration. There's no need for that."

"That's my decision to make, not yours," she said.

"You're right about that," he conceded reluctantly. "But you know, you're actin' a lot like Satan."

"Oh, please—"

"No, hear me out for a minute," he said. "Think about it. He's got lots of folks who care about him. Folks who are ready and willing to help any way they can. But he won't let anyone close enough to ease all those irrational fears he's got floatin' around in his head. So he just paces around that damn pen, lonely and scared all the time, and he's nothin' but a hayburner. He's more dangerous than he's worth."

"My fears are hardly irrational, McBride. The man in question fractured my son's skull and injured me too many times to count."

"I understand that, darlin', and I'd love to have an hour or two alone with him and show him what it feels like to be afraid and hurt and unable to defend himself. I don't suppose I'll get that lucky, but if you'll stay here at the Flying M until this is resolved, you'll have a lot more people than me lookin' out for you and Brandon."

"Zack—"

"No, dammit. Let me finish. We McBrides don't always agree or get along real well with each other, but when there's trouble, we circle the wagons and face it together."

"I'm not a McBride."

"You don't have to be. It's enough that I'm willing to tell 'em all how I feel about you and Brandon. Shoot, the whole town of Sunshine Gap will back us up without a question."

"You'll all be safer if Brandon and I just leave."

"We don't look at things that way here. We're a community. If one of us is in trouble, we're all in trouble. If your ex sets one foot in this town, we'll know he's here long before he can even find the ranch."

"That's lovely, Zack, but my answer is still no."

He studied her mulish expression and came close to cussing a blue streak. What would it take to get through to her? "This kind of a life is not fair to you or to Brandon. You can't run for the rest of your lives."

"If we don't run, the chances are very good that we won't have any rest of our lives to worry about. We'll both be dead."

There was just no reasoning with her. She made him so mad he could rip chunks of bark out of a pine tree with his bare hands, but that would hardly convince her to trust him. The bleak resignation in her eyes and her voice told him it was time to retreat. He could always try again in the morning.

Pitching the dregs of his coffee onto the ground, he got up and went to retrieve the sleeping bags. He'd hoped while they'd been packing that they might be zipping the bags together to make one cozy bed to share. After so much arguing, he figured the last thing she'd want to do was snuggle with him anytime soon.

He handed her a small tarp and a bag, she carried it around to the opposite side of the campfire from his, spread it out on the ground, yanked off her boots and slid inside without even saying good-night. Sometimes he really hated being right.

* * *

"No, let me go!" Brandon shouted.

Lori looked up from the open suitcase on her bed, a sick feeling of dread racing from the pit of her stomach to her heart and then to her whole body.

"Leave me alone. Mommy, he's here again! Mommy, help me!"

Dropping the pile of clothes in her hands, she took her pistol out of the nightstand, turned the safety lever off and ran to the living room. His face contorted with rage, Hugh stood over a cowering Brandon, his right hand lifted in preparation to strike.

Lori raised the pistol and assumed the stance she'd practiced a thousand times at the firing range. "Stop it, Hugh. You're never going to hit him or me again."

His eyes widened when he first caught sight of the gun, but he recovered immediately. He let out a mocking laugh and uncurled his raised fist to gesture at the pistol. "Put it down, Lori," he said in his soft, Kentucky drawl. "You know you don't have the guts to use that thing. Is it even loaded?"

Ignoring his taunt, she motioned for Brandon to get out of the way. He obeyed instantly, racing into the apartment's kitchen as they'd rehearsed since Hugh's last abduction attempt. She heard him unlock the backdoor and knew he was ready to run for help if she gave him the signal.

"It won't do any good to fight me." Hugh took a step toward her. "In fact, you're only making it worse for yourself and Brandon by carrying on this way."

"Stay back. It's loaded and I *do* know how to use it. Dammit, don't make me shoot you."

"You know you're going to lose, darling," he said as if she hadn't spoken. "Why not just give in and take your punishment? Then we can all start over with a clean slate. We'll be a happy family again."

God, he looked so impossibly huge, so confident, so invincible, she wouldn't be surprised if bullets bounced off him the way they did Superman. Sweat dripped down her sides and her heart felt as if it might pound itself right out of her chest. "I mean it, Hugh. I won't take this from you anymore. I don't have to."

"You'll take whatever I say you'll take," he said, smiling as he took another step toward her.

It was the smile that steadied her hands. To the unaware, it looked perfectly friendly and normal, but she and Brandon both knew that it masked evil intentions. He took another step. She lined up the sights, held her breath and carefully squeezed the trigger.

The blast nearly deafened her without the protective ear muffs she'd used in target practice. Hugh faltered. His eyes widened in surprise and he raised both hands to the rapidly spreading red stain high on the side of his chest. Blood immediately covered his fingers. He slowly sank to his knees.

"You'll pay for this," he snarled. "You and that boy will die for this."

There was blood everywhere, always more blood, and his hateful voice echoed again and again and again. "You'll pay for this. You and that boy will die. You and that boy will die. You and that boy will die."

"No!" Lori screamed. "No, no, no!" Then she began to whimper. "Oh, please stop. Just stop and leave us alone. Leave us alone, damn you."

Big hands closed around her upper arms, lifting her, gently shaking her. "Lori, wake up. It's only a dream, darlin'. You're safe."

The voice came from far away, and the only thing that registered at first was that it didn't belong to Hugh. Still in the grip of terror, she shook her head and tried to twist away from the hands anchoring her in place. "No, please, let me go. For God's sake, let me go."

"Shhhh," the new voice said. One of the big hands rubbed over her back, pressing her against a hard chest. Strong arms closed around her, bringing comfort and warmth to her shivering body. "You're safe, darlin'. Brandon's safe. Everything's all right now. Just wake up."

She inhaled a deep, shuddering breath, and the scent of the man who held her penetrated the nightmare fog in her brain. It was a good smell. A safe smell. But she was suddenly even more terrified to open her eyes. What if this was just some trick of Hugh's to disguise himself?

The man rocked her back and forth, crooning to her as if she were a frightened child. She certainly felt like one. "It's all right, sweetheart. I'm here. You're safe. Everything's all right."

Something deep inside her tore loose at his tenderness. She sobbed against the pain of it, instinctively tried to rein in the emotions assaulting her, then nearly drowned in an uncontrollable wave of weeping. His arms tightened around her and the rocking continued, as did the stream of soothing words.

Dear God, she was so tired. Tired of being wary and alone and afraid. Tired of being the only source of safety in the whole world for Brandon. Tired of never having a home or friends or family—anyone she could trust.

It felt so good to lean on someone. To be held and comforted. To let down her guard and allow someone else to be in charge just for a minute or two.

Every sob that shuddered out of her ripped off another piece of Zack's heart. His spine felt permanently bent from holding her in this position and the front of his shirt was plastered to his skin with hot tears, but he wouldn't have let go of her for anything on this earth. He'd never heard such gut-wrenching cries come out of anyone's mouth, except maybe, when Jake's beloved Ellen had finally succumbed to breast cancer.

He could only hope these tears would be healing for Lori. If what he now suspected was true, she would need every bit of strength she could muster in the next few days. He finally had the last missing piece of the puzzle, and knowing what he'd have to do now made him want to bawl right along with her.

At last she throttled down to an occasional hiccupping sniffle. Eyes nearly swollen shut, nose red as a third-degree sunburn, she slowly peeled herself away from him, averting her face as if it embarrassed her to have him see her this way. After rubbing the heels of her palms into her eyes, she turned away and wrapped her arms around herself.

"I'm sorry," she whispered.

"No need to be. We all have nightmares sometimes."

She gave a jerky nod and swiped at her eyes with her palms again. "Yeah. I, uh, guess so."

"Care to tell me what that one was all about?"

She gulped, then shook her head. "No. It's not important."

"Sounded like it was," Zack said. "Usually is when you shoot somebody."

Her hair flared out behind her when she whipped her head around and stared at him with a horrified comprehension. Damn. He'd hoped, even prayed that he'd misunderstood her frantic, nightmare ramblings. He hadn't.

"Isn't that what happened?" he asked when she didn't speak. "You shot Brandon's dad. Didn't you?"

Mashing her lips together, she slowly nodded.

"Did you kill him?"

"I don't know," she said, her voice raw and harsh.

Aw, hell and damnation, it all made sense now. Her uneasiness around him, especially after she'd learned he was a cop. Her attempts to keep Brandon away from him and the rest of the family. He'd ignored plenty of warning signs because he'd been thinking with the wrong part of his anatomy.

She wasn't just hiding from her ex. She was in trouble with the law. Big trouble. And he was a first-class chump.

Cursing under his breath, he lunged to his feet and shoved his hands into his front pockets where they couldn't get him into trouble. He paced around the campfire, then turned to face her. She raised her chin and returned his scrutiny, but her quivering lower lip betrayed her show of bravado for the lie it was.

Exhaustion had etched lines into her face. Jeez, did she

have to look so damn defenseless? Well, tough cookies. He couldn't think about that.

"I want the truth, and I want it now," he said.

"I've told you the truth."

"All of it," he insisted.

Her throat contracted in another gulp and her eyes looked as if they might swallow up her whole face. "Wh-wh-what do y-y-you m-mean?"

"Start with any outstanding warrants for your arrest and we'll go from there."

Lori's heart wrenched painfully. He knew. Oh, God, he knew. But how? Not that it mattered. Nothing had gone right since she'd left California, where no one had paid the slightest bit of attention to her. Every drop of saliva in her mouth evaporated, and her heart pounded so hard, breathing was painful. She couldn't have spoken if he'd jabbed her with a sharp knife. She swayed, then braced her hands on the ground on either side of her hips. She couldn't possibly afford to faint.

Zack came toward her, cursing, long and loud, using the most colorful combinations of obscenities she'd ever heard. She gaped at tendons standing out on his neck and the vein throbbing in the center of his forehead. It didn't seem possible that this furious giant could be the same man who had held and comforted her with such tenderness only moments earlier.

Maybe she *should* faint. Then she wouldn't feel it when those big fists smashed into her nose or her ribs or wherever he chose to hit her. She couldn't possibly stop him; she'd never been able to stop Hugh, and Zack was nearly twice his size. Or he seemed so at the moment. Raising one hand, he shouted something at her, but she couldn't understand the words because of the roaring in her ears.

She could only stare at him with morbid fascination while the blackness gradually filled her field of vision. Just before it blotted out all the light, she covered her head with both arms and prayed she would live through this beating for

Brandon's sake. Dear God, Brandon needed her now more than ever.

She came to, stretched out on the sleeping bag with her feet propped up on a log, a cool cloth on her forehead and surprisingly little pain. Zack was down on one knee beside her, studying her face with the most worried, regretful eyes she'd ever seen. She wanted to sit up and assess the damage, but she was afraid to move with him still so close.

"How do you feel?" he asked, his voice soft and subdued.

"I'm, um...okay, I guess. How long was I out?"

"Just a couple of minutes. I'm sorry. I shouldn't have yelled at you like that. I don't usually have such a lousy temper."

She surreptitiously lifted one hand to the side of her face and cautiously pressed along her eye socket, cheekbone and jaw in search of bruises. Though she'd been as discreet as possible, the movement must have drawn his attention. His eyes widened and his swarthy complexion paled.

"Good Lord, you really think I'd *hit* you?"

She struggled to sit up, catching the damp cloth in one hand. Making no attempt to hide her actions, she checked out the other side of her face, her arms, wrists and ribs. No pain whatsoever. "You were so...angry."

"Hell, yes, I was angry, but I don't hit anybody if I don't have to. And I'd never, ever hit a lady." He rubbed one hand down over his face. "This is *me,* Lori, and I care about you. We've made love."

"That never stopped Hugh. In fact he would have hit me extra hard for trying to cover my head just now. I only shot him because I had to, Zack. I couldn't take any more, and I couldn't risk letting him get his hands back on Brandon."

"What are you wanted for, Lori?"

"I don't know for sure. Murder if he died, I suppose. Assault or attempted murder if he didn't."

"What happened?"

"I thought an angel must have been looking out for us during the divorce, because we got the only judge in the whole state Hugh couldn't buy. I was finally free of him, I had my little boy and a job waiting tables, and I thought we could finally start a new life. But he wouldn't leave us alone. Protection orders didn't stop him from breaking into our apartment, destroying our stuff and beating us for refusing to go back to him. Nothing did.''

"Aw, jeez, Lori.''

She ignored his interruption. After holding all of this inside for so long, it felt surprisingly good to finally share it with another human being. She needed to tell him the rest before she completely lost her nerve.

"Then he started trying to abduct Brandon. I guess he knew that if he had my son, he'd also have me. When it became clear that the law couldn't or wouldn't protect us from him, I bought a gun and I learned how to shoot it. I'd saved every penny I could, hoping to get away from him for good. I was packing to leave when he broke in and tried to take Brandon for the third time. He started coming at me, and when he wouldn't stop, I shot him.''

"Where did you hit him?''

She thumped the upper left quadrant of her chest. "I didn't hang around long enough to find out if he lived or died. I just grabbed Brandon and ran like hell. We've been running ever since.''

"Have you looked for an obituary?''

"Yes, but I never found one. His family owns the local newspaper, and the few stories they printed about what happened were brief and distorted. I have no idea what the other media reported.''

Zack muttered something she didn't quite catch, then sat on the log he'd used to prop up her feet. She couldn't see his face, but his shoulders looked so rigid, she was afraid to ask what he was thinking. The silence went on and on until she thought she would have to let out a primal scream or lose what little was left of her mind. Before she could do it, however, he braced his elbows on his knees and turned halfway around to meet her gaze.

His eyes were filled with regret, but there was no mistaking the determination she saw in them as well. "You know I have to find out if you're wanted, and if you are, I'll have to turn you in."

"No, Zack, pl—"

"I don't have a choice. I'm a law enforcement officer. I swore to uphold the law, and that's what I have to do."

While she desperately had hoped Zack would be different from all the other cops she had dealt with over the years, she had known he might react this way. Still, actually hearing him say the words out loud filled her with an aching, unbearable sense of defeat. It had taken every scrap of courage, intelligence and strength she possessed to stay out of Hugh's clutches this long. Now, she was simply too depleted to fight anymore.

Her throat closed around a huge, razor-edged lump and her eyes burned with acid tears she refused to shed. She had tried so hard. So damn hard. And she had failed.

She wouldn't have minded it so much if she had only failed herself; prison couldn't possibly be any worse than what she'd already endured at Hugh's hands. Failing Brandon was another matter entirely. She couldn't bear even to think about what would happen to her little boy if she wasn't there to protect him from Hugh's wrath. And she couldn't just give up.

"All right," she said quietly. "I know I've put you in an awkward position, and I'm sorry for that. But you have to know that if you turn me in, you'll be signing my death warrant as well as Brandon's."

"I'll make sure you get a good lawyer, and—"

She cut him off with a bitter laugh. "I don't need a lawyer, Zack. I need a damn SWAT team."

"You've gotta have a little faith in the criminal justice system."

"Says who? Besides giving me a divorce and custody of Brandon, it's never helped me once. Never given us any real safety or justice. And now it's going to kill both of us and you're going to help it along."

"Dammit, Lori, that's not fair."

"So sue me."

"Very funny."

"May I ask for one small favor?"

"What is it?"

"Will you let me get Brandon before you turn me in? This is really going to upset him."

"Do I have your word that you won't try to escape once you've got him?"

After a moment's consideration, she nodded. "I promise."

"All right. Let's get some sleep then and we'll find him in the morning."

While Zack built up the fire, Lori crawled back into her sleeping bag and gazed up at the full moon, wondering how anything could look so beautiful when her whole world was coming apart.

"Hugh what, Lori?" Zack called from the direction of his own sleeping bag. "What's his last name?"

"VanZandt. Hugh VanZandt."

Zack's only response was a soft curse, but it was enough to tell her he'd recognized the name. Any serious horseman in America probably would. His Thoroughbreds had won two Kentucky Derbies and a Triple Crown in the past five years. So now Zack knew exactly what kind of money she'd been up against. Would it help him understand why she had run away?

Chapter Eleven

Zack watched Lori closely the next morning, partly out of concern for her well-being, partly out of a need to avoid his own confused feelings about everything she'd told him, and partly out of fear that she might be feeling desperate enough to do something irrational. He really didn't think she'd go anywhere without Brandon. But even though she'd given him her word, he wasn't completely sure what she'd do once she had the kid back.

She looked even more tired and stressed out than he felt, and he wondered how she was managing to stay in the saddle. She did it, though. She stuck to that gelding's back over the roughest terrain like she had velcro on her behind. She was quiet, but not surly. It was more like she was just hanging on with sheer guts and determination.

He admired that, even while he felt angry that she hadn't trusted him with her past sooner. He realized things had happened fast between them, but she'd had plenty of opportunities to tell him the truth. That she hadn't done so hurt and confused him more than anything else in this whole mess. It raised too many questions he couldn't answer. Or maybe he just didn't want to answer them.

Had she slept with him because she really felt something for him? Or because she needed to distract him from wondering about her background? Or because she wanted him to feel obligated to her somehow? No, none of that made any sense. She hadn't pursued him; he had pursued her.

If her troubles with Hugh were completely resolved, would she be at all interested in staying here with him? Or would she go back to California when the movie was finished? The questions continued, driving him nuts while the horses continued climbing the side of the mountain.

Midmorning, he heard a faint, but piercing whistle coming from somewhere beyond a copse of trees straight ahead of them. That was where he thought it had come from, anyway. He stopped his horse and listened intently, trying to make certain of the direction. Yeah, that was it, all right.

He turned back to look over his shoulder at Lori. "There's a meadow beyond those trees, and I think Grace and the kids are there. Watch out for stray calves. My horses are trained to go after 'em without waiting for a rider's signal.''

She nodded, and they silently rode toward the meadow. The closer they got, the sounds came more clearly. That was Grace's obnoxious whistle, all right. Steven and Riley each had their own cow-moving yips. He heard other voices, as well, but couldn't single any of them out over the bawling protests of the cows and calves.

Once they were clear of the trees, it was easy to pinpoint the herd's exact location by the cloud of dust kicked up by so many heavy, plodding hooves. He reined in and waited for the others to emerge from the forest on the opposite side of the meadow. Lori followed suit, and he glanced down at her, inwardly grimacing at the ferocious pain that sliced through his chest at the sight of her wan, exhausted face.

Dammit, he didn't deserve to feel this guilty when he was just doing his duty. For God's sake, he only had her word that any part of the story she'd told him was true. In the eyes of the courts, what she'd done had been nothing short of taking the law into her own hands, which had been bad enough. The fact that she'd run away without calling an ambulance for VanZandt only made it all look worse. If it truly had been a case of self-defense, she should have turned herself in.

And yet, he'd seen how real her terror was and how real Brandon's fear was. There was no doubt in his mind that both of them had been savagely abused at some time. Abused women and children often died at the hands of their abusers. And he really couldn't imagine her shooting anyone unless she honestly feared for her own life or Brandon's. She just wasn't wired that way.

So maybe VanZandt had needed shooting. As a man who loved Lori and her son, Zack easily could buy into that idea. As an officer sworn to uphold the law, he couldn't ignore the possibility—however slight he thought it was—that Lori had committed a terrible crime.

As famous as VanZandt was in the horse world, Zack found it odd that he'd never seen a mention of his being shot in an industry magazine or in the regular press. Before he could ponder on that one for long, the Flying M's lead bull lumbered into view, his bell clanking loudly with each step. Lori tensed, her gaze eagerly scanning the trees as if she expected Brandon to come trotting out any second.

Zack gave her a warning glance. "Cows can be real dumb. If you want to get out of here before noon, don't make any sudden moves or you'll spook them all back into the woods and we'll have a hell of a mess rounding them up again."

"All right," she said quietly.

The noise increased and the dust cloud thickened as more and more cows and calves entered the meadow. One by one the riders came into view, waving ropes and yelling at the stragglers. Grace spotted them first and trotted her horse over to see what they wanted. After listening to Zack's abbreviated explanation, she went back to the herd and sent Brandon to talk to them next.

Zack figured the kid must have guessed something of what was going on. Walking his mount at the slowest possible pace, he shot first wary, and then hostile glances between his mother and Zack. When Lori told him the same brief version of why they had come, he scowled ferociously, but his chin quivered and his eyes glistened with unshed tears.

"Aw, Mo-o-o-m," he said with a whine that set Zack's back teeth on edge, "not *now*. I'm having so much fun, don't make me go. Nobody'll find me up here."

Zack opened his mouth, but Lori gave him a quelling look.

"We'll discuss this later, Brandon," she said. "I don't blame you for being disappointed, but we're not going to argue about this. Now, please get your things and let's go."

Brandon's chin raised in defiance for a moment, and his eyes glittered with rage. Lori met and held his gaze without flinching, and the fight went out of him in less than a minute. His head lowered and his shoulders slumped, he turned his horse back toward the herd, muttering a string of cuss words Zack recognized only too well. Better watch his mouth around that kid in the future.

The ride back down to the ranch passed uneventfully. Under better circumstances, Zack would have enjoyed camping out for a night with Lori and Brandon, and he promised himself to do just that when this mess was resolved. Maybe they'd even spend a weekend at the old homestead cabin when Dillon and Blair were done using it.

Yeah, that was it. Lori and Brandon were acting glum enough to pass for a couple of death row cons waiting for the gas chamber. He needed to keep a positive attitude about the whole situation and look for solutions instead of more problems. If Lori was wanted, he'd have to detain her, all right, but he could also help her.

Shoot, Nolan Larson, his sister Alex's next-door neighbor, was supposed to have been one hell of a successful defense attorney in L.A. before he'd moved to Sunshine Gap.

Nolan practiced family law up in Cody now, and he'd seen plenty of spousal and child abuse cases. He was a good guy, and Zack knew he'd be willing to help Lori and Brandon for free if necessary.

Then there was his brother Cal's fiancée, Sandy Bishop. She was the head nurse and Jill-of-all-trades at the Sunshine Gap clinic. Zack had worked closely with her for years, and he could count on her to take X rays of both Lori's and Brandon's previous injuries. By the time any extradition orders were carried out, Zack figured they could build a solid case for Lori's defense.

As soon as the horses were taken care of, he'd radio the sheriff's office in Cody and get the facts. Then they could all start dealing in reality. And then maybe Mr. Hugh VanZandt would start looking less invincible.

Lori wracked her brain for some way to escape all the way back to the Flying M. Yes, she'd promised Zack she wouldn't do that, but she felt no guilt. She'd already proved she would do anything to protect Brandon. How much more trouble could she possibly get into for breaking a promise? Not enough to worry about.

Unfortunately, Zack was not a cop who lacked vigilance. They were all filthy and tired by the time they turned his horses into their pasture, but he insisted on driving a pickup back to her tiny trailer in the movie company's village, collecting their few possessions and taking them back to his place. He even found her pistol and kept it.

She glared at him for that, but she couldn't exactly blame him for doing so. She'd admitted to shooting one man with it. What was to stop her from doing it again? Since he was the only thing standing between her and Brandon and their freedom, probably not much.

The tension between them expanded and expanded like a giant, puffy marshmallow that sucked all of the oxygen right out of the pickup's cab to make itself grow. It was almost a relief when Brandon finally emerged from his sulking long enough to figure out there was something more wrong than he'd realized. Sitting in the middle of the bench seat, he nudged Lori with his elbow.

"What's going on, Mom?"

"Zack knows...everything, Brandon," she said quietly.

Eyes rounded with surprise, Brandon shot a fearful glance in Zack's direction, then looked back at Lori. "Everything?"

She nodded.

"What's he gonna do?"

"He has to turn me in, honey."

Brandon immediately started shaking his head. "No. You can't let him, Mom. They'll put you in prison."

"Hold on there, Brandon," Zack said. "There's no need to panic just yet. Let me go radio the sheriff's office in Cody and we'll see what's what."

"I already told you what's what," Lori said tightly.

"You gave me your side of the story," Zack said, "but you were missing a few important details, such as whether or not you'd killed a man. You can understand why I might need to know the answer to that one, can't you?"

Lori pointedly turned her gaze to the side window. In all honesty, she did understand why Zack felt he had to check out her story, but that didn't mean she had to make it easy for him to destroy what little safety and security she'd been able to provide for herself and her son. Brandon slid his hand into hers and gave it a tight squeeze.

She squeezed back, and blinked hard at the sudden tears fighting to escape her control. No one talked for the rest of the drive. At Zack's house, they all carried in a load from the pickup. Lori and Brandon huddled together on the sofa, giving each other strength and support.

Zack turned to her, his expression grim. "May I see your divorce papers now?"

"Why?" she asked. "You don't even believe I'm divorced?"

His eyebrows came together in a disgruntled-looking V.

"I don't know what to believe anymore. I wish I did, but I don't. So will you please just let me see the damn papers?"

"Well, sure, why not?" She dug them out of the appropriate tote bag and shoved them at his midsection. He accepted them without a word, then quickly flipped through the pages of the decree and custody agreement. His shoulders relaxed a bit as he scanned the legal language that confirmed at least a part of her story.

"All right," he said, handing them back to her. "You two stay put. I'm just going out to the Blazer to use the radio. I'll be back in a few minutes."

Unable to give in without one more attempt to make him understand, Lori lunged to her feet and held out her palms to him. "Zack, please. If you loved me at all...if you had any feelings for Brandon, you wouldn't do this."

His nostrils flared and his expression hardened again. "If you had any feelings for me, you wouldn't ask me to ignore my duty."

Without another word, he went outside. Lori returned to sit beside Brandon and put her arms around him when he started to cry. Zack returned in less than five minutes, his expression more baffled than anything else.

"What is it?" Lori asked.

"Good news, I think." Zack sat in the overstuffed chair adjacent to the sofa, leaned forward and propped his elbows onto his widespread knees. "You're not wanted for anything."

Lori and Brandon gasped, then asked in unison, "What?"

"Even cops have computers now," Zack said. "According to the FBI's data bank, there are no warrants for your arrest anywhere in the U.S."

"How can that be?" Lori gaped at him, then shook her head to clear it. "I shot him, Zack."

"Are you sure you hit him?"

"Of course, I'm sure. There was so much blood, he must have needed medical help, and don't doctors have to report treating a gunshot wound?"

"Yeah," Zack said. "They're supposed to."

"Then how can there be no warrants?"

Zack frowned thoughtfully. "Maybe he refused to cooperate. If the victim won't file a complaint, there's no case. No case, no warrants."

"Unless he'd died, right?"

"Yeah. If he'd died, there would have been a full homicide investigation. Given your history with him, you'd probably be at the top of the suspect list. I think it's pretty safe to assume he's alive."

Her stomach knotted at hearing those words. Brandon started crying again. She gave him a reassuring hug, then surged to her feet. "Since I'm not wanted for anything, I'm free to go. Would you mind giving us a ride to Cody?"

Surprised by her request, Zack stared at her. "Why would you want to do that? You're off the hook."

Laughing bitterly, Lori shook her head. "As long as Hugh is alive, I'll never be off the hook. There's only one reason he wouldn't press charges against me for shooting him."

"What's that?"

"He wants to punish me himself."

"It's been four years."

"It wouldn't matter if it was four decades, Zack. Hugh does not forgive and he certainly doesn't forget. He just hasn't been able to find us before this."

"And he probably won't be able to find you now. I doubt if he even saw that film clip on TV, and he can't access the FBI's computer—"

"Says who? He's got lots of friends in law enforcement. He's probably got somebody inside the FBI watching for an inquiry about me or Brandon or his shooting. You might as well have put up a billboard for him." Lori passed one hand in front of her face as if she were reading a sign. "Here she is, VanZandt! Come and get her!"

"Aw, come on," Zack protested, though he felt sick at the thought that he might needlessly have put her and Brandon in danger. "Don't you think maybe you're actin' just a tad paranoid?"

"It's not paranoid when someone really is out to get you." She crossed the room to the pile of luggage beside the entertainment center and picked up a couple of battered duffel bags. "Now, will you please drive us to Cody?"

"Dammit, you don't have to go on hiding from the jerk. Stand your ground, stay here and do your job. Let me worry about protectin' the two of you. I promise, nothing will happen—"

"Don't make promises you might not be able to keep." She looked over her shoulder at Brandon. "Come on. I can't carry all of this by myself and we've got to get out of here."

Brandon climbed to his feet and tucked his hands into the opposite armpits. "No, Mom. I don't want to leave."

Lori huffed, then glared at the kid. "I don't either, but—"

The kid returned her glare in spades. "No. I'm not going anywhere."

"You knew before we ever left California, that we would only be here for a short time, Brandon. I realize you've had a lot of fun, but we can't stay. You know it as well as I do."

Brandon's chin came up and Zack had to smile when he perfectly mimicked the ultrapatient tone she had used on him. "No, Mother. I'm sick of always hiding and moving. I'm sick of never going to school or having any friends. I'm sick of never having a home."

"Listen to him," Zack said.

She shot him a withering glance and snarled, "*You* stay out of this, McBride. You've already caused us more than enough trouble." Then she took a couple of long, deep breaths and turned back to Brandon. "I'm sick of all of that, too, honey. But you know what your father is like. If anything happens to me, you'll end up with him again. I'm not willing to risk that."

"Well, I am!" Brandon shouted. "Zack's right, Mom. We have to stand our ground."

"Brandon, please. Be reasonable."

"You're the one who's not being reasonable." Propping his fists on his narrow hips, Brandon stuck out his chest and raised his chin another notch. "I mean it, Mom. I won't go with you this time, and you can't make me. We have to stay here where we've finally got some friends to help us."

She stared at him as if she didn't recognize him anymore, then dropped the duffels as if her fingers had suddenly turned to soggy noodles. Her shoulders slumped and her eyes filled with tears. She swallowed noisily and swiped furiously at her eyes with the backs of her hands.

"What if…" She paused and cleared her throat before starting over. "What if one of our friends gets hurt trying to protect us? Have you thought of that?"

Brandon's face paled, but before he could dwell on the idea for more than a second or two, Zack butted back into the conversation. "Don't worry about that," he said. "We'll have everybody in Cody and Sunshine Gap on the lookout for the guy. He probably won't even get close to the ranch."

"You can't guarantee that," Lori said.

"Well, hell, I can't guarantee the sun'll come up tomorrow mornin', either." He waved an arm toward the mountains. "Some of those mountains are volcanoes, and I can't guarantee that one of 'em won't erupt and wipe out the whole ranch. I can't guarantee I won't drop dead of a heart attack tonight. But I'm not gonna live in fear of what *might* happen. I'd go crazy."

"Are you implying that I'm crazy?"

"Not really." He gave her a quick, coaxing smile. "Of course, I can't guarantee that you're not."

Brandon grinned and Lori rolled her eyes in apparent exasperation. Encouraged by the dissipating tension, Zack approached her and cupped his hands around her face.

"The only thing I really can guarantee is that I'll do my damnedest to keep both of you safe. Trust me on that much, will you?"

She looked into his eyes for the longest time, though what

she was looking for, he couldn't say. In the blue depths of
her eyes, he saw fear—raw, horrible fear. But he also
glimpsed a spark of hope. Before this was over, he intended
to fan that spark into a gut-deep conviction that she and Brandon really could have a safe and happy life, preferably with
him.

Finally she gave him a jerky little nod, then pulled away
from him and went to Brandon. Propping her hands on his
shoulders, she shook him once, as if making sure she had his
complete attention. He looked up at her, his eyes trained on
hers with an intensity Zack almost found spooky.

"All right, Brandon. We'll stay for now," she said, "but
I want you to promise me that you'll follow every single rule
Zack and I give you to keep you safe."

He nodded eagerly. "I will, Mom. I promise. Cross my
heart and hope to die."

She pulled him against her then, closing her eyes, rubbing
the side of her face against the top of his head and hugging
him as if it might kill her to let him go. The anguish in her
face gave Zack's heartstrings a vicious wrench and brought
a burning sensation to the backs of his eyes. Lord, she literally was trusting him with everything in this world that
mattered to her.

He would die before he would let her down.

Fred Wilkins drummed his fingers on top of the least clut-
tered spot on his desk and eyed the telephone with an odd
sense of reluctance. He'd been a cop for twenty years and a
private investigator for five more, and his instincts were
screaming at him not to deal with this particular client. The
guy was loaded, well-known and extremely well-connected,
but he also seemed a little wacko.

But it wasn't his job anymore to make those kinds of judg-
ments. Pleasing his clients paid the bills now, and this particular client would pay outrageous fees for the information
Fred had just received from an old pal who'd gone to work
for the FBI. In fact, with the fee he would get, Fred figured

he could buy a small lake cabin and a decent boat to use on the weekends.

He wanted the cabin and the boat, and if he didn't turn the information over, and this client found out, the situation could get very ugly, very fast. Besides, the client already had a good idea where the woman and boy were. Fred's information would only confirm what he already knew. Where was the harm in getting paid for work he'd already done?

Before he could talk himself out of it again, he picked up the handset and dialed the client's number. The man answered on the third ring. As always, his cool, inflectionless voice with its soft Southern drawl made Fred's skin crawl. Even knowing about caller ID, it gave him the creeps when the man used his name before he could identify himself.

"Mr. Wilkins."

"How are you today, sir?"

"Forget the pleasantries. You must have something new or you wouldn't have called. What is it?"

"A hit on the FBI's data banks. The sheriff's office in Cody, Wyoming, requested information on any outstanding warrants for the lady. That's the same place the film clip came from."

"I'm aware of that, Mr. Wilkins."

"Do you want me to go out there? If she's not in jail, I can bring her back here for you. The boy too, if he's with her."

"No, thank you. You've done exactly what I've paid you to do. I'll finish this myself. Your check will be in the mail this afternoon."

The phone clicked in Fred's ear, and he realized the client had hung up on him. Cursing the man's arrogance, Fred hung up, too, then wiped his hand on his trouser leg. He picked up the photo the client had provided to aid in the search.

The woman looked about twenty-five; the boy was a toddler. She was a brunette, and beautiful. Though her full lips smiled like a beauty queen's, there was a haunted, or maybe it was a wounded light in her eyes—

Unwilling to finish that thought, Fred shoved the photo back into the file, then crammed the file into the open drawer of the cabinet beside his desk. Poor lady.

No matter what she'd done to his client, Fred sure wouldn't want to be in her shoes.

Chapter Twelve

Brandon squirmed out of Lori's embrace and gave her one of his jeez-don't-get-all-mushy-on-me expressions that usually made her smile. This time it made her want to hold him even tighter. She wiped her hands on the sides of her jeans and waved toward the pile of luggage.

"We should take our things back to the trailer," she said. "And get some sleep."

Before she could move a foot, Zack stepped in front of her. "I want you to stay with me."

An automatic protest rose to her lips. Laying his hands on her shoulders, he slowly shook his head. "A five-year-old could break into one of those tin cans and you'll be a lot harder to approach without warning out here than you would up at the main house."

"All *right!*" Brandon said, his voice filled with relief. "What's for supper?"

Zack flashed him a grin. "Tell you what, pard. You go put your stuff into the back bedroom on the right and grab a shower, and we'll see what we can scrounge up in the kitchen. Help yourself to some towels in the linen closet.''

Brandon wasted no time in obeying. Lori gazed after him, trying not to take her son's obvious preference for a man's protection as a personal affront. It hurt anyway. After all, she'd managed to keep them both safe and together for four years. Shouldn't that count for something in Brandon's eyes?

As if he could read her thoughts, Zack gave her a sympathetic smile, then slung one arm around her and ushered her into the kitchen. He made a quick phone call, pulled a couple of frozen pizzas out of the freezer and put them in the oven. Lori set the table and helped him make a salad. Neither of them talked much, but considering how much conflict had passed between them during the past two days, the silence felt surprisingly comfortable.

When Brandon joined them in the kitchen, the pizzas and salad quickly disappeared. Zack insisted that he would do the dishes while Lori tucked Brandon into bed. By the time she returned, he'd made a pot of coffee and put an extra leaf in the table, where he sat making notes on a legal pad.

"What's going on?" she asked.

"Family meeting." He tipped his head toward the front door when the sound of pickup doors slamming reverberated through the house. A moment later, she heard a soft knock, the door opened and more than one set of heavy footsteps came toward the kitchen. Smiling with what looked like satisfaction, Zack got up and started pulling coffee mugs out of the cupboard.

Cal McBride entered the room first, followed by Jake, Dillon and Marsh. Each man gave her a nod, grabbed a coffee mug from Zack and took a chair at the table. By the time everyone was settled, she felt like a small alien being among all of the broad shoulders, big arms and hands and deep, rumbling voices.

Zack cleared his throat to gain the others' attention. "We've got a problem, fellas, and I need your help."

His cousins and brothers leaned forward, listening intently

as he gave them a rundown of the situation. Lori quickly began to understand what he'd meant when he had told her that when they had trouble, the McBrides circled the wagons and faced it together. From the instant Zack had said he needed help, none of the others questioned whether or not they should get involved—they already *were* involved. And they didn't so much as blink at the prospect of facing a potentially dangerous opponent for the sake of a woman and boy they barely knew.

Realizing the full extent of their compassion and generosity stunned her. Humbled her. Touched her so deeply, she was afraid she might burst into tears of gratitude. Only the fear that she might miss something important prevented her from doing so.

That, and seeing a transformation come over Zack. While he'd answered his brothers' and cousins' questions, the cowboy/small-town cop had vanished. In his place sat a hardheaded strategist who could have built an outstanding career in the military or any law enforcement agency the government possessed.

"Lori and Brandon will stay on the ranch until we nail this guy. Brandon will have an adult with him at all times, even when he's with the boys," he said. "I want a guard at the main driveway, and anyone who steps onto our land has to have a photo ID, and a legitimate, logical reason for being here."

Marsh made an okay sign. "The production company should be doing that anyway. I'll handle it."

Zack made a check mark on his list. "I want one of the ranch dogs to stay out here with Lori."

Dillon nodded. "You got it. I'll bring Farley over in the morning."

Zack turned to Lori. "Do you have any pictures of Hugh?"

She shook her head.

Jake said, "I've got one up at the house in a magazine. There was an article about his last Derby win."

"Good," Zack said. "Make us two hundred copies of it. You and Marsh can show it to everyone on the ranch and in the movie company and tell 'em we're lookin' for him."

"I'll pass some around in town," Cal said.

"I knew you would," Zack said. "Take some over to Cody, too. Concentrate on the airport, restaurants, bars and motels."

The meeting continued. The other men made a few minor suggestions and left. Lori had no doubt whatsoever that each of them would carry out his assigned tasks or die trying. They were just so...honorable. It was an old-fashioned word, but she couldn't think of another one that described them half as well. Of course it described Zack, too, and she wondered if he had a clue as to how special that made him. He was the kind of man she hoped Brandon would become someday.

Feeling as if her heart had climbed into her throat, she watched him scoot back his chair, stand and gather up the empty mugs. He carried them to the sink, loaded them into the dishwasher and turned it on. Then he turned back to face her, his hands propped on his hips.

"So, what do you think?" he asked.

Lori pushed herself to her feet and slowly crossed the room to stand in front of him. "I think your plan sounds very professional. Very thorough."

"Do you feel safe?"

She raised one shoulder in a helpless shrug. "I don't know if I'll ever feel safe as long as Hugh is alive, but I believe you'll do everything in your power to protect us."

"Damn straight." He raised one hand and gently brushed the tip of his index finger under her eyes. "Aw, sweetheart, don't cry. I can't stand to see any woman cry, but when you do it, it just rips my insides out."

She hadn't realized she was crying, but it didn't matter. She laughed, then sniffled and gave him a watery smile. "Tough. I always cry when I'm touched. You and your family really touched me tonight."

His neck and ears reddened. "We'd do it for anyone who needed our help."

"I know. That's what's so amazing about all of you."

He pulled her into his arms. She slid her own arms around his waist and rested her head against his chest. His arms tightened around her back, nestling her more firmly against him.

"I just hope you all know what you're doing," she said. "I'm still afraid someone is going to get hurt."

"We'll be careful, darlin'."

"Promise me you won't underestimate him?"

"You bet."

She looked up at him. "What if he doesn't show up here while they're shooting this movie?"

"We'll deal with it." Zack's fierce smile chilled her soul and reassured her at the same time. "Your running days are over."

Closing her eyes, she savored the idea. "That sounds wonderful, but—"

"No buts, woman. You've carried this load all by yourself for too long. It's time to let somebody give you a hand."

"It's been so long since I dared to hope I would ever be free of him."

Zack stroked her hair, then tucked a finger under her chin, lifting it and urging her to meet his gaze. "You start hoping right now. You and Brandon are going to live normal lives again. Trust me on that."

Her heart sped up at the solemn intent in his eyes, and the unspoken words she knew he'd wanted to say. But they both knew she had too many other things to figure out at the moment to make any promises about the future. She would have kissed him then, but she didn't want to start something she couldn't finish.

She pulled away from him before temptation got the better of her. "I, um, I'd better get some rest. Is it all right if I use the room next to Brandon's?"

His dark brows came together in a scowl. She knew he'd

hoped she would stay in his room. At the moment, she certainly wanted to, but she couldn't do that while Brandon was in the house. It probably wasn't a sensible thing to do, anyway.

But oh, how her heart longed to ignore all logic and good sense and grab whatever joy and pleasure she could find with Zack. At least some of her inner turmoil must have appeared on her face. Zack's scowl softened into a rueful smile and he gave her a nod of understanding.

"Yeah," he said. "I'll help you move your stuff in."

Once that was finished and he turned to leave, she brought up the subject she'd been wanting to discuss since he'd announced she wasn't wanted for anything. "I want my gun back."

He hesitated, then turned back to face her. "That's not a good idea."

"I didn't ask for your opinion or your permission. It's my property and I want it back."

"What about the kids? Do you have any idea how many kids are killed every year in accidental shootings?"

"Yes, I do, and I would never leave a gun unattended."

"All it takes is a second of inattention—"

"Don't play games with me. You and your family have guns here, and I'm sure you've impressed all of the safety rules on Riley and Steven. Give me enough credit to believe I've done the same thing with Brandon."

"We'll protect you—"

"I need to be able to protect myself," she insisted. "I know how to use it."

"When's the last time you practiced with it?"

"Just before we left California. I've made it a habit to go to a firing range at least twice a month." He still hesitated, and she frowned at him. "I'm not a child, Zack. Stop treating me like one."

"I know you're not a child," he said. "It goes against my grain, that's all. You've already shot a man once and you're understandably jumpy as hell. That's a dangerous combination. If one of us startled you, you might accidentally blast him to kingdom come.''

''I wouldn't do—''

''You don't know that, and I don't, either. Let me think about it, all right?''

''No. It's not all right. Your behavior is condescending and controlling, and I resent it.''

''I'm just doing what I think is best.''

''That's right. You're doing what *you* think is best, but you're not listening. You're making decisions for me that I want to make for myself. Are you hearing me now?''

''Honey, they're hearin' you in Cody.''

Pretending to ignore her ferocious glare, Zack beat a hasty retreat to his bedroom. Dang woman could talk him into almost anything, but she didn't need to know that. He stripped, tossed his dirty clothes into the hamper and stepped into the shower. By the time he cracked his door open and slid into his bed, he knew he wouldn't sleep, even though he was exhausted.

It didn't matter that Lori was just down the hall. He still worried about her every moment she was out of his sight. And though they'd only been lovers a short time, he missed having her beside him. She might have come to him if Brandon was somewhere else, but he wasn't sure she would have. She was so angry with him now.... Jeez, what a situation he'd gotten himself into.

He wanted to do what was right for everyone involved, but he kept running into these damned, hazy areas he wasn't sure what to do with. He hated it when that happened. He trusted his brothers and his cousins without question. He wanted to trust Lori the same way, but he didn't have enough history with her to do that yet.

People were unpredictable at best. It took time—with some people it took a long time—to know when or how much they might exaggerate things. He didn't doubt that Lori's ex was a mean, dangerous, possibly even a crazy individual. He just didn't know exactly how mean, dangerous or crazy Hugh

VanZandt was in reality. After all this time, would he really come after her? It seemed unbelievable that anyone could harbor such a deep, long-lasting hatred for anyone as wonderful as Lori.

On the other hand, Zack sure as hell didn't want to take any risks with her safety or with Brandon's. Hour after hour he lay there, staring at the ceiling, trying to figure out more ways to protect them. If VanZandt did manage to breach their security and threatened either Lori or Brandon, Zack knew he'd likely have to shoot the SOB, but God, he hoped it wouldn't come to that.

Through the opening he'd intentionally left in his door, he heard a muffled noise that made his neck hair stand up. He sat up, listening intently. Was that Lori? Or Brandon?

He climbed out of bed. Yanked on a pair of jeans. Stepped into the hallway. Listened again. Lori was sobbing.

Reaching her door in three long strides, he turned the knob and hurried across the room. Her whole body was tightly curled around her pillow. Oh, man, she was having another one of those nightmares. Poor little gal put on such a brave front all day long, but her fear leaked out of her at night.

"Lori, darlin'," he said, gently squeezing her shoulder. "It's just a dream. Wake up, honey."

She started violently at his touch, then slowly raised her head and squinted into the darkness. "Wh-what?"

"It's just a dream," Zack repeated. "A nightmare."

Vaulting into an upright position, she threw her arms around his neck and clung to him. He heard her breath coming in hitching little gasps, felt the fine tremors vibrating through her rigid muscles. Nudging her over, he slid into the bed and gathered her close. Stroking her hair, he murmured soothing nonsense in her ear, and knew moments of heart-wrenching tenderness while she slowly relaxed into his embrace and succumbed to her desperate need for sleep.

She snuggled against him with such complete trust, it reminded him of the way Melissa used to fall asleep in his arms when she was a toddler. Her warm, seemingly boneless little body had aroused every loving, protective instinct he owned. Those same emotions rose up inside him now, accompanied by a nearly crushing sense of responsibility.

God, what if he'd unleashed something horrendous by checking on warrants for her arrest? What if he couldn't protect her? What if he couldn't protect Brandon?

No, he couldn't afford to think that way. It was late and he was tired, a sure recipe for irrational, middle-of-the-night doubts. Hugh VanZandt was not some indestructible monster. He was just a man, vulnerable as any other. If he showed up at the Flying M, they would deal with him in whatever way proved to be necessary.

Nevertheless, Zack spent the rest of the night in Lori's bed, holding her while she slept. It felt good to be needed, if only to chase Hugh the Jerk out of her dreams. When she woke, she'd probably be mad at him again. He didn't want to waste any opportunity to be this close to her.

The next morning, Lori awoke to an empty room, but with the distinct impression she hadn't been alone very long. Though she had a fuzzy memory of a nightmare, she felt surprisingly well-rested. Shaking her head at the contradictory impressions, she climbed out of bed, dressed and went to check on Brandon.

His room was empty, but the bed was made in his usual, haphazard way. She closed his door and followed an enticing aroma of coffee to the kitchen. A note propped up on the counter informed her that Zack and Brandon were up at the main house checking on security arrangements.

She wadded it up and tossed it in the trash can. Wretched man probably wanted her to think he'd simply forgotten about returning her gun. Yeah, right. Fat chance of that. If he thought *she* had forgotten about it, he was sadly mistaken. And if he didn't return it within the next twelve hours, she would take steps to get another one, even if she had to steal it.

She poured herself a thermal mug of coffee and strolled

out to visit the horses. Most of Wade's were still in Cody.
She talked to the few left behind, scratched ears and blew
kisses at them, then moved on to check out Zack's babies.
They trotted to the fence to greet her, soaking up all the
attention she was willing to give them. And he thought *her*
charges were spoiled. Hah!

Sipping the last of her coffee, she ambled to the last pen
and studied Satan, automatically angling her body sideways.
He was one beautiful creature. She was so used to seeing
him go into his nervous-pacing, ears-laid-back, teeth-bared
routine whenever anyone approached his pen, it took her a
minute to figure out what was different about him today.

When she did, she couldn't help smiling. It was just a
small thing, really. Satan was standing still. Better yet, with
his ears and his eyes pointed directly at her, he looked more
curious than hostile.

She sidled closer to the fence, propping her left elbow on
the top rail. Satan flicked one ear, but the rest of him remained motionless. She made a clucking noise with her
tongue. Satan snorted and shook his head, but he settled back
down in a few seconds.

Her mind racing with questions and possibilities, Lori
called softly to the big gelding. "Hey, there, Satan. What's
up with you? Are you just in a good mood today, or what?"

The horse tilted his head slightly to one side, as if he were
trying to understand everything she said. She clucked at him
again. He took a couple of prancing steps sideways.

She held out a hand to him, wiggling her fingers invitingly.
"Why don't you come on over here and let me pet you, big
boy?"

Satan lifted a hoof as if he might actually do it, but then
his head jerked up, his ears swivelled toward the other horse
pens and he let out a neigh that gave Lori goose bumps. One
hand clasped to her chest to keep her heart in place, she
whirled around to see what had frightened the animal. From
the other side of the barn, Zack and his cousin Dillon stepped

into view, accompanied by a medium-size dog with a mottled, shaggy coat, long ears and a droopy tail.

Satan immediately started pacing. The closer the two men came, the more agitated the gelding behaved. Lori held up her palms and made shooing motions.

"Guys, go back behind the barn and be quiet for a minute." she said.

Zack and Dillon exchanged questioning glances, then shrugged and retraced their steps. When they disappeared from sight, Satan calmed down and resumed his previous stance. Lori spoke to him again, clucked at him, wiggled her fingers at him, and received the same curious responses she had before.

When she called Zack and Dillon back out, Satan became agitated the instant they stepped into sight again. Her suspicions confirmed, Lori decided to do the horse a favor and hurried to meet the men. Now that she knew Satan was only afraid of men, she might be able to help him. The thought made her smile.

"What are you doin' out here?" Zack demanded.

She stopped and stared at him for a long moment before answering in a tone dripping with sweetness. "Good morning, Dillon. Zack. How are you this morning?"

Zack scowled at her, but had the grace to flush. "Mornin', Lori. We're just fine, thank you very much," he said, mimicking her tone. "And how are you?"

"Fine, thanks," she said. "And where is my son?"

"Helping Marsh clean up the kitchen before Grace gets back. She's fussy about messes in her territory."

Lori shot a glance toward Zack's tack room and rolled her eyes toward heaven. "Do you honestly think you have any room to talk?"

Dillon made a choking sound and turned his face away, but not fast enough to hide a grin from Lori. She hadn't had much contact with him before, and his badly scarred face and curt manner could be intimidating. But that grin and strangled laugh revealed a man she thought she could learn to like. She winked at him, and received a wink in return.

"And who is this?" she asked, holding out the backs of her fingers for the dog to sniff.

Going down on one knee, Dillon stroked the dog's head. The dog gazed up at him with a slavish sort of devotion in its eyes, one of which was a startlingly light shade of blue, while the other was brown. Dillon motioned for her to come closer.

"This is Farley," he said. Petting the animal again, he reached out and grasped Lori's arm. "Farley, this is Lori. Friend. Stay with her."

At Dillon's nod of encouragement, Lori stroked Farley's head. "Hi, Farley. I'm pleased to meet you."

Farley licked her hand, then gave her a doggy grin. Lori petted him again. "I think we're going to get along just fine."

Dillon straightened to his full height, then reached down to help Lori up. "He's a good dog. Some Blue Heelers aren't real friendly, but Farley's got a little Lab in him and he loves kids. He and Brandon took to each other right away. I don't know if he'd attack anyone, but nobody'll sneak up on you. He senses somethin' wrong, you'll know it right quick."

"I'll appreciate having him around."

Dillon gave her another wink. "We'll take good care of you and your boy. Keep your chin up."

"Thanks, Dillon, I will."

"Well, I've got to go and give some more roping lessons to those idiot stunt people," he said with a grimace. "Only one with a lick of coordination's that little gal who rides the Harley. Wish me luck."

Zack waved him off, then turned back to Lori. "All right, fun's over. What were you doin' with Satan?"

"Nothing much. Just visiting." She gave him a bland smile and set off toward the house.

Zack kept pace with her. "Why don't I believe you?"

"Beats me," she said. "Could it be your overly suspicious nature?"

"Since I don't have one, I doubt it." Grabbing her hand, he pulled her to a halt. "Come on, Lori, tell me. Why did you make us leave and then come back?"

She pulled her hand away and crossed her arms over her chest. "Perhaps we could arrange a trade."

"What kind of a trade?"

"You give me back my gun, and I'll tell you what you want to know. It'll be worth your while."

Giving her a thoughtful frown, Zack scrunched his mouth up to one side, then slowly shook his head. "It's tempting, all right, but I'll pass. I still don't think it's a good idea for you to have one. You're just gonna have to trust me to take care of you."

"You're asking for the one thing I'll never be able to do," she said. "With or without your help, I'll take care of myself and Brandon."

After studying her intently, he let out a disgruntled sigh, turned away and left her without another word. She repressed the urge to scream or throw something at him. Trudging back to the house, she told Farley she didn't care if she never saw Zack McBride again. Farley gave her another one of his doggy grins and acted as if he didn't believe her. She really couldn't blame him. She didn't believe her, either.

When she heard a pickup's engine in front of the house several hours later, she gave up all pretense of not missing him and hurried to the front door to greet him. But it wasn't Zack. Wade and Grace jumped out and hurried toward the house.

Lori opened the door for them. Grace came inside first, swept Lori into a fierce hug and passed her on to Wade. Smiling self-consciously, Lori offered to get them something cold to drink.

"Not for me, thanks," Wade said. "I just stopped by to let you know Manny's coming back to work."

"Are you sure he's ready?" Lori asked.

"The doctor says so," Wade replied. "I'll keep an eye on him, of course, but I don't want you worrying about your job. Zack told me what's been going on with you, and you've got more than enough to cope with right now."

"That's...very sweet of you, Wade. Especially when I left to get Brandon without any explanation—"

He waved away any apology she might have made. "Forget about it. I just wish you'd told me this before. I understand why you didn't, but I wish we could've been more help to you."

"You and Manny have been wonderful," Lori said. "I can't just sit here every day, though. There must be *something* I can do for you and Manny."

Wade nodded. "You can take care of the horses we're not using in Cody if you want. When we come back to the ranch, there'll be plenty you can do. But take the time you need to get your life back in order. No matter how long it takes, you'll always have a job with us."

Since her throat felt too tight to speak, Lori gave him a teary smile and nodded. He awkwardly patted her shoulder, then asked to use Zack's phone to return some business calls. After directing him toward the kitchen, Lori invited Grace to join her on the sofa.

Before they were settled, Grace asked, "What more can we do to help you?"

"Nothing," Lori replied. "I already feel guilty enough about bringing trouble here and exposing all of you to danger."

Grace shrugged. "Aw, don't worry about that. With a family this size, there's always some kind of trouble goin' on. We don't run from it, and you don't have to, either."

"What if one of you gets hurt? What if it's one of your boys?"

Grace grimaced, then looked Lori directly in the eye. "Hey, don't even start that what-if stuff. You play that game long enough, and pretty soon you won't have the nerve to get out of bed in the morning. Stand your ground and damn the consequences.''

"You sound just like Zack," Lori grumbled.

"In this case, Zack's absolutely right. I don't blame you a bit for takin' off when you did. Sometimes that's the only solution a woman's got. But you're not alone, now. Let us help. In fact, I think you should leave Brandon with me for a while."

"What?"

"You heard me. Let me keep Brandon at the main house. He'll be safer up there than he would be out here."

"What makes you think that?" Lori demanded.

Grace reached over and squeezed Lori's left hand. "Now, don't get all offended. I'm not criticizing you. I'm just trying to look at the situation objectively."

"What's your point?"

"We'll never be able to keep those boys apart, and between me and Jake and the rest of the bunch, there's always an adult around to keep an eye on 'em. And if you and Brandon are split up, it'll be a heck of a lot harder for your ex to grab both of you. Make sense?"

Lori nodded reluctantly. "I guess it does. I'm just not used to being away from him."

"I know. But I'll bring him out here to visit you, and I promise we'll take real good care of him." Grace patted her hand, then stood. "Let's go pack his stuff."

It only took a few minutes to gather Brandon's things. Grace and Wade hugged Lori again and left, and the sudden quiet of the house drove Lori back outside to visit the horses again.

Farley trotted along beside her while she did her own and Zack's chores. When she filled Satan's water trough, the gelding watched intently, but made no fearful or threatening moves, not even when she straightened up and looked right back at him.

"We're two of a kind, big guy," she murmured. Satan snorted and bobbed his head a couple of times, as if he agreed. She smiled, then added, "Maybe I'll never be able to heal myself, but I'll do what I can for you."

He bobbed his head again and took a couple of prancing steps sideways. Chuckling softly, Lori headed back toward Zack's house, Farley following her as faithfully as a shadow. The more she thought about it, the more she liked the idea of working with Satan.

For one thing, it was something tangible she could do to at least try to repay Zack for his kindness. For another, it would give her something to do to fill up the days ahead. If she had too much empty time on her hands, she would probably worry herself into a breakdown. Last, but definitely not least, working with Satan would focus her attention on the horse instead of on Zack.

They would be alone in the house again now. Though she was still angry with him for bossing her around and not returning her gun she knew he could coax her back into his bed without much effort. That simply wouldn't do. He'd said he had strong feelings for her, but she knew he was caught up in the drama of her problems with Hugh. Or perhaps he was simply trying to replace the wife and daughter he'd lost with her and Brandon.

When this was all over—if it ever was—he would discover that. She wouldn't make it any harder on him to end their affair than necessary. It would be much, much easier for all of them if Zack never knew she was in love with him.

Chapter Thirteen

Two weeks passed, and Zack felt edgier than a convict waiting for the results of his parole hearing. For days he'd been all primed and ready to slay Lori's dragons, but no dragons had appeared. Not that he really wanted any trouble from Hugh VanZandt, of course. If it was going to happen at all, though, Zack wished it would hurry the hell up and happen so he could get it over and done with.

When the Good Lord had handed out patience, Zack figured he must have been standing in the wrong line. Waiting for something he couldn't control drove him nuts. Always had and probably always would. If it was this bad for him, it must be a hundred times worse for Lori and Brandon. Maybe a thousand times worse.

Knowing he needed to get away from the ranch for a while, he drove into town to visit his little brother. At three o'clock on a weekday afternoon, Cal's Place was usually quiet, and today was no exception. When Zack stepped into the restaurant, Cal waved him to a table near the back of the room and had a glass of iced tea waiting for him when he got there.

"How's it goin'?" Cal asked when Zack sat down across from him.

"Lousy," Zack said. "It's hard to stay sharp and focused for longer than a few days."

"I know what you mean," Cal said. "You think VanZandt even knows Lori and Brandon are here?"

"Hard to say. I've been tryin' to find out more about him, but other than his big racing wins, he's a man who avoids the press."

"You don't suppose Lori might've…imagined he'd come after her? Or maybe just let it get all blown up in her mind?"

Zack had already asked himself that question so many times, he didn't have to give it any prolonged consideration now. "Anything's possible, I guess, but my gut says no. I'd love to go pay that SOB a visit in person. But if he's as crazy as he sounds, and he doesn't know Lori and Brandon are here, I'd hate to tip him off."

Nodding, Cal stroked his mustache the way he always did when he was thinking hard about something. "You've got a point there, all right. What if he doesn't show up by the time they're done shootin' the movie? You're not just going to let this go on and on, are you?"

"No way." Zack rested his elbow on the table, glanced all around to make sure nobody else was listening and leaned closer to Cal. "Keep a secret for me?"

"Sure," Cal said.

"I want to marry Lori."

Cal chuckled. "That's not much of a secret."

"What do you mean?"

"We all figured that out when you called the meeting at your house. A blind man could have seen you were in love with her."

Zack's face grew hot at the thought of his family discussing him behind his back. But, what the hell. It happened all the time. "So, what did you guys decide about her?"

Cal shrugged. ''That you could do a lot worse. You know how it goes. As long as you're happy, we'll be happy for you.''

''Are you still showin' VanZandt's picture around?''

Cal nodded. ''You bet.''

''And you haven't seen *anybody* new in town.''

''Just a couple of female reporters.''

''They ask any questions about the wranglers?''

''You know damn well I would've told you if anyone had done that. I'm not stupid, you know.''

''Never said you were. I'm just...frustrated and scared I'll miss somethin'. Know what I mean?''

''Yeah, I do.''

Sylvia Benson, Cal's most experienced waitress, came into the staging area and started refilling supplies for the evening shift. Zack figured she was probably eavesdropping, but she was just the kind of busybody who might help him catch VanZandt if he did show up.

''Well, tell me about the lady reporters then,'' Zack said. ''Just in case.''

''There's not much to tell,'' Cal said. ''They hang around in the bar sometimes and interview the movie folks when they come in for a beer after work.''

''Ever see either of 'em with a man?''

Sylvia snorted, then grinned at Zack. ''They're both nice enough gals, but a little on the homely side. Next to them, even I look pretty darn good.''

Cal grinned, then shrugged. ''Let's just say I doubt either one of those ladies dates much.''

Zack sighed, then took a swig of iced tea. He knew he was grasping at straws, but it was either that or go completely nuts.

''So, how's Lori doing?'' Cal asked.

''How do you think? She's nervous and twitchy and cranky as a cow with sunburned teats. It's killing her to have Brandon staying with Grace all the time.''

''What you both need is a little fun,'' Cal said.

"Fun? *Now?*"

"Hell, yes. Now's when you need fun the most. It'll keep your head clear, your muscles relaxed and your reflexes quick."

"Got any ideas on where I might find some fun?"

Cal scowled at him. "Cut the sarcasm. I was just about to suggest that you take the old pinball machine home with you. When you get tired of that, you can borrow my video games."

Zack thought about it for a moment before nodding his agreement. "All right. Thanks, Cal. Sure can't hurt to give it a try."

They both got up then. Cal loaned Zack his pickup to haul the pinball machine home and promised to drive the Blazer out to the ranch later to trade back. Eager to show Lori their new toy, Zack peeled out of the alley behind Cal's Place and sped out of town. The more he pondered Cal's remarks about having fun, the more he realized his little brother was absolutely right.

He and Lori had been on the verge of building something really special together, but now they weren't even sleeping in the same room. They'd allowed this situation with VanZandt to dominate their whole lives. In doing so, they had given the SOB more power over them than he deserved.

It was time for that nonsense to stop.

Lori stood in the center of Satan's pen, crouching slightly to make herself look less threatening as she held out one hand to him. Poised on the verge of flight, Satan watched her, eyes and ears trained on her while he struggled to decide how dangerous she might be.

"Easy, boy," she crooned. "It's only me."

Satan bobbed his big head and blew out a nervous snort.

"I know it's scary, sweetie, but I promise I'd never hurt you." She took a tiny step closer to him.

His glossy hide shivered, but he didn't move otherwise. Encouraged, Lori took another tiny step toward him. Satan fled, running around the pen in a vain attempt to get away from her. Sighing, Lori straightened up and rubbed the small of her back with both hands. Over the past two weeks she'd learned the hard way that, while the gelding wasn't actively hostile to her the way he was toward men, that didn't mean he was ready to let her jump on his back and go for a ride.

She'd left him treats and sung to him. She'd spent hours sitting outside the pen in a lawn chair talking to him, then sitting on the fence, then stepping just barely inside the gate, then moving to the center of the pen, and she still hadn't gotten within an arm's length of him. The sad thing was, he obviously wanted contact, but he just couldn't conquer his fear long enough to let her touch him. But now that she'd told Zack about Satan's real problem and demonstrated his ability to improve, he had a much better chance of living out his lifespan.

"It's okay, Satan," she called softly. "There's always tomorrow."

Farley suddenly sat up, both ears standing straight and his neck bristling, a low, steady growl coming from deep in his chest. In the space of a heartbeat, adrenaline surged through Lori's body. She hurried out of the pen and grabbed the small backpack she'd started hauling around to carry her pistol, which had "magically" appeared under her pillow the day after Grace took Brandon to the main house. Yanking at the zipper, she squatted beside the dog.

"What is it, boy?"

Farley barked a couple of times, then charged into the brush beyond Satan's pen. Sucking in deep breaths, Lori pulled the pistol out, checked the clip and the safety. Still squatting, she swivelled left and right on the balls of her feet, holding the pistol in both hands, scanning. Satan became agitated, but she didn't know if he'd simply picked up on her fear or if he'd sensed the presence of a man nearby.

The nearest phone was in the barn. In terms of distance, it wasn't far away. In terms of the agonizing minutes it would take her to get there, it might as well be in Boston. She could still hear Farley barking, but she couldn't see him.

Pistol pointed skyward, she broke into a crouching, zig-zagging run. When she reached the barn, her lungs screamed for oxygen, and she let out the breath she'd unintentionally been holding since leaving Satan's pen. Pausing to gather her wits before entering, she heard another sound—the rumble of a pickup's engine coming up Zack's drive. She crept to the end of the barn and cautiously peeked around the corner facing the house.

To her horror, she recognized Grace's truck rolling to a stop. Grace and Brandon climbed out and turned toward the house.

Lori stepped out into the open. If Hugh was out there, she didn't want Brandon in sight.

"Grace, Brandon, don't go in there," she called softly. Both turned back around and smiled when they saw her. She glanced all around herself, then ran to meet them. "Grace, please, get him out of here now."

"Mom," Brandon protested. "I just got here."

Grace's gaze focused on the gun in Lori's hand. "What's wrong?"

"Farley took off into the bushes. He was growling and barking like he was after someone."

Brandon stiffened and lost three shades of his tan. "Is he here, Mom?"

"I don't know, honey."

"Maybe Farley was after some*thing,*" Grace said. "It could've been an animal, you know. Farley loves to chase coyotes, jackrabbits and even deer."

As if he'd heard his name mentioned, Farley trotted into the driveway, his bushy tail wagging in a manner of unmistakable pride. Brandon's shoulders relaxed and his color quickly improved. He dropped to his knees and held out his arms. Farley sprinted toward him, knocked him over onto his back and proceeded to lick his face.

"I suppose that could have been it," Lori said with a sigh. "I'm so jumpy anymore, it probably was just an animal."

Laughing, Brandon tried to fend the dog off, but Farley was a persistent creature. Lori finally dragged him off her son. Brandon and Farley moved away and started a game of fetch with a stick.

Indicating the dog with a tilt of her head, Lori asked, "What do you think?"

"Coyote." Grace smiled sympathetically. "The waiting's getting to you, huh?"

A lump rose in Lori's throat. She nodded, exhaled a deep breath and tucked the pistol into the waistband of her jeans at the small of her back. "Yes. I, um…guess it is."

Grace reached out one hand and patted Lori's shoulder. "Hey, don't beat up on yourself for jumpin' at a false alarm. You don't know if that guy's out there or not. It's not time to let your guard down yet."

"I know," Lori said, "but it's hard. Sometimes I find myself wondering if I've wasted four years of our lives running and hiding for no reason."

"I don't buy that. If I were in your shoes, I'd sure listen to my instincts, and that's all you've been doing."

"But what if I'm really just paranoid, Grace?"

"Well, if you are, you're darn selective about it. I mean, at least you're not afraid of everybody. Only your ex."

Lori gave her a weak smile, then swept one hand toward the house. "Want to come in and have some coffee?"

"Wish I could, but I've got a thousand things to do today. I just brought Brandon over because I think he was missing you a lot, and all of the boys were ready to take a break from each other."

"Uh-oh. Is he wearing out his welcome?"

Grace grinned. "Not at all. I'll come back for him tonight. By then they'll have started missing each other."

"Maybe we should plan to separate them on a regular basis," Lori suggested. "I could come and get Brandon every morning or afternoon—"

"Let's just play it by ear for now. I think you're spending too much time out here by yourself. They're gonna shoot that big chase scene tomorrow. Want to come with us and watch Dillon ride for the cameras?"

"I don't know. Maybe. Let me talk to Zack about it when he gets back from town and I'll let you know."

Grace agreed and drove away. Lori watched the pickup until it was out of sight, then turned to her son. Hair tousled in the wind and a smile as wide as his face would allow, he threw the stick with all of his strength, looking happier and healthier than she'd ever seen him before. Her heart contracted at the sight of his delight when Farley raced after the prize.

Unable to stop herself, she went to him and gathered him into a big, warm hug and kissed the top of his head. "I've missed you, sweetie."

He rolled his eyes at the hated endearment, but hugged her back anyway. "I've sorta missed you, too, Mom."

"Only sorta?"

He grinned. "Well, Mrs. Kramer doesn't make me do the dishes. She's a good cook, too."

"Oh, yeah?" Lori gave him a mock glare. "Well, maybe I'll have to make you do extra dishes while you're here. I wouldn't want you to forget how."

"No way." Brandon wiggled out of her arms and ran to meet Farley, who dropped the stick at his feet and gazed up at him, hopefully wagging his tail.

Brandon threw the stick again. The dog raced after it. In spite of Grace's assurances and Farley's relaxed demeanor, Lori anxiously scanned the area for any signs of an intruder. Maybe she was becoming irrational and paranoid, but her skin prickled with gooseflesh and she simply couldn't shake the conviction that Hugh was indeed out there somewhere. Silently watching and waiting for her to let down her guard.

Zack arrived home to find Lori and Brandon singing along with a golden oldies radio station and baking chocolate chip cookies. If the unmistakable aroma hadn't drawn him to the kitchen, their cheerful voices would have. Neither noticed him at first, and he leaned one shoulder against the doorjamb and watched them with a tightness in his chest that was emotional rather than physical.

Their laughter and obvious love for each other warmed him. At the same time, it made him feel lonelier than he could ever remember feeling. He wanted to be part of their circle of affection. He wanted them to stay here forever. He wanted them to love him as much as he loved them.

Brandon looked up and saw him. The boy's immediate smile of welcome drew Zack into the room. The next thing he knew, he was spooning chocolate chip cookie dough onto a pan and belting out "Sweet Caroline" with Neil Diamond and his fellow bakers.

For the rest of the day the three of them played pinball and ate cookies, made a horse tape with the video camera and ate cookies, went out to do the chores, ate steaks for supper and cookies for dessert. It was a lazy, fun-filled day, one they all desperately needed after being on edge for so long. Without a word spoken, they became a family, if only for this one day. He never wanted it to end.

When Grace arrived to take Brandon back to the main house, he hugged his mother and then Zack, clinging at the last moment as if he wanted to say something, but didn't have the right words. Zack's arm locked the boy's head against his chest for a moment, playfully rubbed his knuckles across the top of Brandon's hair, then dropped a quick kiss there. Brandon pulled back and smiled up at him as if he were some kind of a hero. It was all Zack could do to turn the kid around and shoo him down the front steps to Grace's pickup.

Lori sniffled when Grace turned the pickup around and gave them a jaunty wave on her way back down the driveway. Zack put his arm around Lori and escorted her back into the house. Turning her to face him, he pulled her into a hug. She rested quietly against him, accepting his comfort for a long, blissful moment before pulling back and gazing up at him with the same sort of hero worship in her eyes that he'd earlier seen in Brandon's.

"Will you make love to me tonight?" she murmured.

He didn't know why she'd changed her mind about being intimate with him again, but he wasn't about to question such a gift. He lowered his head and kissed her, slowly and tenderly at first, then with a driving, greedy passion he could barely control. Control didn't seem to be real high on Lori's list of priorities at the moment, however. She met him kiss for kiss, caressed the back of his neck with her hands, rubbed her breasts against his chest like a cat twining around its owner's legs, demanding attention.

"Keep that up and we're not even gonna make it to the bedroom," he muttered against her lips.

Her low, throaty laugh finished off what restraint he had left. Clamping one arm around her rump, he yanked her flush against him and let her feel how much he wanted her. She wrapped herself around him, her strong arms and legs pulling him closer yet, as if she would absorb him completely into her body. He'd be lucky to make it to the sofa.

Lori felt her back make contact with the carpet and eagerly popped open the snaps on Zack's shirt. How on earth had she ever resisted this man for two whole weeks, she wondered, gliding her palms over the hard contours of his chest. And why had she ever thought resisting him was a good idea? She must have been insane.

When he had hugged her son with such tenderness, and even kissed his head, she had lost her heart all over again. Given the chance and a little guidance, Zack would make a wonderful father and a terrific husband. If she couldn't have forever with him, she could have this one night, maybe even two or three nights if she was lucky.

It wouldn't be much longer than that, though. Hugh was out there somewhere. Somewhere close. She could smell him and his hatred in the air. She would have to face him, of course. But in the meanwhile, she would enjoy this time with Zack and store up a few more memories that no one, not even Hugh, could ever take away from her.

By the middle of the night she'd lost all track of how many varieties of sex from Zack's crazy list they had already shared, but she was too exhausted to try any more. She vaguely remembered Zack carrying her into his bedroom. She snuggled against him now in the middle of his big bed, still floating somewhere in the ozone from her last climax.

The arm wrapped around her shoulders tightened in a gentle hug. Then his fingertips burrowed into her hair and played with one strand, then another. His lips brushed the top of her head, much as they had kissed Brandon. His chest rose and fell on what sounded like a supremely satisfied sigh. She smiled and rubbed her cheek against him, felt his fingers twining through her hair. His deep, quiet voice vibrated against the ear she had pressed to his chest.

"I love you, Lori. Brandon too."

His simple, heartfelt declaration made her heart thump painfully against her ribs. She took a quick breath to steady her voice. "I know that...now."

"Does that mean anything to you? Anything at all?"

"Of course it does. I wouldn't be here with you like this if I didn't care for you."

"I'm not talkin' about caring for each other. I'm talkin' about being in love. Forever."

"I know. But we've already been over this, Zack. You know I can't make any promises about forever."

"Because of VanZandt?"

"He's the main reason."

"How many other reasons are there?"

"I don't know. I can't think about them until I know Hugh will leave us alone."

Zack raised up on one elbow, shifting her onto her back and looming over her. "Forget him. Think about what a great day the three of us had together. Think about how many of those we could have if we were married."

"Oh, Zack—"

"No. Don't give me one of your hopeless monologues here. I love you and your son, and I'm pretty darn sure that both of you love me. Let's just make a commitment and get on with our lives. If VanZandt shows up, we'll deal with him, but let's not waste any more time because of him."

Lori slid out from underneath him, pulled the sheet up to her neck and sat up. "No. You've already become one of his targets because of me. Don't ask me to sign your death warrant by marrying you."

"Are you *always* this melodramatic?"

"Only when it's necessary."

"And why is it so necessary right now?" he demanded.

"Because you're not listening to me," she retorted. "You're being stubborn and selfish, and you think you know everything, but you don't, dammit."

"What don't I know about Hugh VanZandt?"

"You're so decent, you can't even conceive of a monster like him. It's bad enough that we've put your whole family at risk by being here. I will *not* single you out for Hugh's sick and twisted mind to focus on."

"Lori—"

"No. Case closed. Don't even think about bringing that up again."

He frowned at her, his dark eyebrows pulled together in a tight V, his beard bristling as if his jaw was clenched hard. Unable to stop herself, she reached over and cupped the side of his face with her hand.

"Try to understand my position for a change, Zack. I love you too much to risk siccing my worst enemy on you. It's not fair of you to ask me to do that."

Covering her hand with his own, Zack shut his eyes for a moment, then gave her the most reluctant nod she'd ever seen. "All right," he said, heaving a sigh. "We'll do it your way for a while. But this is not gonna go on forever. If he doesn't come here soon, we're gonna go after him."

"And do what?" she asked faintly.

"We're gonna sit him down and have ourselves a little talk. And then we'll take it from there. I mean it, Lori. You've lived in fear of that SOB long enough, and it's got to stop."

Chapter Fourteen

Zack took Lori and Brandon out to see the production folks shoot the big chase scene the next morning. It was the first time he'd stood around and watched the whole process. He found it fascinating for the first couple of hours. After that, it began to wear thin, except for when his cousin Dillon galloped his palomino gelding across the hills as a stunt double for the lead actor.

While he considered himself the best horse trainer in the family, Zack freely admitted that Dillon was by far the best rider. Stick him on a horse and let him run like that, and it was pure poetry in motion. Shoot, if he wanted to, Dillon could probably ride a buffalo and make it look good.

Between takes Zack contented himself with holding Lori directly in front of him with his arms around her waist and checking out the crowd around them. He'd been told that reporters would be allowed to watch the day's shooting, but he felt surprised and a little uneasy at how many strange faces there were. None of them looked particularly threatening or interested in Lori and Brandon.

He had to hide a grin when he spotted the two women Cal and Sylvia had described. In all honesty, they *were* a tad homely, but not as much as Sylvia had led him to expect. On closer inspection, he decided they weren't really homely after all. It was more a matter that they obviously didn't spend much time or energy on their looks. A little makeup, better fitting clothes and some decent haircuts would probably do wonders for both of them. He laughed at himself for thinking such things. Who did he think he was, anyway? A beauty consultant? Still, there was something odd—

Lori tipped her head back and gazed up at him. "What's so funny, McBride?"

He grinned and shook his head. "Trust me, you don't want to know."

She rolled her eyes at him and tipped her head back down. Zack rested his chin on the top of her head and hugged her tight. Her warm, womanly fragrance teased his nose. He inhaled deeply, remembering how she had snuggled into his arms last night, even after they'd had that intense disagreement.

That had never happened with Billie, especially when she thought he wasn't listening to her. He'd never been able to convince her that listening to and agreeing with everything she said were two different things. She was one hell of a grudge holder, too. Thank God Lori was more reasonable. Better yet, in a roundabout way, she'd even admitted she loved him.

Damn, but he wished this thing with VanZandt was done. Lori would probably marry him if she didn't have a constant threat hanging over her head. Even while it frustrated the devil out of him, he also admired her concern for the safety of the people around her. Well, somehow, they would work it out. They just had to.

Scanning the crowd again, he spotted Jake's pickup bouncing up the dirt road. He was supposed to stay at the house today and take care of some ranch business. What the heck was he doing up here? The pickup shuddered to an abrupt halt. Jake jumped out and glanced around as if he were looking for someone. When he spotted Zack, Jake trotted toward him.

"You got an emergency call," Jake said. "Warren Fisher's been drinking again, and it sounds bad this time. He's holding his wife and two of his kids hostage."

Zack looked into his brother's eyes and read the grim truth of what Jake hadn't said. "What about the third kid?"

Jake grimaced. "Little Matt's the one who got out and ran for help. He's okay physically, but he's damn shook up."

Zack reluctantly released Lori and scanned the crowd one more time. An uneasy sensation that he'd missed something hovered at the back of his mind, but he couldn't have said why. As far as he could tell, everything looked okay.

"I'm sorry," he said to Lori.

She gave him a rueful smile. "It's all right. When duty calls, you have to go."

Turning to Jake, Zack said, "Will you give Lori and Brandon a ride back to my place?"

"You bet. Get moving, bro. Those folks need you."

Zack took off at a run, climbed into his Blazer, radioed the Cody office for backup and drove as fast as he dared on the narrow, winding road. This was the first time in his memory that he'd seriously resented duty's call. For one thing, he'd really been enjoying himself with Lori and Brandon. For another, he couldn't shake the feeling that something was a little out of whack. If anything happened to Lori or Brandon while he was gone....

Well, he couldn't change things now. He had a job to do. The best he could hope for was to take care of Warren and get back home as soon as possible.

Lori arrived back at Zack's house half an hour later with a grumbling, crabby Brandon at her side. She understood his disappointment at having their day out with Zack interrupted;

she felt that way, too. But the instant Zack left, she had started to get the willies. It was silly, and it bothered her to realize how much she had started to depend on his protection, when she was perfectly capable of protecting herself.

Farley greeted them effusively. Jake checked out the house before Lori and Brandon went inside. After a few reassuring comments, he headed back to the main house. Lori went into the kitchen in search of something to fix for lunch. Brandon entertained himself by using Zack's video camera to drive her bonkers while she made tuna sandwiches and sliced apples. Lord, from that angle, he was probably getting a great shot straight up her nostrils.

"All right, put that thing down and wash your hands," she said, making a face at the camera's lens.

Brandon grudgingly obeyed. She carried their plates out to the deck, then settled herself on one of the benches at the weathered picnic table. It was blessedly quiet and peaceful, with only the popping of insect wings, an occasional birdcall and a breeze rustling the grass to interrupt the silence. The air was warm, the sunshine bright, and she knew she could happily live out the rest of her life right here.

Though Zack's stubbornness occasionally made her want to shriek with frustration, she had to give him full credit for good intentions. He had so much confidence in his own abilities and he was so used to taking charge, he simply tended to forget that other people had abilities, too. As character faults went, it really wasn't so terrible.

Brandon joined her, wiping his hands on the sides of his jeans. Farley trotted around the house and dropped a stick at Brandon's feet. Brandon reached for it, but Lori shook her head at him.

"Finish your lunch, first. Then you can play with him." She pointed to the other side of the deck. "Lie down, Farley."

Farley picked up his stick and carried it to the spot she had indicated. After tromping around in a tight circle three times, he lowered himself to his belly, laid his head on his front paws and shot her such a dirty look, she had to laugh. Brandon chuckled, too, easing the tension between them.

Munching away on their sandwiches and apples, they made small talk between bites. When Brandon started eating the second half of his sandwich, Farley jerked up his head and growled. Neck hair bristling, he jumped to his feet and, barking maniacally, tore into the woods.

Brandon's faced paled. "Oh, jeez, Mom."

"It's all right, honey. He did the same thing when Grace brought you over here the other day, and it was just a coyote, remember?"

"Did anybody ever see the coyote?" Brandon asked.

Lori shrugged. "Not that I know of, but—"

A piercing cry of pain that could only have come from Farley cut her off. Brandon moaned. Lori gave his shoulder a quick squeeze, told him to stay put and ran into the kitchen to call for help. She picked up the phone, but heard no dial tone.

The uneasy sensations she'd felt earlier returned, only now they had grown into something approaching full-fledged dread. Her heart pounded, her lungs didn't want to accept a complete breath, and her skin suddenly felt damp with sweat. Her gun. Her backpack was in the living room, and she had to get to her gun.

Forcing a deep breath into her lungs, she hung up the phone and ran through the doorway. A large woman Lori had seen at the movie set that morning stood inside the entryway with one arm extended. Lori's backpack balanced on the end of her index finger, and the woman's smile was sickeningly familiar.

Lori halted so fast she nearly fell over. The other woman grabbed the back of her own hair, tugged it off and tossed it behind the door. Oh God, it couldn't be, but it *was* Hugh.

"Hello, Lori," he said. "It's been a long time."

Stunned speechless, she gaped at him. Her throat constricted on an involuntary gulp. Hugh's smile widened.

"What's this? The last time we were together you had

more than enough to say." He stepped closer, and it was all she could do not to back up. "Aren't you happy to see me? Aren't you glad to know you didn't murder me?"

Lori shook her head. The action cleared away the shock of seeing him enough to unfreeze her vocal cords. "Run, Brandon!" she screamed. "Run! He's here!"

"Lori, Lori, Lori, was that a nice thing to do?" Still smiling, Hugh crossed the room in a blur of motion and took her left arm in a punishing grip. "Surely you knew I would want to see my son after all this time."

She kicked at his shins and swung her right fist at his damnable smile. He ducked, let go of her arm and wrapped his own arm around her waist with crushing strength, lifting her onto her tiptoes. She fought him anyway, still yelling at Brandon to run. Her foot connected with an end table, tipping it over and spilling the stack of magazines it had held onto the floor.

Hugh cursed, then whipped her around and wrenched her arm up behind her back. The excruciating pain in her shoulder and elbow stole her breath, but she couldn't give in to it. He frog-marched her into the kitchen.

His eyes wide, his face white and his whole body trembling, Brandon stood just inside the sliding glass door that opened on to the deck. "S-s-stop it," he said. "D-d-don't h-h-hurt her."

"Still stuttering, son?" Hugh laughed. "What a shame. I really did hope you would at least learn to speak well while we were separated, but you're still an idiot."

"Leave him alone!" Lori stomped the heel of her boot onto the top of Hugh's sneaker. He cursed again and yanked her arm even higher in retaliation. Lori gasped. "Go, Brandon. Get Jake. Hurry."

Brandon shook his head. "I won't l-l-leave you, M-M-Mom. I c-c-can't."

"Isn't that sweet?" Hugh sneered. "By the way, Brandon, you should know that I'll kill her if you try to leave."

"He'll kill me, anyway," Lori said, panting against the

agony in her arm. "Get out of here, Brandon. That's an order."

Brandon shook his head again, but he didn't speak. His right hand fluttered oddly, drawing Lori's gaze to the counter. He was trying to show her something, but what? Not the cookie jar or the toaster. The video camera? Did that little red light mean it was recording? Had Brandon turned it on? She studied his face and he gave her a slight nod. She winked at him.

"All right, Hugh," she said. "What is it you want?"

"I want you to pay for everything you've done to me."

"Everything I've done to *you?*" she demanded. "I could have shot you ten more times and I still wouldn't have paid you back for all the black eyes and broken ribs you gave me."

"Ah, but *you* deserved it, Lori. I didn't. Now, let's go." He pushed on her arm, forcing her to walk in front of him. "The sooner you get what's coming to you, the sooner we can go back to being a happy family."

"We were never a happy family," Brandon said, his eyes filled with loathing.

"We're not going anywhere with you," Lori said.

"Yes, you are, darling. I have a small plane waiting in a field not far from here. We'll stop in Reno and get married again, then go straight back to Kentucky and get on with our lives."

Lori turned her head around and glared at him. "I wouldn't marry you again if you were the last man in the universe. Not that you ever were much of a man to start with."

Hugh's lips still smiled, but his eyes burned with fury. Fast as a startled Thoroughbred, he brought his fist up, threatening her with it. "See what you do, Lori? You bring this kind of thing on yourself. If you would only learn when to keep your big mouth shut, you wouldn't have to go through all of this, would you?"

"Go to the devil, you bastard!"

"Tut, tut. That's not polite and you shouldn't say it in

front of an impressionable child. And don't tell me you would prefer that...cowboy lover of yours to a man of my means and sophistication.''

''I'd take Zack McBride over you in a heartbeat. He's twice the man you could ever hope to be.''

Hugh half turned her around and kissed her so hard her front teeth drew blood on the inside of her lips. When he finally pulled back, she spat obscenities at him and writhed like a wild thing. He was bigger than she was, but she'd done more hard physical labor in the past four years than he'd done in his whole useless life. Desperation gave her an added boost of strength, and when her free hand flailed into the telephone hanging on the wall, she grabbed the handset and smashed it directly over her head into Hugh's face.

There was a crunching sound when it made contact with his nose, and a stream of warm blood gushed down the back of her neck. Howling with pain, Hugh relaxed his grip on her arm for just a second, but it was all she needed to pull herself free. She ran to the table, yanked out a chair and slammed it into his legs. Hugh howled again and bent over, clutching one hand to his nose, the other to his knees.

Knowing she needed to get herself and Brandon up to the main house before Hugh recovered enough to catch them, Lori took Brandon's hand and charged onto the deck, down the steps to the yard and around behind the horse pens. Satan greeted her with a loud whinny, which would have thrilled her had he chosen to do that at any other time. Now, however, it would only tell Hugh which way they had gone.

She couldn't help looking at Satan with longing. The big horse was powerful enough to carry both of them for miles and miles, if only he would allow them to ride him. In a few more weeks, that might have happened, but he wasn't ready yet.

Instead, she grabbed a bridle from the tack room and hurried into a pen holding some of Zack's horses. Of course, they all shied away from her, whether from the frantic vibes she must be giving off or the smell of the blood on her shirt,

she didn't know. In case it was the former, she willed herself
to calm down and cautiously approached a roan mare she'd
ridden several times.

Lori caught her on the second try, slipped the bridle into
place and frantically fastened the buckles. Then she hurriedly
led the horse out of the pen, shut the gate and gave Brandon
a leg up onto the mare's bare back. Swinging herself up
behind him, she headed for the nearest pasture that would
lead them toward the main house.

They had barely started when she heard Satan scream. Lori
glanced back, wincing when she saw Satan throwing himself
against the fence, ears pinned back and teeth bared, tail slic-
ing the air like a whip. Oh, God. Hugh wouldn't hurt his own
horses, but she doubted he would blink at hurting one of
Zack's. Especially one who dared to get in his way at a time
like this.

"Mom, come *on*," Brandon said. "Let's *go*."

She knew he was right. Turning back around, she lifted
the reins and heard the unmistakable sound of a revolver
being cocked.

"Don't move." His lower face and shirt red with blood,
Hugh stepped onto the path, his right hand extended and
gripping a thirty-eight. "Don't move, or I swear to God I
will blow both of you off that nag."

Everything inside Lori froze at the sound of his voice. She
didn't need to see his face to know he'd gone beyond fury
now, and straight into madness.

Oh, God, she needed help. Zack would come. She knew
he would. He'd promised and he always kept his promises.

By the time Zack sent Warren off to jail with the deputies
from Cody, and Warren's wife and kids to the Cody hospital
to have their injuries treated, his skin was crawling with ap-
prehension. He didn't believe in ESP or any of that psychic
stuff, but he *knew* Lori and Brandon were in some kind of
trouble. He didn't know how he knew, and he didn't care.

The only thing he cared about was getting to the ranch as soon as possible.

He was still two miles out when Grace's voice came over his CB radio. "Home base calling Zack McBride. Zack, you there?"

Zack grabbed the microphone and pressed the talk switch. "Yeah, Gracie. What's up?"

"Steven tried to call Brandon a while ago, but nobody answered. He got worried and dragged Jake down there with him. They found a real mess, Zack. Broken stuff everywhere, and…quite a bit of blood."

Zack's gut roiled, but he took a deep breath and maintained control of himself. "Any idea how long they'd been gone?"

"Jake didn't think it was more than a few minutes. The blood was still really fresh."

"Anything else, Grace? Any clue where they might've gone?"

"Yeah, somebody left the video camera on and caught the whole thing. Hugh was one of those female reporters."

"Where did they go?" Zack snapped.

"Jake thinks they're headed for George Pierson's place. Hugh said he'd parked a small plane in a field not far from here, and George has the only field around that's flat enough for a plane to taxi on."

"I know the one. I'm almost there now. Where's Jake?"

"He took Marsh and Wade and went after them not two minutes ago."

"Good. Tell him I'm goin' in first and I want him to make a silent approach."

"Will do. Good luck, Zack."

"Over and out." Zack hung the microphone back on its hook and tromped on the gas pedal. He hadn't seen any sign of a small plane in the area, but God knew he easily could have missed one. Just like he'd missed VanZandt. He had been right there, right under everybody's nose and undoubtedly thumbing his own nose at all of the security precautions.

Zack took a death grip on the steering wheel and stomped the accelerator even harder. After seeing firsthand the damage a man out of control could inflict on his family, he felt sick. He'd promised Lori he would protect her and Brandon. A lot of blood at his house meant somebody was hurt, which meant he'd already failed to keep his promise. How could he ever live with himself if either of them died because of his failure?

Dammit, she'd tried to tell him. Tried to get it through his thick skull that Hugh VanZandt was a dangerous man. So why hadn't he listened to her? Why had he always patronized her and accused her of being melodramatic? If it would bring Lori and Brandon back, he would rip out his stupid tongue and stomp it into the dirt.

But who would have figured on any man being crazy and devious enough to go around dressed like a woman for weeks, just waiting for the chance to grab Lori and Brandon? Hindsight was such a joy when you discovered you'd been right, such agony when you'd been wrong. Man, had he ever been wrong.

But when he got his hands on Hugh VanZandt, he was going to pay. Big time.

Sitting between Hugh and Brandon in the front seat of Hugh's rental car, Lori sent silent prayers toward heaven, toward Zack, toward the Flying M, anywhere they might possibly do some good. At the same time, she watched the road ahead, looking for any opportunity—however small—to escape. Brandon pressed himself against her side, and she could feel him trembling. She put her arm around his shoulders and rubbed her hand up and down his arm, trying to reassure him.

Hugh ranted about making her suffer when they got back to Kentucky, but she was beyond listening to him. He drove with one hand and held his gun with the other, poking it into her ribs. Lori ignored it, too.

He could only kill her once, and she'd rather make him do it quickly, here in Wyoming, than let him take her somewhere else where he could torture her before finishing the job. Above all else, she would *not* let him leave here with Brandon. Once she was dead, God only knew what he would do to her son.

She watched for a sharp curve in the road, anything that would force Hugh to slow down. There weren't any. She cast a longing glance at the keys dangling from the ignition. If she grabbed them and threw them out of the open window, would Hugh kill her on the spot? No, the keys wouldn't come out while the engine was running. What else could she do?

Moving carefully, she slid her free hand along the back of the seat and silently popped the lock on the passenger door. Brandon looked up at her, his eyes wide with alarm. She tilted her head toward the door, then silenced him with a look when he opened his mouth to protest.

She braced her right foot on the floor, then threw her weight against Hugh's side, forcing him to use both hands to control the car. She reached for the keys with her right and switched off the ignition with one quick flick of her wrist. The power steering and brakes died with the engine, the car's hood aimed straight for the opposite side of the road.

The front tires came to a jolting halt at the bottom of a shallow ditch. Lori leaned to her right and opened the door latch. Hugh grabbed a fistful of her hair, cutting off her opportunity to escape, but she pushed Brandon out of the car, shouting, "I love you, honey. Run to Zack. He's our only hope."

Brandon took off with the determination of an Olympic runner. His fist still gripping her hair, Hugh stepped out of the car, dragging her across the seat and shouting, "Brandon, come back here!"

"Go, Brandon, go!" Lori yelled, stifling a scream of pain when Hugh yanked her up beside him. Where it wasn't bloody, his face was bright red. His nostrils were flared. His eyes were maniacal. But strangely, she felt no real fear for herself. Now that Brandon had escaped, she could handle what happened next.

Hugh could beat her, torture her, kill her if he wanted, but she wasn't going to go down easy. No, she was going to fight him with every single second she had breath and make him pay the biggest price she could for his sadistic pleasures. Now that she knew what being with a good man was really like, she had too much to live for to allow this pathetic nutcase to take it all away from her.

He shook her as if she were a puppy he could carry around by the scruff of the neck. "That wasn't very smart, Lori."

She grinned at him. "Hey, it worked for me. And for Brandon."

He frowned as if her grin had confused him. She supposed it probably had. He was much more used to seeing her cower away from him. How long would it take him to learn that the old rules no longer applied?

Hugh cursed viciously. She glanced in the direction of his gaze and saw a dust cloud heading toward them at a fast clip. Her heart surged with hope. It was Zack. It had to be Zack. Before she could catch a glimpse of the vehicle, Hugh shoved her none too gently back into the car, started the engine and drove back onto the road.

Spotting Brandon running down the middle of the road, Zack slammed on his brakes and jumped out of the Blazer before the dust had even started to settle. He scooped Brandon into his arms and held him close. The kid was shaking all over, sweating and crying, and he clung to Zack like someone who'd been plucked out of raging flood waters. God, but he loved this boy.

When Brandon's jerky breathing eased, Zack set him on his feet and went down on one knee in front of him. Brandon was obviously terrified and shaken, but he looked okay otherwise.

"What happened, Brandon?"

The boy sobbed, "Mom p-p-pushed me out of the car so he wouldn't g-g-get me. She told me to find y-y-you. That you're our only h-h-hope."

Zack's stomach twisted at the thought of Lori alone with Hugh. What if he'd already killed her? "How long ago, Brandon?"

"Just n-n-now. And he's still got her, Zack. He's takin' her to his plane and he's got a gun. He's gonna k-k-kill her. I know he is."

"Not if I can help it." Zack surged to his feet and caught sight of a dust cloud approaching from behind.

A moment later Jake stopped his pickup behind the Blazer. Marsh and Wade got out with him. Zack quickly filled them in on the situation, then asked Wade to take Brandon back to the ranch.

"No, Zack," Brandon protested. "I want to help you save Mom."

"I know you do, and you're a brave kid, but I'll have a better chance of saving her if you're not there."

"Why?"

"Because you're the most precious thing in the world to her. She'll sacrifice her own life to save you, and your dad knows it. If you're there, he'll find a way to use it against her."

Brandon sniffled, then nodded. "Just save her, Zack. Please."

"I'll do my best."

Zack led Marsh and Jake back to the Blazer. Opening the rear door, he handed out Kevlar vests, rifles and ammunition while he explained his plan. Then they all piled in and raced after Hugh and Lori. None of them spoke again, but Zack took comfort in Jake's and Marsh's presence. If something happened to him during this confrontation, the others would save Lori or die trying.

Without a word of warning, Hugh yanked the steering wheel to the right and mashed the gas pedal to the floor. Lori braced one hand on the dash and covered her face with her other arm. The car sped down into the narrow ditch, crashed through a barbwire fence and bounced across a huge, empty pasture.

An impossibly small, red-and-white airplane sat at the far end, shielded from the view of anyone passing on the road by a shelter belt of pine trees. She glanced from side to side, frantically searching for an avenue of escape. Hugh had his pistol buried in her ribs again, and she suspected that this time he would shoot her if she tried to thwart him. Still, she inched her right hand toward the passenger door latch.

"Don't even think about it," he said. "You won't make it. Do you suppose that's your *lover* following us? Perhaps I should take care of him right now, so you can watch him die. You'd like that, wouldn't you?"

"Leave Zack alone," she said.

"You know I couldn't possibly do that." Hugh gave her his most chilling smile. "He used my property."

"I'm not your property. I'm not even your wife anymore."

"You think not? We were married in the sight of God. The state of Kentucky hardly has the authority to separate us. Only death can do that. That's what you promised."

"And you promised to love, honor and cherish me," Lori said bitterly. "It you had kept your promise, maybe I would have kept mine."

He laughed uproariously. "Snippy to the end, aren't you? I've missed your smart mouth—"

"What you've missed is having me for a punching bag. Have you found a replacement? Or have you gone back to torturing helpless animals?"

"Don't push me."

They were almost to the plane. He glanced into the rear-view mirror, then uttered another vicious curse. Lori looked over her shoulder. She nearly fainted with relief at the sight of Zack's Blazer hurtling into the pasture through the gaping hole in the fence. She'd *known* he would come for her. She just hadn't been sure about *when*.

Hugh braked to a halt beside the plane, put his arm around her waist and dragged her out of the car. She twisted and writhed, bit, kicked and literally dragged her heels across the grass, hoping to slow him down enough for Zack to help her.

Hugh put his gun to her head and threatened her with unspeakable tortures, but she refused to stop fighting. Zack was here now, and everything was going to be all right. She believed that as she hadn't believed in anything for years and years. She loved Zack McBride, and she intended to have a future with him if she had to kill Hugh with her own bare hands.

Zack skidded to a halt ten yards away, whipping the Blazer's back end around until the passenger side faced Hugh. He stepped out, and came around the front end of the vehicle. Using both hands, he held his pistol at arm's length. With his Stetson hat, beard, badge, jeans and boots, he looked big, confident of his authority and as tough as any lawman out of the Old West.

He waited a full thirty seconds before speaking, letting the tension grow and expand. When he did speak, his voice was low and professional, but it left no doubt whatsoever that he meant business. "Let her go."

Hugh's arm tightened around her waist, nearly cutting off her ability to breathe. "I'm not done with her yet. When I am, you can have what's left."

Zack stepped closer. "Let her go."

Hugh shoved his gun under Lori's chin. "Back off, or I'll kill her right now."

"Do it and you'll be dead before she hits the ground."

"Well, I feel lucky today. Maybe I'll just take that risk."

Marsh and Jake came out from behind the Blazer, their rifles aimed straight at Hugh. "I wouldn't," Jake said. "Zack might miss, but I sure as hell won't. And Marsh here could hit a fat head like yours from a hundred yards with one eye closed and the other one blind."

A lack of oxygen made Lori's vision waver and turn gray around the edges. Wishing her nails were long and sharp instead of short and neatly clipped, she clawed at Hugh's arm. He flinched, and loosened his hold just enough for her to breathe.

"Ooooh, I'm so scared," Hugh jeered. "Who do you hicks think you are? The Earp brothers?"

"We're your worst nightmare, VanZandt," Zack said. "Let her go. *Now.*"

Hugh jammed his gun more firmly against the curve where the base of her chin connected to her neck. "Go to hell. She's *mine,* and you're going to pay for touching her."

"Where's your ugly girlfriend, Hugh?" Zack asked. "You know, the other lady reporter you were hanging around with in Cal's Place?"

"That was my assistant, Jerome. He truly was an ugly woman, wasn't he? Impossible five o'clock shadow."

"Where is he now?"

"On his way to Reno," Hugh said. "I sent him on ahead so he could make wedding arrangements for Lori and me."

"She divorced you, VanZandt. What do you want with a woman who publicly rejected you?"

"Don't you see, that's just it? I'm a VanZandt. She's a nobody. *She* can't reject *me.* I won't have it."

"Give it up," Jake said. "You're making a fool of yourself."

Hugh violently shook his head. "No, that's what *she* has done to me. Divorcing me, having me arrested for child abuse, can you even imagine the humiliation that caused me? Then she took my son away from me. I'm nothing but a laughingstock in my hometown, and it's all *her* fault. She'll pay for that. I *have* to kill her." His gun hand trembled, and Lori closed her eyes as if that would somehow save her if he accidentally pulled the trigger.

"Aw, you don't want to do that," Marsh drawled. "Everybody'll think it's just another cheap murder-suicide thing. Why don't you be more original?"

"What do you mean?" Hugh's hand steadied and he looked at Marsh with apparent interest. Style had always been terribly important to him.

"If it was me, I'd write one hell of a suicide note, saying how much I adored her and how I couldn't live without her and all that kind of thing, you know? Then I'd go off and kill myself in some really gruesome way. Everybody'd blame her for driving you to despair. Now *that's* what I'd call punishment."

"You're just trying to trick me," Hugh said, jamming the gun hard into Lori's throat, making her gag at the pressure on her windpipe.

She shoved the gun away long enough to call out. "Brandon?"

"He's fine, Lori," Zack said. "On his way to the ranch."

"Shut up," Hugh shouted. "Throw your guns into those bushes and back off, or she dies right now."

Lori's vision wavered again, but she saw Zack and the others carefully toss their guns into the brush. Hugh pulled her backward, closer to the plane. His arm around her waist tightened again. Black spots danced in front of her eyes and she clawed him again. Pinched and twisted his arm. Kicked back against his legs. But she was so tired, she felt as if she were making every movement through a pool of mud.

Using her last reserves of strength, she managed to wrap her fingers around Hugh's gun hand and sink her nails bone deep in his flesh. This time she must have hit at least one sensitive patch of nerves. He yelped and jerked the gun away from her chin. His arm loosened for a second. She inhaled a deep breath and let her body go limp as a wilted tulip.

Zack watched VanZandt pull Lori toward the plane, watching for an opening—any opening. Lori was pitching such a fit, he was terrified for her safety. VanZandt's elevator was missing so many floors, there was no guessing what the SOB would do.

Lori suddenly went limp, forcing VanZandt to drag her. He staggered under the burden of so much dead weight, but caught his balance and continued dragging her closer to the

plane. Zack surreptitiously moved forward, readying himself
to spring, watching for the opening he wanted so desperately.

He finally got it when VanZandt had to figure out how to
get Lori into the plane. The instant he stopped dragging her,
she fought him like a crazed grizzly sow protecting a cub.
VanZandt couldn't control her and the gun, too. Zack
launched himself into the air and brought the other man down
in a flying tackle.

Lori found herself rolling on the ground in a tangle of arms
and legs she couldn't sort out. Where was the gun? Where
was the damn gun? An elbow connected with her right eye,
snapping her head back so hard, her neck popped. Strong
hands closed around her wrists and pulled her aside.

She looked up into Jake's worried eyes and nearly burst
into tears. But there was no time for that. Her breath came
in painful hitches and she couldn't seem to find her voice.
She frantically pointed at Zack and Hugh.

"You want me to get in there and help Zack?" Jake asked.

She nodded and pointed more insistently.

Jake grinned at her, the big dope. "I'd be glad to take a
few whacks at that jerk for you, hon, but this is something
Zack really wants to do for himself. I'd hate to spoil his fun."

"Get him, Zack," Marsh hollered. "Hit him again."

Oh, Lord, this was one of those idiot male things, but Jake
and Marsh were forgetting the gun. *Calm down,* she told
herself. *Calm down and breathe, dammit.* She did breathe
and she did calm down, but her throat must have been dam-
aged by the repeated jabs from Hugh's gun. She still couldn't
speak.

She looked at the two men rolling over and over, cursing
and punching each other with ferocious force. Hugh finally
collapsed with a grunt and lay absolutely still. Bruised and
battered, Zack pushed himself to his feet, propped his hands
on his hips and sucked air into his lungs.

To Lori's horror Hugh raised his thirty-eight and fired it
directly at Zack's chest. Zack toppled over backward, both
hands clutched over his breastbone. She opened her mouth

and tried to scream, but all she heard was the echoing blast of the gunshot and the curses of Marsh and Jake as they ran to Zack.

She scrambled toward the bushes where the McBrides had tossed their guns. A moment later she heard an engine start, then the distinctive roar of a propeller whirring to life. Oh, God, it was her worst nightmare come true. Hugh had killed Zack, and now he was going to get away again. He would come back for her and Brandon again and again and again.

The plane started to taxi across the field. She shoved bushes aside, right and left, frantically searching for a rifle. By the time she found one, the little plane had reached take-off speed, and she knew it was already out of range. She fired at it anyway, over and over until the trigger only clicked. Marsh came to her, gently removing the gun from her hands. She sank to her knees, her eyes filling with bitter tears that no amount of blinking could ever hope to hold back.

"Hey," Jake shouted, "he's not gonna make it."

Lori jerked her head up, hastily swiped at her eyes and saw the plane's left wing slice into the branches of a massive pine. There was a loud crack as it hit the trunk. The fuselage shuddered, hovered for an instant, then slowly tipped over backward and dropped like an eagle diving for prey. The severed wing tumbled after it.

The ground shuddered, and the horrible sound of crunching metal filled the air. A blinding flash of light came next, followed by a deafening explosion. Lori shook her head in amazement while the reality of what she'd just seen and heard sank into her brain.

Hugh was dead. She was free. Brandon was free. Hugh was dead.

But so was Zack. He'd taken a bullet for her, and he had to be dead. Sobbing, she got up and stumbled toward him, needing to hold him one last time. When she reached his side, however, she found him struggling to sit up and cursing

Jake, who was trying to restrain him. Gaping, she knelt beside him, fearing that she'd finally lost the rest of her mind.

"Wh-wh-what's going on?" she asked, her voice barely above a whisper. "Hugh shot him in the chest, but there's no blood?"

Zack gave her a tight-looking smile. "It's all right, darlin'. I had a vest on."

"A vest?" She was so confused, nothing made any sense.

"A Kevlar vest, Lori," Jake said. "Like the cops wear?"

"Oh." Her head felt weird, a little…spacy, but she held on to the conversational thread. "You mean a bulletproof vest?"

"That's right," Zack said. "I probably got some cracked ribs, but it stopped the bullet. Lori? Are you all right?"

The spacy sensation intensified so much she felt disconnected from her body. "I think—" Her vision turned completely black, and the last thing her brain registered was Zack's grunt of pain when she collapsed on top of him.

Chapter Fifteen

Wearing a big grin, Jake ambled into Zack's bedroom one evening when things had settled down at the Flying M. "Hey there, little brother, it's only eight o'clock. What are you doing in bed so early?"

Disgusted that he'd been caught in a moment of weakness, Zack sat up straighter and restrained Farley from trying to get up and greet Jake. Lori had brought the dog in to keep him company while they both recuperated, Zack from three broken ribs and Farley from four stab wounds. The dog needed rest in order to heal. Since he'd been wounded in defense of Lori and Brandon, Zack intended to see that he got it. It was about all Lori would let him do now anyway, and the inactivity was starting to drive him nuts.

"What do you want, Jake?" Zack asked, barely maintaining a civil tone.

Jake went on as if he hadn't spoken. "It's not like you're in major plaster, and it's been five whole days since you

busted those ribs. Guess you needed a vacation or you'd be
up and around by now.''

It was a lie, and they both knew it, but Zack played along
with him. It was a rancher's way of acknowledging a serious
injury in a way that wouldn't make the guy who was laid up
feel any worse than he already did. Zack grumbled, ''Well,
I *would* be up and around if it wasn't for Nurse Nightingale
out there.''

Jake glanced toward the doorway. ''Lori's taking good
care of you, isn't she?''

''Of course she is,'' Zack replied. ''But if she keeps this
up, she's gonna kill me with kindness. Dang woman will
hardly even let me go to the bathroom by myself. She's
worse than Mom when it comes to fussin' over an injury.''

Jake's eyes glinted with amusement. ''Aw, you poor guy.
I don't know how you can stand lying there with a sweet,
gorgeous woman eager to fulfill your every little whim. I
know I'd sure hate every minute of that.''

''Shut up, Jake. You don't know what you're talkin' about.
It was great at first, but she's startin' to drive me loony.''

Lori breezed into the room, carrying a tray loaded with
coffee and freshly baked cookies. Zack gulped, hoping she
hadn't heard him griping. It wasn't that he didn't appreciate
everything she'd done for him. It was just…too much. Especially when her flittin' around, fluffin' his pillows and such
got him all turned on and his damn ribs wouldn't let him do
anything about it.

Jake thanked Lori for the goodies she offered him, then
said, ''Your shiner's getting pretty colorful. Does it still
hurt?''

''Not much.'' She wrinkled her nose at him. ''The worst
is definitely over.''

Before he could reply, the phone on Zack's bedside table
rang. Zack shifted his weight in preparation for turning to
answer it. Of course, Lori beat him to it. From his armpits
to his waist, he was wrapped up so tightly, he could barely
breathe, much less twist his torso.

Lori handed him the receiver. He raised it to his ear and said, "Zack McBride."

The soft, feminine voice on the other end of the line stole what little breath he still had. "Daddy? It's me."

Zack's eyes stung and a lump lodged in his throat. "Melissa? Is that you?"

Jake and Lori whipped their heads around and stared at him, their eyes full of questions. Zack clamped the receiver between his ear and his shoulder and motioned for Lori to sit beside him. She did so, automatically reaching out to hold his hand. God, but he loved her for knowing he needed that.

"Yes, it's me." Her voice wobbled as if she were fighting tears. "Aunt Grace called and said you'd been shot. Are you going to be okay?"

"It's just a few busted ribs, honey. I'll be fine."

"Thank God," Melissa murmured. "When Aunt Grace told me, I really felt bad that I hadn't talked to you for so long or thanked you for the presents you've sent me. I'm sorry, Daddy."

"I appreciate that, but I was wrong about…well, most of the things I said to you the last time we were together. I'm sorry, too. It's wonderful to hear your voice, honey."

"Do you think I could come for a visit sometime?"

Zack's heart thumped against his rib cage, but he felt no pain. He'd wished, but hadn't dared to hope he ever would hear Melissa say these things to him. "Anytime you want. Or I'll come to you if it's easier. I, uh, owe your mom an apology, too."

There was a long silence on Melissa's end, and Zack could almost see her eyes widen in surprise. One part of him wanted to laugh; another part felt sad that he and Billie had subjected their daughter to so much conflict and anguish in her short life.

"That's great, Dad. When Aunt Grace called, Mom was really upset, too."

"Well, heck, I should've gotten myself shot sooner," Zack said with a chuckle.

"That's a terrible thing to say," Melissa scolded, but he could tell she was half laughing.

Tears flooded his eyes, but he wasn't ashamed of them. Why should he be? Lori's face was pretty soggy, too, and even Jake hadn't been able to stifle a sniffle or two. "I've missed you, baby."

"Me, too. I'll let you know when I can come there, okay?"

"Okay. I'll talk to you soon."

Zack hung up the phone and cleared his throat, praying his eyes would dry up fast. Lori released his hand and stood. Jake stood, too, grabbed a cookie and said he had to get back to his office. Lori ushered him out, and Zack heard them visiting all the way to the front door. Grateful for the chance to collect himself, he swiped at his eyes, then grabbed a tissue from the bedside table and blew his nose.

He regretted hanging up the phone. Now that he'd lost the connection to Melissa, he had a million questions he wanted to ask her. And he should have set a date for her to visit. Of all the times to turn wishy-washy, but he'd been so surprised that she wanted to come back to the Flying M, and so scared.

Scared? Of a fifteen-year-old girl? Well, not scared of Melissa herself, so much as he was scared of screwing things up and losing her all over again. For good.

But he wouldn't have to do it all alone, this time. Lori would help him. He smiled at the thought of her kicking him under the table, pinching his arm or turning a warning scowl on him. However she did it, she wouldn't hesitate to rein him in if he started getting out of hand.

She returned to his room, her expression sober, hands shoved deep into her front jeans pockets. "Congratulations, Zack. You must be thrilled."

"I am, but you don't look very happy."

"We have to talk." She took the chair Jake had vacated.

He didn't like the air of finality in her manner, or the rigid tension in her neck and shoulders. He forced himself to reply in a calm, reasonable voice. "All right. What do we need to talk about?"

"I have to go back to Kentucky to settle Hugh's estate."

Zack's gut twisted into what felt like one huge knot. "You were divorced. Why would you have to do that?"

"According to his lawyer, Hugh never bothered to change his will. That means Brandon and I are his only heirs, and I'm the executrix of his estate."

"We can hire a lawyer to handle it for you. Alex's neighbor could do—"

She interrupted with a firm shake of her head. "No. This is something I need to do myself, Zack."

The knot in his gut twisted again. His chest was so tight, breathing hurt like a son of a gun, but it had nothing to do with his ribs. "You're not leaving. I want you to marry me as soon as we can arrange it. There's no waiting period in Idaho. We'll just zip across the border and find a justice of the peace."

She gave him a wry smile. "Why would you want to do that? So I can go on driving you crazy?"

His neck and ears suddenly felt hot. "Oh. You heard that?"

"Uh-huh." She pulled her hands out of her pockets and leaned toward him. "But don't worry about it. I really think it's time we took a break from each other. Marriage should be a rational decision. Everything's happened so fast, and it's been so intense, we both need to step back and reassess our feelings."

"But, Lori—"

"No buts, McBride. If this relationship is going to go anywhere, you've got to learn to listen and accept it when I tell you what I want and what I need."

"We can't even discuss it?"

"You're not discussing. You're telling me what to do. I won't live that way."

He let out a disgruntled sigh. "Okay. I'm sorry I came on

so strong. I guess I was…afraid you'd leave me for good. Like Billie did.''

"That's not what I want," she said. "I just need to go back to bury all the old hurts. I want to face it all and be done with it so I can make a fresh start.''

Zack's tension eased, allowing him to smile at her. "All right. How about leavin' Brandon here with me? He'll have fun, you'll get done quicker and easier, and I'll know for sure you're comin' back.''

"As a hostage?" She scrunched up her mouth in a thoughtful pose, then slowly nodded. "I suppose that could be arranged.''

"Better yet, why don't you wait a few more days and I'll come with you? There's no reason you have to go alone, is there?''

"Yes," she said automatically. "This is something I have to do for myself.''

"You're still mad at me for letting you down, aren't you?"

She let out a huff practically dripping with exasperation. "We've been over and over this issue. None of what happened with Hugh was your fault. You saved my life, and I'm grateful to you for your help. Now drop it, will you?''

"But—''

"You're not listening to me again, Zack.''

"Okay, okay," he grumbled. "I'm never gonna hear the end of that, am I?''

"Not until you get it right.''

He grinned and crooked a finger at her. "Why don't you come over here and give me another lesson?''

She grinned back at him, then got up and slowly crossed the room. Taking her hand, he pulled her down to sit on the dogless side of the bed. He dropped a gentle kiss on the black eye she'd received while rolling on the ground between Hugh and himself. Lifting his head, Farley eyed them with what looked like suspicion, then slowly slid off the bed and limped out of the room.

"It's not that I don't mean to listen, darlin'," Zack said. "But every time I see that shiner, I feel terrible that he got to you at all."

"I know, but it's over, Zack. Or it will be if you'll let it be over. You don't have to be perfect to be my hero."

She kissed him then, and he felt a deep, healing peace settle over him. Jake had been an impossible act to follow, and his other cousins and siblings were all so bright and talented, he'd always felt that he needed to be perfect or darn close to it, in order to get his share of attention, praise and affection. Especially since he far preferred raising horses over raising cows, a preference neither his dad nor his uncle had ever understood or tolerated well.

But here was this sweet, wise, loving woman he adored, who told him without any prompting, that he didn't have to be perfect. The idea was liberating. If he didn't have to be perfect, maybe he could stop expecting perfection from the people he loved the most. Like Melissa and the rest of his family. Like Lori and Brandon. Or even himself.

Ignoring the pain in his ribs, he moved off the pillows and pulled Lori down beside him. They kissed and cuddled, and he finally fell asleep, knowing that more than anything else in the world, he wanted to spend every night for the rest of his life holding her in his arms. He needed to find a way to convince her she belonged with him.

And he would, just as soon as his damn ribs stopped hurting every time he tried to move.

When he awoke the next morning, however, Lori was gone. Instead of the hearty breakfast he'd come to anticipate, he found a note on the kitchen table.

Dear Zack,
I've decided to go ahead and finish what I need to do in Kentucky. I left Brandon with Grace so you could sleep in. She'll be checking on you. The morning chores

are done. I'll be fine, so don't worry. I'll call once a day
until I can come back.

Love,
Lori

Zack reread the note twice, struggling to rein in the sudden
fear clawing at his heart. Damn. He'd thought he'd have a
few days to talk her into letting him come along. Dang
woman shouldn't go off like that all by herself, and he wasn't
just being a chauvinistic, overprotective idiot, either. The
cops in Reno had picked up VanZandt's pal Jerome, but they
hadn't been able to hold him. And a wealthy man like
VanZandt probably had a lot of other people indebted to him,
people who would hate Lori for taking away their benefactor.
She needed someone to watch her back.

On the other hand she'd told him she needed to go to
Kentucky by herself. Maybe this was her way of testing him.
He was supposed to listen to her wishes and respect them.
Which meant that he should stay home and twiddle his
thumbs while he waited to hear from her, right? Well, *right?*

He crumpled the note, threw it in the trash and stomped
back to his bedroom, muttering, "Like hell." He didn't mind
Lori being independent, but he did mind her being reckless
with her safety. He pulled a dusty duffel bag off the shelf in
his closet, stomped back to his dresser and started shoving
underwear, socks and a shaving kit inside. After adding a
clean pair of jeans and a couple of shirts for good measure,
he grabbed the phone and dialed the main house.

"Grace? It's Zack. How long ago did she leave?"

"About an hour," Grace answered. "Is there a problem?"

"I'm going after her. Is Blair around?"

A moment later, Blair DuMaine came on the line. "Hi,
Zack. What's up?"

"I need to get to Kentucky fast. Do you or any of your
Hollywood pals happen to have a jet I can borrow?"

Thanks to some violent thunderstorms in the Midwest,
Lori spent the night in a Chicago hotel. She caught an early

flight out the next morning, arriving in Lexington at ten o'clock. When she stepped out of the small plane, the heat and humidity wrapped around her like a soggy blanket. By the time she crossed the tarmac and entered the air conditioned terminal, she could feel her hair curling out of control and her clothing sticking to her skin in numerous places.

Eager to finish this trip, she located the little red sedan she'd rented and headed for the horse farm. This was the Bluegrass country where houses were estates and trees, grass and flowers were incredibly lush and beautiful and horses were long-legged, pampered Thoroughbreds. The old, familiar sights, sounds and smells filled her with uneasiness, making her feel as if she had stepped back in time. Back to a place where she'd felt small, scared, helpless and...alone. So utterly alone.

The closer she came to Hugh's farm, the more difficult breathing became. Her chest ached. Her thoughts flitted uncontrollably from one awful memory to the next. She repeatedly told herself that Hugh was dead, and she had nothing more to fear. But that didn't stop the anxiety from growing and growing until she had to pull over, park the car and get out.

Resting her bottom against the hood, she bent over and gripped her knees, fearing a panic attack was imminent. Tears of anger and frustration filled her eyes, but she blinked them back and forced air in and out of her lungs. Dammit, she'd thought she could do this. She *had* to do this. Otherwise, Hugh might haunt her for the rest of her life. If only Zack was here....

She shook that useless thought from her head, straightened up again and tried to form a coherent plan. Zack wasn't here and he wouldn't be coming—not unless she asked him to. After making such an issue of it, she didn't believe she could do that. But it would be so much easier if she had a friend with her. Someone she could trust.

Gathering her courage, she climbed back into the car and set off again. This time she found a rock station on the radio and cranked up the volume until she couldn't hear her own thoughts. The technique worked well enough, even when she turned at the huge sign announcing VanZandt Thoroughbreds and drove up the long, oak-lined drive.

A rental car nearly identical to hers sat in front of the house, a white colonial mansion reminiscent of Tara in *Gone With the Wind*. Wondering who the gray car might belong to, she parked beside it, reluctantly climbed out and took a moment to look around. Nothing had changed. Absolutely nothing.

Surely, Hugh could walk out that front door at any moment. Lord, even thinking about how he used to look gave her the creeps. Setting foot in that house again would be like going back to visit a prison. Dear God, she didn't want to do it. Dammit, she'd known it would be this way, even though logic alone should have been enough to convince her that Hugh couldn't hurt her anymore.

The uneasiness she'd experienced while driving returned, stronger than before, bringing with it a crushing burden of anxiety that threatened to swallow her alive. Her chest hurt as if someone had branded her heart with a hot poker. She swayed, then grabbed the open car door to regain her balance.

Oh, this was ridiculous. Coming back to the VanZandt farm alone had nothing to do with being strong and independent. It was all about protecting her pride and proving to herself as well as to Zack that she really didn't need anyone—not even him. But that wasn't true anymore. She needed him to hold her hand.

She'd learned to trust him. He'd done everything within his power to help her and she knew deep down that he would have taken that bullet for her, vest or no vest. She loved him. She loved knowing she could count on him to be there for her and for Brandon. No matter what.

He'd badgered her into reclaiming her life. So why not go back to Lexington, call Zack and ask him to come and help her through this one last step to freedom? Why not, indeed?

Smiling and meaning it for the first time since she'd left

Wyoming, she tossed her purse into the passenger seat. A footstep scraped the paved driveway behind her. Adrenaline rushing through her system, she whirled around to face whoever was there, raising her hands to ward off an attack. None occurred.

Instead, big, gentle hands reached out and grasped her shoulders. "Lori, it's me. Are you all right?"

She looked up into Zack's eyes and felt her heart squeeze down tight, then fill to bursting with joy. "I'm fine. You just...startled me."

"I'm sorry. I didn't mean to do that."

Happy tears flowed from her eyes, and she would have thrown herself against him and hugged him if not for his broken ribs. "I was going to town to call you. What are you doing here?"

A frown crinkled his forehead and deepened the crow's-feet around his eyes. "Aw, *jeez,* honey, don't cry. I know you didn't want me to come with you, and I really was listening. Honest."

She swiped at her eyes. "Then why are you here?"

"I got to thinkin' that Hugh probably had some buddies around, and I was afraid they might try to hurt you. I just couldn't stand the thought of you havin' to face somethin' like that all alone again."

"Oh, Zack," she murmured, fearing that she might have to hug the daylights out of him in spite of his sore ribs.

He cupped her face between his hands and wiped away her tears with his thumbs. "Shoot, woman, we all need a little backup sometimes. When Melissa called, I was damn scared. I needed someone to hold my hand and you were right there to do it for me. Won't you let me do the same for you?"

"Stop, plea—"

"I can't." His voice was low, rough and utterly earnest. "Not until you understand. I know you're capable of handlin' darn near anything, Lori. And I promise I won't try to take over or boss you around. I won't even say a word if that's what you want. I know you have to do this, but dammit, woman, you don't have to do it all alone.''

Sniffling, she gave him what must be an awfully soggy smile. "Yes."

He went on as if he hadn't heard her. "I love you, Lori, and I think you love me. Please don't be mad at me for comin' here and don't ask me to go home without you. As long as I'm alive and kickin', I swear you won't ever have to go through any of this hard stuff all by yourself again."

Lori cleared her throat and raised her voice. "Zack, I said *yes.*"

"Yes?" Narrowing his eyes, he warily studied her. "Yes, you're mad at me? Yes, you'll let me stay? Yes, what?"

"Yes, you may stay. Yes, I love you, too. And *yes,* I'll marry you. Any time, any place you want."

His eyes widened, and a slow, sexy smile stretched his mouth as wide as it would go. He lowered his hands to her waist as if he intended to pull her against him, broken ribs or no. Then he paused and directed his gaze toward the horse paddocks for a long, quiet moment before looking at her again. A worried little crease settled between his dark eyebrows.

"Are you sure, Lori? Really sure?"

"Aren't you?"

"Damn right, I'm sure. I want my ring on your finger so bad I can hardly think straight. But this is your show, darlin', and I don't ever want you to have any regrets. If you need more time, I'll wait."

She let her gaze wander from the house, to the stables, to the paddocks, then looked at Zack again. "I'm absolutely, positively sure."

"Good. Now that I know the secret to dealing with women, I'd hate to waste any more time."

The wicked amusement glinting in his eyes made her feel wary, but she smiled at him anyway. "Okay, I'll bite, McBride. What's the secret to dealing with women?"

"The way I see it, they're really not much different than

horses. A soft voice, a gentle hand and respect for their feelings are all it takes to make them happy.''

She raised an eyebrow at him. ''You think so?''

''Yeah. Did I leave somethin' out?''

She considered giving him an attitude adjustment on general principle alone. But then, she supposed she would have another forty or fifty years to set him straight. Shaking her head, she linked her hands at the back of his neck. ''Nothing too important. Why don't you quit while you're ahead?''

''What's that supposed to mean?''

''Just shut up and kiss me, Zack.''

He tipped back his head and laughed, that deep, rich sound she had come to love. ''All right, darlin'. I'm always happy to oblige a pretty lady.''

*   *   *   *   *

This July don't miss
the next installment of Myrna Temte's series,
HEARTS OF WYOMING
Turn the page for a preview...

Coming in July 1999
Myrna Temte's rollicking
HEARTS OF WYOMING SERIES
continues with Book #4, the story of
Cal McBride
in
THE GAL WHO TOOK THE WEST

only from Silhouette Special Edition
Here's an exciting preview...

Chapter One

"Sure is dead around here, boss," Sylvia Benson groused, settling her wide rump onto a bar stool. "I swear I thought that shift would never end."

Cal McBride gave his tired waitress a sympathetic smile, fixed her a weak whiskey ditch and set it in front of her on the bar. "Wednesdays are always quiet, Syl."

She took a swallow from her drink and made a face. "You call that a drink? How'd you ever pass bartender school?"

"Hey, you old bat, it's free and it'll keep you sober. What more do you want?"

Sylvia's bray of laughter would have drowned out the juke box had anyone bothered to put money in it. Cal was enjoying the break from the same five songs everybody tended to play. The two second-rate cowboys shooting pool at the far end of the room were more interested in their game than they were in music.

Shaking her pudgy finger at Cal's nose, Sylvia said, "Listen, kid, I'm old enough to be your mama, so let's have a little respect here, shall we?''

Cal chuckled and shook his head. In the ten years he'd owned Cal's Place, the best—and often the only—bar and restaurant in Sunshine Gap, Wyoming, he and Sylvia had worked out a friendly bickering routine. He'd inherited her from the previous owner, and while she was loud, nosy and occasionally crude, the customers loved her.

She was also loyal, dependable and such a skilled waitress, she could carry dinners for four people without a tray. She didn't take much guff off of anyone, but her heart was as big as Yellowstone Park. Cal intended to keep her on his staff forever if possible. In a town as small as Sunshine Gap, good help was harder to find than customers on a Wednesday.

Sylvia lit up, inhaled a drag and blew out a stream of smoke, then took another swig from her drink and banged the glass back down on the bar. ''I'm tellin' you, Cal, we need some *action* in this town, or we're all gonna die of boredom.''

''Once those movie folks start showing up, we'll have more business than we can handle.''

''You *hope*,'' Sylvia said.

Suddenly the roar of a motorcycle engine ripped through the momentary silence. Cal exchanged a surprised glance with her, then dried his hands and stepped from behind the bar to check it out.

He opened the front door and watched a big, chrome-studded bike make an illegal U-turn at the end of the block and come back toward the bar. A small, secret part of him envied the rider for the freedom the gleaming, red-and-black Harley-Davidson represented. He shoved that part back down inside himself where it belonged.

He had too many commitments in Sunshine Gap even to dream about taking off on a bike like that. He wouldn't mind getting a closer look at it, though. A guy didn't see many motorcycles this far from the interstate. This was more of a pickup and horse trailer kind of town.

The bike slowed, its engine noise dropping to a throaty grumble when the driver turned into a space barely five feet from Cal's door. With a flick of a wrist, the driver silenced the engine. He rocked the bike back onto its kickstand, then swung his right leg over the saddle and stood upright.

He was a short, wiry little fella, and he wore black leather chaps over a pair of jeans, hiking boots, black leather gloves and a matching jacket that looked at least two sizes too big for him. The pool-playing cowboys joined Cal in the doorway, watching with interest while the driver pulled off his helmet.

To Cal's surprise, a delicate, decidedly feminine face emerged. The woman had big blue eyes, a slightly square chin and the cheekbones of a fashion model. Setting the helmet on the seat, she yanked down the jacket's zipper and fanned the open sides, revealing a skin-hugging tank top as red as her helmet.

She reached up toward the back of her head, yanked out some kind of a clip and a sun-streaked light-brown ponytail fell past her shoulders. It was a little mashed down, but Cal figured it ought to be real pretty when it was combed.

Then she peeled off her jacket and draped it over the handlebars. Her arms were tanned and slender, but with muscles as well-defined as an Olympic athlete's. Cal barely had time to wonder about that when she leaned down to poke around in a storage compartment behind the seat. Her jeans pulled tight across her backside, delineating every curve for her fascinated audience.

"Damn," Ronnie Black breathed in Cal's left ear, stretching the word into two syllables.

Joe Wright gave a low whistle in Cal's right ear, then drawled, "Oh, honey."

"Honey?" Cal snorted. "That's trouble on two legs, boys."

Ronnie leaned closer to Cal, his gaze trained on the

woman's sweetly rounded bottom. "Bet they're great...legs, though."

As if to confirm Cal's assessment, however, the woman straightened up, shot them an irritated glance and propped her fists on her hips, "What're *you* bozos looking at? Haven't you ever seen a woman before?"

Cal wished she hadn't done that. He really did. Most guys with half a brain would run like hell from a woman with a temper. Unfortunately he wasn't one of them.

Call him a fool, but he'd always found a woman with a temper...exciting. Challenging. Alluring. He shifted his weight to his right leg and tugged at the bottom of his vest, but it didn't stop the message his libido sent to his body. Even now, right here on Main Street in front of God and everybody, he could feel himself getting excited.

It didn't matter. This woman might be the stuff of late-night fantasies, but he was well past the age when he might have acted on that sort of foolishness. Every time he tended bar, he heard story after story about love gone wrong, and most of them started with some idiot who didn't know when to keep his pants zipped. That was just sex, of course.

And love? Well, it sure hadn't brought much happiness to anyone he knew. After seeing all of the tears and anguish falling in love had caused in his own family, Cal wanted no part of it. But as he took a closer look at the sexy, hot-tempered woman standing before him, he couldn't help sensing that life in Sunshine Gap would never be the same....

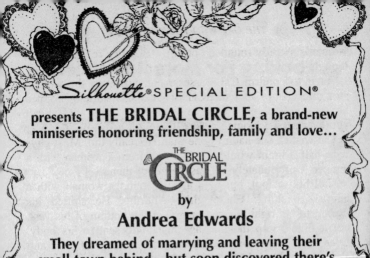

Silhouette® SPECIAL EDITION®

presents **THE BRIDAL CIRCLE**, a brand-new miniseries honoring friendship, family and love...

THE BRIDAL CIRCLE

by

Andrea Edwards

They dreamed of marrying and leaving their small town behind—but soon discovered there's no place like home for true love!

IF I ONLY HAD A...HUSBAND (May '99)

Penny Donnelly had tried desperately to forget charming millionaire Brad Corrigan. But her heart had a memory—and a will—of its own. And Penny's heart was set on Brad becoming her husband....

SECRET AGENT GROOM (August '99)

When shy-but-sexy Heather Mahoney bumbles onto secret agent Alex Waterstone's undercover mission, the only way to protect the innocent beauty is to claim her as his lady love. Will Heather carry out her own secret agenda and claim Alex as her groom?

PREGNANT & PRACTICALLY MARRIED
(November '99)

Pregnant Karin Spencer had suddenly lost her memory and *gained* a pretend fiancé. Though their match was make-believe, Jed McCarron was her dream man. Could this bronco-bustin' cowboy give up his rodeo days for family ways?

Available at your favorite retail outlet.

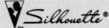

FORTUNE'S Children™

**The Fortune family requests
the honor of your presence at the weddings of**

The Brides

Silhouette Desire's scintillating new miniseries,
featuring the beloved Fortune family
and five of your favorite authors.

The Secretary and the Millionaire
by Leanne Banks (SD #1208, 4/99)

When handsome Jack Fortune asked his dependable assistant to
become his daughter's temporary, live-in nanny, Amanda Corbain
knew almost all her secret wishes had come true. But Amanda
had one final wish before this Cinderella assignment ended....

The Groom's Revenge
by Susan Crosby (SD #1214, 5/99)

Powerful tycoon Gray McGuire was bent on destroying the
Fortune family. Until he met sweet Mollie Shaw. And this sprightly
redhead was about to show him that the best revenge is...
falling in love!

Undercover Groom
by Merline Lovelace (SD #1220, 6/99)

Who was Mason Chandler? Chloe Fortune thought she knew
everything about her groom. But as their wedding day
approached, would his secret past destroy their love?

Available at your favorite retail outlet.

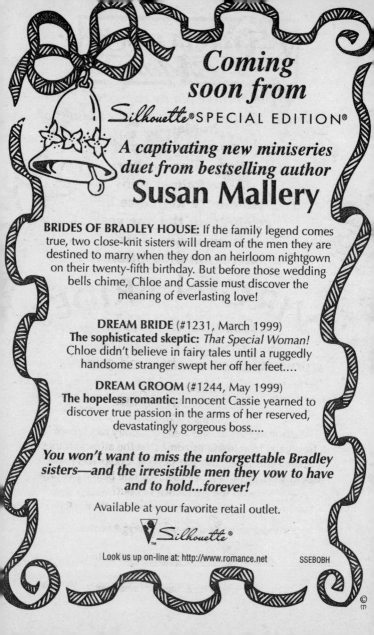

Coming in May 1999

BABY *Fever*

by
New York Times Bestselling Author

KASEY MICHAELS

When three sisters hear their biological
clocks ticking, they know it's
time for action.

But who will they get to father their babies?

**Find out how the road to motherhood
leads to love in this brand-new collection.**

Available at your favorite retail outlet.

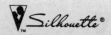

World's Most
Eligible Bachelors

**Available April 1999 from
Silhouette Books...**

The Greek Tycoon
by Suzanne Carey

The World's Most Eligible Bachelor: Extremely wealthy Theo Petrakis was built like a Greek god, and his reputation as a ladies' man—and confirmed bachelor—was no mere myth.

Gorgeous tycoon Theo Petrakis lived life to the fullest, so when he came up against the utterly proper Esme Lord, he found adventure in teaching the American beauty his wicked ways. But one tempestuous night had left them with rings on their fingers and a faint recollection of wedding vows. Was their marriage for real...or just their passion?

Each month, Silhouette Books brings you a brand-new story about an absolutely irresistible bachelor. Find out how the sexiest, most sought-after men are finally caught.

Available at your favorite retail outlet.

PSWMEB8

SILHOUETTE®

Desire is celebrating the 10th Anniversary of

MAN OF THE MONTH

For ten years Silhouette Desire has been giving readers the ultimate in sexy, irresistible heroes.

So come celebrate with your absolute favorite authors!

JANUARY 1999
BELOVED by Diana Palmer—
SD #1189 Long, Tall Texans

FEBRUARY 1999
**A KNIGHT IN RUSTY ARMOR
by Dixie Browning—**
SD #1195 The Lawless Heirs

MARCH 1999
**THE BEST HUSBAND IN TEXAS
by Lass Small—**
SD #1201

APRIL 1999
BLAYLOCK'S BRIDE by Cait London—
SD #1207 The Blaylocks

MAY 1999
LOVE ME TRUE by Ann Major—
SD #1213

Available at your favorite retail outlet, only from

Silhouette®

Silhouette ROMANCE™

**In March,
award-winning,
bestselling author
Diana Palmer joins
Silhouette Romance in
celebrating the one year
anniversary of its
successful promotion:**

VIRGIN BRIDES

*Celebrate the joys of
first love with unforgettable
stories by our most beloved authors....*

**March 1999:
CALLAGHAN'S BRIDE
Diana Palmer**

Callaghan Hart exasperated temporary ranch cook
Tess Brady by refusing to admit that the attraction they
shared was more than just passion. Could Tess make
Callaghan see she was his truelove bride before her time
on the Hart ranch ran out?

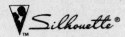

Silhouette®

Available at your favorite retail outlet.

Look us up on-line at: http://www.romance.net   SRVB99